THE TROUBLE WITH MAGIC

TRUDI JAYE

TANIA HUTLEY

Magic Types

Earth magic – the ability to manipulate, transform, and use earth, stone, minerals, etc.

Animal magic – an affinity with animals. The ability to connect with and manipulate creatures, and transform flesh. The ability to heal.

Fire magic – the ability to control fire and create heat.

Water magic – the ability to control water and ice, and draw moisture from the air.

Air Magic – the ability to control air, including the air in someone's lungs. Some can control weather. Air magic can be used to locate people.

Plant magic – an affinity with plants. The ability to manipulate and grow plants. The ability to use plants to make magical tinctures and potions.

Archivist Magic – Archivists are researchers and guardians of knowledge. Creators and custodians of grimoires. Most archivists develop the ability to use spells from the grimoires they handle.

Veritas – A user of mind magic. Traditionally a seeker of truth charged with administering justice in the magical community. A rare power that is a heavy burden for the witch born with it.

ONE

The top of a ladder is a sucky place to be when a magical shockwave hits. But that's where I am, cleaning rag in hand, loud music pumping from the stereo.

Power sizzles, stinging my flesh, and I gasp.

The shockwave wakes the trapped magic inside me. I grit my teeth, instinctively fighting against the surge. My magic has been locked down for so long, I don't know if I can control it. Whatever happens, I can't let it out.

The ladder wobbles.

Dropping the cleaning rag, I shoot out a hand to steady myself on the ceiling beam I was wiping. Instead of wood, my hand hits a rusty old nail. The sharp point rips open the skin on my palm. It hurts like hell.

"Shit!"

My calloused hands aren't exactly delicate or lady-like, but the nail has torn through my roughened skin, deep into my flesh. Blood flows from the ragged wound, and for a moment, I'm frozen. The rush of power in my blood holds me spellbound.

Literally.

My magic struggles to break free of the powerful council bonds holding it dormant. The released blood calls to my magic, both the earth and animal sides. It throbs inside me, pushing against its restraints. Pulsing in time to the song by *The Flaming Buttholes* that's pumping out of my stereo system.

But how can my magic be surging? The crushing bonds the Blood Council placed around it have held it in place for years. I've cut myself hundreds of times in the years since the spell was cast with no reaction. I don't understand what's happening.

And then another wave of magic hits me and I can't think of anything other than the need to control and contain my magic before I hurt someone.

The magic is insistent. Urgent.

Dangerous.

With one hand, I stumble down the ladder, cursing the urge to clean drywall dust off the walls that led me up there in the first place. Desperately holding the power in, I'm relieved to feel the council bonds tightening back around the magic, helping me fight it. I press the wound into my *Death Metal Forever* T-shirt, wrapping the fabric around my hand to constrict the blood flow. *Better*. As the bleeding subsides, so does the power inside me. I let out a long breath, releasing some of the tension holding me rigid.

There's a pause in my favorite song, the musicians catching their breath before launching into the climax. In the silence, I hear somebody banging on the front door. They're pounding hard, probably using the side of their fist. How long have they been knocking? When the lead singer's gravelly voice starts up again, it all but drowns them out.

I won't do what ya want. I won't be what ya make me. Hard as ya try, ya still can't break me.

The power is all but gone and my panicked heartbeats are slowing. I probably shouldn't open the door before I've bandaged the cut on my hand, but whoever's banging isn't letting up. It sounds like they're trying to break the door down. It must be urgent.

With my injured hand pressed against my T-shirt, I stride into the hallway and pull the door open.

Big mistake.

Agnes Postlethwaite—AKA the demon neighbor from hell—is standing on the doorstep. All five feet of her trembles with outrage. Damn. My roommate Jess is good at dealing with the old battleaxe. Me, not so much. People skills aren't exactly my super power.

"Sapphira Black, I'm sick and tired of coming over here." Agnes has to shout to be heard over the music, and the best thing that's happened to me all day is that the singer has just launched into the climax of the song. He's now screaming, *'You're a butthole,'* over and over. Perfect timing.

"Turn off that horrible noise and stop hammering at all hours," shouts Agnes. "Or I'll call the police."

"I was cleaning, not hammering," I yell back, glancing at the antique grandfather clock behind me. "And it's three o'clock in the afternoon. When am I supposed to play music?"

"That's not music, it's an abomination."

I shrug, not prepared to argue with her about this yet again.

"What if I were giving a piano lesson?" She looks down her long beaky nose at me, disapproval etched into her face. She's made it obvious she doesn't like anything about me. Not my music, what I do for a living, or the way I look.

Too bad for her.

During the week, I work as a stonemason. On weekends I work on my house, rebuilding the rooms that were damaged in the explosion. I have three pairs of jeans I wear on rotation, and washing them never gets all the building dust and mortar out of them. The ones I've got on could stand up on their own.

But I'd rather wear filthy jeans and a blood-smeared death metal T-shirt than look like Agnes. She's wearing brown slacks with creases ironed down the front of the legs, a matching brown cardigan, and a blouse with ruffles. *Ruffles!* She's probably about fifty, twice my age, but her gray hair makes her look older. It's styled in such perfectly-crafted waves, I can count how many curlers she must have used.

My thick black locks are pulled into two messy pigtails, one on each side, and probably covered with white drywall dust. Agnes and I couldn't be more different. Still, I had nothing against her until she went to the police to tell them about an argument she heard me having with Mom before her death. I already feel terrible for losing my cool and screaming at Mom, without Agnes trying to convince the police it was something sinister instead of a normal family disagreement.

Since then, I haven't been able to look at Agnes without getting steamed.

"I keep the volume down for you all week," I yell. "Now you want me to tiptoe around on Saturdays too?"

"You could employ a little courtesy." Her nostrils flare as she focuses on my hand. "Are you *bleeding?*"

When I look down, blood is trickling over my hand, shockingly red against my skin. The magic surges again, fighting against its bonds. My mother's ring feels hot on my finger. Her blood inside the clear crystal orb is glowing, as though drawing from the power inside me.

My magic is begging me to use it. I'm a witch, after all.

Something dark curls up inside me. I *used* to be a witch. Now I want no part of it.

"Are you going to do something about that?" Agnes glares at me with beady eyes, judging me yet again for not doing what she considers the proper thing.

She's a mundane through and through, with no idea about witches or magic, but I have a feeling if she found out it'd be the last straw. She'd vote herself in as the head of the witch-burning committee of Druid Park Drive, and I'm the first one she'd throw on the fire.

With a final crescendo of dueling guitars, the song ends. In the silence, all I can hear is my magic, still thrashing against its bonds in a ferocious battering of frustrated energy.

"I was about to bandage it when you knocked," I tell her, gritting my teeth against the renewed surge of magic. "Better go and do that." I start pushing the door closed.

The first notes of next song fill the air behind me. It's called *Thrill Me*, and it starts off a little quiet, with a pulse like a heartbeat and a single electric guitar winding up slowly. But I think Agnes can tell it's going to get loud again, because she steps forward and catches the door before it shuts.

"Not so fast. I'm turning off that stereo." She pushes the door all the way open and barges in, charging past me like she owns the place.

Seeing as I heft rocks for a living, I should have been able to stop her easily, but the magic is making my reactions sluggish, so instead I just watch with my mouth open. I'm shocked that she thinks it's okay to barge in here. There's even a little part of me that's impressed by how badass she is.

Then my responses kick in.

She's in my home, and I sure as hell didn't invite her in. This is my place. My sanctuary. And with my magic surging, I don't have time for her outraged self-righteousness.

"Stop," I snarl. "You're like a clucking chicken, poking your beak into my business." I grab her arm. As soon as my wounded hand touches her, smearing my blood on her bare skin, I realize my mistake.

Too late.

The heat in my veins turns to fire. I try to erase the image of Agnes as a beaky, squawking chicken, but that's the picture in my head. I can't change it. The image is clear.

The magic bursts out of me. My earth magic is strong on its own, but intertwined with my mother's animal magic it feels like a freight train tangled up with a roller coaster. They tear out of me so fast and hard, I have no chance to control them.

It's the animal magic that pours itself into Agnes.

One moment I'm holding the cool flesh of my piano-teacher neighbor, the next there's a chicken in my arms. The bird flaps and pecks me, but I'm already letting it go. My muscles have turned to water and my legs can no longer hold me. I collapse to the floor, trembling all over, the after-effect of the magic I've just released for the first time in five years.

But my earth magic is still charged, still crackling the air around me. It's so strong, so *wild*, it makes my hair stand on end. As desperately as I try to pull it back in, I'm too weak to contain it.

My breaths come faster. The world around me blurs

and both my head and heart pound in time to *Thrill Me*, which has built to be every bit as loud as the intro promised.

With nowhere else to go, my earth magic slams into the stereo system. The machine explodes with a deafening bang. I cover my eyes as bits of plastic fly across the room. When I open them, smoke is pouring out of the twisted wreckage. Hell, I *loved* that stereo.

At least all the magic is spent.

Except that the council didn't just bind my magic, they also banned me from using it. So the fact that my beloved high-performance audio equipment looks like a failed science experiment and my poultry-shaped neighbor is flapping frantically down the hall...well, that's going to make things really complicated.

Shit, shit, shit. In the sudden silence, my ragged breaths compete with the chicken's squawks.

What am I going to do? How am I going to fix this?

I was born with my father's earth magic, but when my mother died in the explosion, somehow I absorbed her animal magic. *Nobody* can control two kinds of magic, especially not power as strong as my mother's. Hence the Blood Council's binding, and the rules around using my magic.

If Magnus Fox discovers the magical binding failed, he might be tempted to find a more permanent solution to keep my magic from creating havoc. One of the council's favorite punishments is turning witches into frozen stone statues, still alive, but capable of nothing more than watching the world go past. Which pretty much sums up how much they suck.

Both Uncle Ray and my cousin Sylvia are council members and would have felt me use the magic. They're my only blood relatives, Ray on my mother's side, Sylvia on my

Dad's, and I'm linked to both of them. I only hope their family loyalty is stronger than their council bond.

Right on cue, my cellphone starts ringing from the pocket of my jeans. It's got to be either my uncle or cousin.

Cursing, I reach for my pocket. But as soon as I touch my phone, a charge of residual magic zaps my fingers, shocking me. I yelp and snatch my hand away. The phone is hot in my pocket and I can smell something bad. Burning plastic?

When I tug the thing out of my jeans, it's so hot I drop it. But at least it's stopped ringing. In fact, I'm pretty sure it's dead. Which means I don't have to talk to anyone, and right now, I'll take any scrap of good news I can get.

I push myself to my feet. In the living room, Agnes is perched on the arm of my couch next to my smoking stereo. I swear she's glaring at me harder than she ever has, which is saying something.

Can chickens blink? Because Agnes sure isn't.

"I didn't mean to change you," I say, still breathless. "I'll find a way to turn you back."

Chicken Agnes is brown all over, with a silver head and pitch-black eyes. At least she's not freaking out anymore. There's a dangerous stillness to her, as though she's devising the best way to murder me.

I can't help myself. "Maybe you should have let me play a little music," I tell her. "Instead of storming over, complaining about every noise."

Agnes glares at me a moment longer. Then she shits on my couch.

TWO

In the bathroom, I clean my wound, gingerly washing away the blood. Some disinfectant and a bandage, and I'm ready to head back out to face the music.

Or the chicken, as the case may be.

Good thing Jess is at band practice today. This would be difficult to explain. She has no idea that magic exists and I plan on keeping it that way.

My living room smells of burnt plastic, so I open a couple of windows to get rid of the toxic fumes. At first I can't see Agnes and my heart leaps into my throat. What if she's escaped? What am I going to do?

Can I leave her as a chicken?

Okay, so even asking that question in my head probably rules me out for receiving any humanitarian awards. But she's a terrible neighbor, always complaining.

My parents used to be friends with the mundanes in our neighborhood. I went to street picnics in Druid Hill Park, and played with mundane kids. But after the explosion, suspicion fell on me, the only survivor. Rumor had it that I'd killed my own parents. Articles in the papers hinted that I was the only suspect, people started looking at me sideways, and mothers hurried their children to the other side of the street when I walked past. Agnes couldn't wait to blab about my fights with my mother, and she helped to brand a grieving nineteen-year-old as a killer.

Instead of supporting me in my time of need, the Blood Council cut me off from everything I'd known. They bound both the earth and animal magic inside me and left me to fend for myself. I had a wrecked house, no job, no money, and I couldn't use magic to help me anymore.

Those first few months on my own, working out how to live as a mundane, just about killed me.

Desperate for money, I advertised for a roommate. Jess turned up and miraculously agreed to move into the half-destroyed house my parents had died in. And getting a job as a stonemason, using my natural affinity for things of the earth, was the one thing the magic I was born with was still good for.

Yeah, I got through it. Doesn't mean I'm not still angry.

There's a flicker of movement behind a pile of paint cans in the corner of my living room. A scratch of claws against tin. Agnes. Hiding from me, perhaps?

"Come out, Agnes," I say loudly. "I can't stand you, and I know you don't like me. But I'll do my best to fix this."

At least I hope I can. Turning her back into a human without doing her any major damage might be all but impossible. But if the bindings that hold my magic in check have weakened, I could definitely try. I mean, the damage is already done, right? And once I've done it, I swear, it's the last spell I'll ever do.

I'll need blood. New blood.

There's a box cutter amongst the well-used, paint-spattered tools in my toolbox. When I hold its blade against the tender flesh of my thumb, it feels cold and sharp.

"You ready, Agnes?"

With a deep breath, I slice into my skin. Not too deep. *Damn* it hurts.

My blood wells, but my magic doesn't. I can't even feel it inside me.

Bad sign.

I stride over to the paint cans, where Agnes is watching. If I smear blood on her, picture her as human, and reach deep, maybe a miracle will happen and I'll be able to pull the magic out again.

But as I reach for the chicken with my bloody hand, Agnes dodges away, squawking and flapping her wings. She half-flies, half-claws her way up my curtains.

"I'm trying to help you." I clamber onto the back of the couch to reach for her. "Want me to change you back? You need to let me touch you."

My fingers barely brush her feathers when my land-line phone rings, making me jump. I lose my balance and fall, landing hard behind the couch. *Crap.*

Groaning, I lift my head. Then I reach my unbloodied hand up to the table next to the couch and lift the handset.

"Hello?"

"What have you been doing, Sapphira?"

I wince. "Nice to talk to you too, Uncle Ray."

"Has something happened to the binding spell? Did you just use your magic?"

The best way to avoid his question is to deflect it. "I felt something weird," I tell him. "A magical shockwave."

"What are you talking about?"

"It almost knocked me off my ladder. And the Council's binding weakened."

"What have you done this time?"

"*This time?*" Sure, when I absorbed my mother's magic, I accidentally destroyed a few things, but that was years ago.

He sighs. "I didn't mean it that way. But using your magic breaks Blood Council law. We can't take that lightly."

"The binding failed. That's not my fault. The spell isn't supposed to wear off." I can't keep the edge from my voice. The council likes to think they're infallible.

"Regardless, you should have contained your magic."

"It was a tiny, harmless spell. No big deal." I cross my fingers behind my back.

"It felt like a lot more than that."

"Maybe what you felt was the shockwave."

He clicks his tongue. "Sylvia would have felt your magic too. I'll discuss with her whether we report the incident to the other council members."

At least he's not planning to ring Magnus before talking to Sylvia. I have confidence that she, at least, will be on my side. "Okay, Uncle Ray," I mutter.

When I hang up, I close my eyes for a moment, wishing the magical world would just leave me alone. Most witches ignore my existence, which is fine by me, except they still expect me to abide by their rules. It feels a little like having to pay rent for a house I've been locked out of.

The sound of Agnes's claws scratching against wood distracts me. She's in the hall now, trying to figure out how to open the front door.

It's been a long time since I was a real witch, but even I know that turning a person into a chicken isn't easy. I'm stunned I managed it, especially without runes, spell ingredients, a grimoire, or any kind of knowledge.

It was a weird one-in-a-million fluke.

The fact that I can't turn her back doesn't surprise me in

the least. I study the cuts on my palm and thumb. Blood is smeared over my hand. It feels sticky. It also feels like mundane blood. There's not the slightest whisper of magic in my ears.

The council restraints have locked down my magic again. Right now, I probably couldn't turn a cockroach into a dung beetle.

THREE

Cleaning up chicken shit and throwing my expensive stereo in the trash become, briefly, my least favorite ways to spend my weekend.

They only get bumped off the top spot on the Sucky-Things-To-Do-On-Saturdays list when I try to catch my annoying neighbor-turned-chicken. It takes a long, frustrating chase through every room in the house, and when I do finally manage to catch Agnes, she squawks like I'm taking her out to be killed for dinner.

I wish.

To keep her from gouging my flesh with her sharp claws, I grab her with both hands, pin her wings to her sides, and hold her well away from my body. It doesn't stop her from craning her neck around, trying to peck my hands.

Some blood has soaked through the bandages I've wrapped around the wounds on my hand, but it isn't so much as humming. I've never felt so empty of magic as I do right now.

At least I have a plan. Although, admittedly, it doesn't

start off well when I realize I can't let myself out my front door without tucking Agnes under my arm where she can peck chunks out of my torso.

"Stop it," I snap. "I'm taking you to my cousin's house. She'll be able to reverse the spell."

Sylvia's not quite as zealous a council member as Uncle Ray, so hopefully I can convince her to keep quiet about the whole thing. After all, if she can turn Agnes back into her normal irritating, busy-body self, there really will be no harm done.

Maybe Agnes doesn't understand I'm trying to help her. More likely, she wants me to suffer. And seeing as she's not co-operating, I can't exactly drive to Sylvia's place. Sharing the cab of my old pickup truck with Agnes would be giving her an invitation to peck out my eyes on the way.

Instead, I walk fifteen minutes down the mercifully quiet Baltimore streets around Druid Hill Park to my cousin Sylvia's place. I need to keep Agnes held out in front of me the whole way. I'm still covered in drywall dust, and probably have blood smeared on my face from swiping escaped strands of hair out of my eyes. Combine that with the fact that Agnes won't stop squawking, and I'm not entirely surprised when a group of tough-looking men cross the street to avoid me.

It's a good thing Sylvia's place isn't far. She's my father's niece, but didn't inherit the earth magic that runs on his side of the family. Instead she got her mother's archival magic. She's the custodian of centuries of magical knowledge, one of the few who can safely handle the oldest and most powerful grimoires.

Her house is warded with the same kind of protection spells as mine, set to repel magical visitors who intend harm.

My dad installed the wards around my house, and it's a testament to the strength of his earth magic that they're still holding, though I'll have to find a way to shore them up again soon.

Sylvia's barrier is strong enough to make my skin vibrate and my teeth clench as I push through it, then climb the front steps of my cousin's brick row house.

Thanks to my job, my arms and shoulders are pretty much all muscle. Still, they're beyond aching. Every time I let them drop closer to my body to give them a little relief, Agnes takes another peck at me. I know it's my fault she's a chicken, but the change sure hasn't improved her temper.

The doorbell is just low enough that I can stand on tiptoe and use one elbow to push it. This house used to belong to Sylvia's parents and I've been coming here all my life, so when Sylvia doesn't answer the door, I grit my teeth, stuff Agnes under my arm, drag my keyring out of my pocket, and fumble to fit the right key in the lock. I've done this a million times—minus the vicious chicken—because I feed Sylvia's rat for her when she goes out of town.

Though I steer clear of most people, I like animals. Ratticus the rat is picky about who he'll let handle him. He's a biter by nature, but comes running whenever he sees me. Since the explosion, when I was filled with my mother's animal magic, critters of all kinds are naturally drawn to me. Locked down or not, the magic still attracts them, and even when I can't feel it, apparently they can.

Except for a certain chicken.

I slip through the door and shut it behind me before letting Agnes go. Sighing with relief, I shake my aching arms out and glower at the chicken as she runs, wings flapping, down the hall. Hopefully she won't crap on the carpet before my cousin can change her back into human form.

"Sylvia? You here?"

My voice is swallowed up in the silence of the house. Sound is absorbed by the plush carpet and the shelves covered in books. Hopefully Sylvia will be home soon. Maybe she's at the library, although Saturday evening is a strange time for her to be at work. I left a message on her cellphone before I left home, and I'd be surprised if she hasn't picked it up by now. Shame my magic turned my phone into a smoking ruin, so she can't call me back.

Still, I feel better just being here. As well as running the library, my cousin owns hundreds of magical books, and a few dozen seriously powerful grimoires. Her magic allows her to contain their spells–or to release them. Hopefully one of those books will have a reversion spell that will turn Agnes back into herself.

The books on the shelves that line Sylvia's hallway are the least magical in the house, but I'm careful not to touch them as I walk past, especially because my hand is throbbing under its bandage. I think I've re-opened my wounds.

For some reason, the house feels creepy today. I'm not sure why, but the silence is thick. Ominous, somehow. And what is that smell? Could Sylvia have let Ratticus's cage get funky?

A bad feeling starts tiptoeing down the back of my neck. "Sylvia? Are you okay?"

Suddenly I feel like I'm watching myself walk down the hall, past the study and hall closet, like I'm in a horror movie and something's about to jump out at me. I glance sharply behind me. Then up, because nobody ever looks up in horror movies, and the scariest things always drop from the ceiling.

There's nothing there, of course. The silence must

really be getting to me. I can't even hear Agnes. Where could she have gone?

At the end of the hall, I turn into the living room. Its tall bookcases are filled to the brim with books of power. They seem more potent than usual, because my skin is tingling, and their covers are trembling with the effort of containing their magic.

A scuffling sound makes my heart leap into my throat, but it's just Ratticus in his cage on the sideboard. He's frantically running back and forth, and his food bowl has tipped over, spilling rat food through the bars of his cage onto the floor.

What could have freaked him out? Hopefully it wasn't Agnes flapping around. I still can't see her anywhere.

"You okay, Ratticus?"

Opening his cage, I place his food bowl back where it's supposed to go. Ratticus normally runs to me, but this time he shrinks back against the other side of his cage.

"Did Agnes upset you?" I ask. Hearing myself talk makes me feel a little less creeped out, as though I'm not really alone. "Where'd that mean ol' chicken go, anyway?"

His cage doesn't look dirty enough to account for the bad smell, although there is something red on his water bottle. What on earth is that?

I'd lean in for a closer look, but I can feel rat pellets under the soles of my Doc Martin boots and I'm grinding them into the carpet. When I step back, I notice a dark stain on the carpet. Sylvia must have spilled something, but it's not like her to leave a mess.

I bend and touch the stain. The instant my fingers brush it, a hot, buzzing shock jolts up my arm and I know exactly what it is.

Blood.

My heart pounds and I jerk around. "Sylvia? Sylvia?"

I spin in a circle, frantically searching the room. There are more stains. Why didn't I notice them before? Droplets have splashed the carpet and hit the spines of some of the books. No wonder they're trembling.

"Sylvia?"

I creep forward to peer into her kitchen. Nothing. Everything there is neat and in its place. Down the hall to her bedroom. Nothing there either. Or in her spare room, or the bathroom. Where could she be?

The only bloodstains are in the living room, and when I return, I notice the biggest stain is directly in front of the bookcase.

My body chills.

The bookcase is the entry to Syliva's athenaeum, the secure room where she keeps her most dangerous grimoires. Her athenaeum is somewhere outside of the mundane world, not in normal space. When Sylvia tried to explain to me where exactly that was, my brain wanted to turn itself inside out.

The grimoires she keeps in there are the ones that have become so powerful, there have been cases of them being able to activate their own spells. Sylvia's archivist power protects her, and the athenaeum has wards and spells to suppress their magic.

I haven't been inside the athenaeum since before my parents died, but I clearly remember its bookcases, which were a lot less packed than the one in front of me. Even with all her safeguards, Sylvia kept the grimoires precisely spaced, giving each book room to cast its shadow so it didn't quarrel with its neighbors.

I'd have thought it would be impossible for one of the

grimoires to hurt Sylvia, but if it did, she could be trapped in there with it. I can't just leave her there.

Heart pounding, I pull out a book from the bottom shelf of the largest bookcase. It looks like the only ordinary novel in the case, a battered copy of *The Lion, The Witch And The Wardrobe*.

The surge of magic that pulses from the book makes goosebumps break out over my skin. When I flip the pages open, a low buzzing noise announces something's about to happen, right before the bookcase shimmers and dissolves. In the empty space where it used to be, the air glows.

Pushing through the glowing air feels like walking through jello. I step through it into a black space. Another step and the room lights up. One more, and the wall seals behind me, enclosing me in Sylvia's athenaeum.

All the grimoires are in their places, neatly spaced in the bookshelves. All except one, on the table.

My stomach clenches.

Sylvia is lying face down on the floor. Blood has pooled around her, and kneeling in it makes my magic surge.

My first instinct is to turn Sylvia's face up and push her blood-matted hair out of the way so I can see her eyes. As soon as I touch her, I know it's too late. Her body is cold. The eye I reveal is soaked with blood, open and staring at nothing.

But, no. It can't be too late. There *must* be something I can do.

My mother could use her animal magic to heal people. Maybe I can figure out how to use it to save my cousin.

I push my hands under Sylvia to lever her over. If I can just get—

The thought disappears as I roll her onto her back.

There's a ragged hole in her chest. It's a sight I've seen once before. A sight that still gives me nightmares.

I need to scream. I need to throw up, to get up and run. To do *anything* other than sit here and stare down at Sylvia's chest. But I can't move. I can't breathe.

Where my cousin's heart should be is a gaping chewed hole, like some unseen monster has eaten through her clothes and bone and skin.

Exactly like the wounds that killed my mother.

FOUR

I must have managed to drag Sylvia out of her athenaeum and into her living room, then call the police using Sylvia's land line, though I barely remember doing those things.

There's a buzzing in my head, too loud to hear anything else. I'm sitting on the floor, my arms wrapped tightly around my knees, trying to hold myself together. It feels like pieces of me are trying to break away, to fly into the air, and I have to clench my arms tight so it doesn't happen.

When someone touches my shoulder, I jerk backward, instinctively trying to get away from them, until I remember where I am. A man in a uniform frowns down at me, and I see him studying the blood on my hands and arms. I recognize that expression.

They're wondering just what happened here, and how I fit into it.

A part of me is telling me to run, that I'm going to end up in trouble again, but it's like it's from a long distance. Everything feels muffled, indistinct.

The police officers ask questions and expect me to answer. They move around, looking through Sylvia's house, examining her body. But I can't watch, I can't talk. My chest is still tight and I'm fighting to breathe. They seem very far away. Unimportant. The only thing I can see is Sylvia.

The gaping hole in her chest. The blood, the terrified expression on her face.

The fact that the spell that killed her is unmistakably the same one that killed my mother.

It's all I can think about. Like there's a tunnel connecting both deaths, past and present, and I'm trapped between them. All I can see is my mother lying dead with her chest torn open, and Sylvia with the same tears in her flesh.

I've been trying to figure out what killed my parents for a long time, and now this. But Sylvia's death raises more questions than it answers.

"Are you hurt?" Another man crouches down beside me. In spite of the question, he doesn't look concerned about my health. His brow is furrowed and his eyes are narrow. He's studying me intently.

"Are you hurt?" he asks again, his tone impatient.

The invasiveness of his scrutiny brings a stab of anger to the surface. Instinctively I grab hold of it. Anger is better than the numb shock that's keeping me frozen.

"No." My tone is curt. "But my cousin's dead." As if he doesn't already know that.

His jaw tightens. "I need you to get up and come outside with me, ma'am. There's an ambulance arriving."

The way he says *ma'am* irritates me. He looks only a few years older than I am, maybe late twenties. He's wearing a suit, like an office worker, though he must be a policeman.

"It's too late for an ambulance," I snap. "She's dead." Then I realize the ambulance is meant for me, and look down at my filthy hands. Though they're covered with blood, my magic has fallen silent. Thank god.

"This is Sylvia's blood, not mine." My cousin's blood is in my hair and clothes, and it's soaked into the bandages on my hand. "I need to get clean. I need a shower."

"Not yet."

"But I need to—"

"First you'll be photographed and examined. You can shower once that's done."

I swallow. Like a recurring nightmare, I remember all this from when my parents died. There were three of us there when it happened. My mother was found in our living room with her heart ripped out. My father in the hall, killed by an unexplained explosion. I'd just arrived home and had barely stepped inside when I was knocked out by the blast. Numbed by shock and grief, it took me a while to realize the police were treating my parent's deaths as a double homicide with me as their only suspect.

This time, I won't assume they're on my side.

"Can I help you up, Ms. Black?" Before I can answer, the policeman grips my arm and pulls me to my feet. He's taller than I realized, his shoulders wide. He towers over me, making me feel small and a little fragile in comparison to his bulk.

I *hate* feeling fragile.

"I can walk on my own." I wrench my arm out of his grip. By his expression, I can tell my strength has surprised him.

"Let's go outside." He motions a policewoman to walk with us. It's much busier outside, with flashing lights playing on the house, and men in blue uniforms swarming around it. The front door and gate are both wide open.

"Wait," I say when we get to the bottom of the steps. "Where's Agnes?"

"Agnes?" He frowns. "Who's Agnes?" He looks around as if expecting to see another dead body.

"The chicken. Where's the chicken? And the rat? Is Ratticus okay?"

"Ms. Black, have you had anything to drink in the last few hours? Taken any drugs?"

"Of course not. My cousin owns a rat called Ratticus. The chicken is... it's my chicken. Agnes is her name. I brought the chicken to Sylvia's place because she was going to..." I shake my head. "I needed some advice about taking care of her. It. The chicken."

"Your cousin was a chicken expert?" His eyes are still narrow, but they're sharp, too. He might be big, but he also strikes me as intelligent.

"Of course not. She...just...knew a lot about all kinds of things."

My brain is whirling, but as he watches me intently, taking in my every word and reaction like he's memorizing them for later, one thought surfaces enough for me to single it out. "Who are you, anyway?"

"Detective Trent. I'm in charge of the investigation." He looks at the policewoman who walked outside with us. "Have we found any animals?"

"The cage in the living room is empty, sir. No animals found alive or dead."

Shit. Now, on top of everything else, I've lost Agnes.

"If you find the chicken, will you tell me right away?" My gaze flicks from the policewoman to Detective Trent and back again. "It's important. You can't let anything happen to her." I don't want to be responsible for my neighbor getting killed, or shut up in an animal shelter.

Or eaten.

The thought makes me shudder. I need to find a way to change her back. Fast.

Detective Trent's frown deepens as he studies me. He's no doubt trying to figure out whether I'm completely off my rocker, or just eccentric.

"So, you brought a chicken to your cousin's house," he says without inflection, as though it's a perfectly normal thing to do. "Can you tell me what happened when you arrived?"

"As soon as I walked in the house, something felt wrong." My voice threatens to crack. The memory of walking down the hallway is so clear and strong. And there was that smell. Should I have been able to tell right away that Sylvia was dead?

"The door was open when you arrived?"

I shake my head. "No, it was locked. I have a key."

"What felt wrong about the house?"

"Just a bad feeling. It's hard to describe, but it felt *off.*"

The detective's expression shifts almost imperceptibly. It's not much, but enough to tell me what he thinks of my bad feeling. Too much of the woo woo stuff for this man mountain, apparently.

"When I went into the living room, Ratticus was upset. He'd spilled his food so I turned his bowl the right way up. That's when I noticed Sylvia's blood." I suck in a deep breath as a fresh wave of horror rolls over me. My cousin is dead. It's like the shock lessened for a few minutes, just so it could come back even stronger and wipe me out again. How can Sylvia be gone?

"Then what happened?" asks the detective.

I can't exactly tell him about her athenaeum. "She was on the floor. I called you. End of story."

"Most of the books on your cousin's shelves are occult in nature," says Detective Trent in a matter-of-fact tone.

"Sylvia collected books. She was a researcher." Of course, they're going to think my cousin was a crackpot. Mundanes can't sense magical power, even when it's so strong that the books quiver with it. To the detective, my cousin's books probably look ordinary. And their subject matter is more woo woo stuff for him to dismiss.

"Was she romantically involved with anyone?"

"Not that I know of."

He studies my face carefully, as though trying to tell whether I'm lying. "Why do you think your cousin's neighbors would see her coming and going at all hours?"

"Are you investigating my cousin's death, or just my cousin?" I point back at the house, my voice rising. "Shouldn't you be trying to find out what did that to her instead of wasting your time with innuendo and gossip?"

"*What* did that to her? Not *who* did it?"

I swallow, bringing my anger under control. I have too many secrets to be able to speak unguarded.

"You saw her chest," I say in a calmer tone. "It looked like an animal tore it open."

He nods, looking toward the road. "There's the ambulance. Let's talk more while they examine you."

"I'm fine, I just need to find my chicken. She must be out here somewhere. I can't let anything happen to her." I start to push past him, but he grabs my arm.

He must have learned something from his previous attempt to hold onto me, because this time he grips my arm tightly with both hands to keep me from wrenching free. I try anyway, and get some satisfaction when his expression tells me he finds it tough to hang on. He nods to the policewoman to help, and she grabs my other arm.

"You'll be examined by the medics," he says through gritted teeth. "Then we'll take you for photographs."

"Look, you can take your photos, then I need to go."

"I'm afraid that's not possible. Ms. Black, I'm taking you to the station for formal questioning in relation to the murder of your cousin."

FIVE

"I need to get out of here." I say for the millionth time. "Agnes isn't safe on her own."

The room they're holding me in has no windows and I'm not wearing a watch, but I know it's the middle of the night. It feels like the detective has been sitting on the other side of the crappy wooden desk questioning me for hours.

Detective Trent's suit jacket is slung over the back of his chair and his tie is loose. He has a manila folder in front of him. The whole time we've been here, I've been obsessed by what's in the folder. My guess, it's all the information they have on me. Like one of those dossiers from a crime show, with a photo of me stapled to the front of printed pages of information. Maybe they have my school grades and copies of old speeding tickets.

"Agnes is the chicken, right?" I'm sure Detective Trent's being deliberately annoying. He's playing bad cop, hoping to get me angry enough that I let something slip.

"You should check whether anyone's found her." The thought of Agnes in someone's chicken run, or worse, their dinner pot, is making me squirm. I really would be a murderer if that happened.

"You're not taking your situation seriously enough. Forget about chickens and rats. Tell me about your cousin." Detective Trent leans back in his chair and runs one hand through his short brown hair, leaving it rumpled. It's crazy for me to feel sympathy for him, but he looks almost as tired as I feel. I doubt this is fun for him either.

"You said Ratticus's cage was empty. He's spent his whole life being fed. I don't know how he'll get by on his own."

Maybe the detective's right and I should be trying to convince him I'm innocent. But they won't believe me, so what's the point? Five years ago, I had a different set of detectives riding my ass. I tried to help them, I tried to convince them. I answered every damn question they had a hundred times over, sure they'd eventually see that I was innocent. And then they turned around and arrested me anyway.

I survived that experience. I'll survive him too.

Before they ushered me into this claustrophobic room, a couple of doctors examined me. They took my blood-soaked clothes and gave me a pair of loose pants and a gray shirt to wear. My most comfortable jeans, my favorite pair to work in, are in an evidence bag, probably being sliced up and tested.

Both the pants and shirt they gave me are so big that I've had to roll up the sleeves and cuffs. I look incredibly dorky. Not that it matters. It's not like I'm about to start flirting with the detective, even if he is tall, square-jawed and annoyingly handsome.

"Those scratches." He nods at my forearms, exposed by the shirt's rolled-up sleeves. "What really happened?"

"How many times do I have to repeat myself? The chicken didn't like being carried."

"Chicken scratches," he says thoughtfully, as though this is the first time I've said it instead of the hundredth. "We're scraping under your cousin's fingernails. Will we find your DNA? If it's a possibility, you should tell me now. Things will go a lot easier for you if you're honest."

"Do they look like scratches from a human?" I can't keep the sarcasm out of my voice. "They're chicken scratches. No matter how many times you ask, there's only one answer." I shove my arms toward him, like it's going to change his mind if he's just a little bit closer.

He just watches me, as if waiting for me to change my mind and admit my guilt.

The silence stretches for a moment, and then I can't help myself. "And while we're being *honest*," I emphasize the word, "here's some *honest* advice. The longer you waste time asking the same questions over and over, the less likely you are to find out what really happened to my cousin."

At first I assumed the grimoire had cast its own spell to kill her, but surely Sylvia's archivist power would make that impossible, even without all the protections of her athenaeum. She was born with the means to control the spells contained in any grimoire's pages, so the only way a spell could have killed her was if somebody cast it at her. And that would explain why there was blood in her living room.

The detective sighs. "We'll be here until you stop talking about chickens and rats, and start telling me something that makes sense."

"Then you'd better order us breakfast." I put my hands on the table, twisting the ring my mother left me in her will. She asked me to always wear it, and I do, though I suspect her blood embedded in it might have helped stir up my bound magic. Still, I like having something of hers close.

"That ring," he says, catching the movement. "Is it yours? Or did you steal it from your cousin?"

"What?" A hot flush of anger surges though me, before I catch the sharpness in his eyes. He's just trying to get a reaction out of me. Probably hoping I'll get mad enough to blurt out something I didn't mean to let slip.

I press my lips together and lean back with my arms folded.

"At least tell us where you killed her," he says. "We know she didn't die in the place we found her. We know you moved the body. So if you don't want to spend the rest of your life behind bars, I'm going to need you to start talking."

"All I know is what I've already told you."

With a resigned expression, he reaches for the manila folder. "Then how do you explain this?" He takes out two glossy crime scene photos and places them side-by-side in front of me.

Bile rises in my throat.

One is my mother's body, partially charred. The other is my cousin.

"They look the same," he says. "A hole in each chest. The flesh torn rather than cut, and their hearts missing. What do you think happened to their hearts, Ms. Black?"

Pressing my mouth into a hard line, I look away. The images from the photos are burned into my brain. If you'd asked me two minutes ago, I would have sworn that my memory of the gaping wound on my mother's body is as clear today as it was on the day it happened. But one glimpse of her photo has proven that's not true. Somehow, the horror of it had softened.

Now it's back, full force.

My chest is tight and my throat feels so thick I can't swallow. But I refuse to let him get to me. There's no way I'll let him win this terrible game. I'm stronger now, tougher. I find a way to pull my eyes back to his, refusing to look back down at the photographs even though it takes all my strength not to.

"You were found with the bodies of your parents, and your cousin," says the detective. "Coincidences like that just don't happen." His voice is soft now. It's low and gentle, like a verbal caress.

I hold his gaze, not saying a word.

He probably thinks he has me, because he leans forward as though hoping I'll share a secret. "You know you can tell me anything, don't you? Even if you did something to them. Maybe it was an accident. Perhaps you didn't mean to hurt them. Things happen sometimes. I know, I see it all the time. It's okay. I'll understand."

His brow has a slight crease of concern. His light blue eyes are perfectly clear, like when you can see the sky all the way to the horizon. He's got wrinkles in the corners like he's used to smiling rather than frowning, and his short, dark brown hair is messy. He has a habit of running one hand through his hair every time he feels frustrated. Over the last few hours, he's been frustrated a lot.

Though my throat is still thick, I manage to whisper back, my voice just as soft. "Fuck you."

He lets out an audible breath as though I've disappointed him. He pushes the photographs back into the manila folder, and my relief to have them hidden makes me feel limp. There's a paperclip on the table that was holding the photos together. The detective picks it up and rubs it between his thumb and forefinger.

"I want to help you, Sapphira." It's the first time he's used my first name and I like the way he says it, rolling around the 'r' on his tongue as though savoring it. Apart from that one quirk, his 'good cop' routine is so lame it should be taken out the back and shot.

Still, it's better than his bad cop act.

"If you want to help me, stop wasting time and find whoever did this."

A question I've been asking myself is how did whatever hurt Sylvia get through her magical protection wards? But that's not exactly a line of investigation the police can follow up.

"You inherited your parent's house, didn't you?" he asks. "And as your cousin's last living relative, you're her sole beneficiary. So that's two houses you own now, thanks to your family's convenient deaths."

I blink at him, trying not to let my shock show. Sylvia's house will belong to me now? What about her grimoires? I don't want her house, and I definitely don't want all that magical stuff.

"It doesn't look good for you," he says in a regretful tone. "You understand that, don't you? Seems you're a dangerous person to know, because your family members keep dying." He pauses, waiting for a reaction, and when I give him nothing he shakes his head. "You only live a few blocks from your cousin, but by all accounts you didn't see each other much, did you? Had a falling out? Argue about something?"

"My cousin and I didn't agree on everything, but we were still close. She was *family*."

"What didn't you agree about?"

It's not like I can tell him how I was ostracized after my magic was bound. Sylvia was one of the few to take my side and support me, but she was still part of the community I'd cut ties with. It was just easier not to see so much of each other when there were so many sensitive subjects to avoid.

"Do you agree with everyone about everything?" I ask.

The detective frowns, but doesn't answer. His hands are on the table, still playing with the paperclip while he studies me with his sharp eyes. I drop my gaze to my own hands. Though I wear gloves when I work, my fingernails are torn. The police scraped under my nails and put whatever they found into plastic tubes for testing. Sylvia's blood would have been under my nails. And yes, I moved her body because I couldn't exactly invite the police into her athenaeum. But they can't convict me for a crime I didn't commit.

Except I've watched enough true crime *Netflix* shows to know they do it all the time.

"I don't know why I expect anything from you," I say, my anger rising again. "You just want the easiest answer. You want me to be the one who did this, because it saves you having to go out looking for the truth."

"There's plenty of evidence against you. It'd save us both time if you admit what happened." The directness of his clear blue gaze, as much as his words, makes my stomach drop. He's not putting on an act. He really thinks I was responsible for Sylvia's death.

Before I can argue, the door flies open. A gray-haired man charges into the room. His expression is murderous and it's all for the detective. "What are you doing, Detective Trent?" he demands.

I lean back in my chair, trying to understand the sudden change in situation. I'm fairly sure the man is someone high up in the precinct, because I vaguely recognize him from my last run-in with the police.

"I'm questioning a suspect, Captain." The detective's back has gone stiff.

"She's a victim, not a suspect." The captain steps to one side and another man appears behind him.

My breath catches. It's Magnus Fox, head of the Blood Council, and the one I hold most responsible for the council's shitty behavior. With his long gray beard, he's always reminded me of Gandalf. Except that Gandalf is a good guy and Magnus is anything but.

The air around him tingles with magic, like static electricity. Whatever spell he's using has turned his irises red: a weird, animal-like effect that's particularly noticeable under the harsh, fluorescent lights of the interrogation room. It's only because I'm looking for it that I see a smear of blood on the side of his curled fist, and a smear on the underside of his wrist, just visible under his sleeve. Probably a rune drawn on his arm.

What the hell is he doing here? It's not like Magnus cares what happens to me.

Maybe he doesn't want a witch, even an outcast one, held by the police? Or is he here to punish me for the magic I've done?

My heart beats faster as a third option occurs to me. What if the police aren't the only ones who think I should be held accountable for Sylvia's death? If the council believes I killed her, I'm in real trouble.

Then I see somebody else behind Magnus and my racing heart calms a little. It's Uncle Ray, and if he's come with Magnus, maybe I'll get a chance to tell my side of the story.

As he squeezes into the small room behind the other two men, my uncle's gaze meets mine and he gives me a nod of reassurance. I let out a long, relieved breath. But my uncle doesn't say a word, and I can't tell anything from Magnus's expression. He's concentrating on whatever spell he's using to manipulate the police captain.

"With respect," says Detective Trent. "We haven't yet established—"

"Ms. Black will be leaving with her uncle and Mr. Fox. Be grateful they've agreed to not press charges over your handling of this case."

"Press charges? I've done everything by the book."

"If you don't want to be demoted to traffic duty, Detective, do as I say."

The detective's expression is puzzled and angry. It's obvious he's biting back more protests, forcing himself not to object further. It always surprises me when magic is so obvious and mundanes still don't recognize it.

When Detective Trent looks back at me, a muscle pulses in his jaw. "Looks like you're free to go, Miss Black." The words are tightly controlled. I almost feel sorry for him.

But hanging in the air, left unsaid, are the words: *I'm not giving up.*

I can tell from his expression he's going to keep trying to prove that I killed Sylvia. A tight knot of emotion sits heavy in my chest, and I struggle to breathe again. I saw that same expression on the face of the detective who thought I killed my parents. He hounded me for months, making my life a living nightmare.

For a moment, the room moves in and out of focus. Memories collide with reality, and I'm back there, being pressured to admit to something inconceivable.

"Saffy, come on," says a familiar voice. I cling to Uncle Ray's words, and use them to pull me back to reality. When I look up, he gestures for me to stand, to move quickly.

He's right. We need to get out of here, and fast.

Whatever spell Magnus is using could die at any second, and as soon as it does, the police captain won't be so sure of my innocence.

Standing up, I sneak a look at the detective. He's staring hard at me, like he thinks I'm some kind of master criminal who's foiled his chances of solving the case.

Though I'm glad to get away, I can't help feeling that walking out of here with Magnus is like stepping out of the frying pan and into a blazing demon fire of hell. The powers of the council are far scarier than anything the police could throw at me.

I don't have a choice. I stand up, and walk out of there with Magnus and Uncle Ray, knowing I'd never have managed to get away by myself.

For so long, I've had almost nothing to do with the magical world. I carved out a place for myself as a mundane, I have a business that's doing okay, and a home that's almost back to being how it was before the explosion.

And now, all that means nothing in the face of Magnus's magic. Now my mother's gone, he's the most powerful witch in Baltimore. If it came to a fight, I'd be helpless against him.

Gritting my teeth, I stride along behind him with my fists clenched and every muscle tight. Whatever Magnus Fox intends to do with me, I can't do a damn thing to stop it.

SIX

Walking out the front door of the police station, the sky is unexpectedly light. The street is still quiet, but there's a jogger going past and a man walking his dog. I thought it was still the middle of the night, but dawn has broken.

Magnus's black BMW and Uncle Ray's silver Jaguar are both parked outside the station in a no-parking zone. Of course, neither of them have been ticketed or towed away.

Uncle Ray nods at Magnus. "Thank you for helping, Magnus. I'll take her home."

Magnus grunts and steps forward to shoot me a sharp, narrow-eyed glare. I get a whiff of something funky, like when a dog needs a bath. Then he lets out a disapproving breath through his nose, turns, and slides into his car. As he drives away, I let my fists unclench. My uncle came through for me. Guess I underestimated him.

Uncle Ray gets behind the wheel of his car and I ease onto the cool, sleek leather of his passenger seat. The car looks and smells brand new. It makes me all too aware how filthy and smelly I am. After the police finished examining me, they let me wash my face and hands, but a tingling in my scalp tells me I probably still have dried blood in my hair. All I want to do is stand in a scalding hot shower until the water runs clear and cold, then crawl into bed and sleep for a year.

"Thanks for getting me out of there," I say.

"Mundane laws don't apply to us, Saffy. You know that."

As if I could forget when I'm with him. Life with magic is so easy compared to living as a mundane. My uncle has no idea what it's like to work, or worry about money, or even to come back to his car and find a parking ticket on the windscreen.

He's my mother's brother, and every time I look at him I see heart-breaking reminders of my mother in the length of his nose and the shape of his mouth. He inherited her side of the family's affinity for animals, though his magic is weaker than my mother's was.

"Do you know what happened to Sylvia?" I ask.

"Sylvia was risking her life with those powerful grimoires. She got careless with one of them." He starts the car, checking in the rear view mirror.

"But how could a grimoire kill an *archivist* on its own? And her heart was torn out, just like Mom's. It would have had to have been a dark magic spell to do something like that, and there's no way Mom would have had a dark magic grimoire." Only an archivist could control a book like that, and they'd never think of using it.

"I warned Sylvia to keep her grimoires securely locked away," he says, shaking his head as he reverses out of the park.

"But she did. She died in her athenaeum."

Did the grimoire I saw on the table in her athenaeum kill Sylvia? The room's wards prevent anyone but Sylvia from removing any book. Even if a person cast one of its spells, they would have had to leave the grimoire behind.

"Her wards must have failed." He frowns. "Going into her athenaeum was incredibly dangerous for you, Sapphira. If the grimoire killed a witch as powerful as your cousin, imagine how easily it could have killed you."

"You think my parents were killed by the same grimoire?"

"They must have been. It's the only thing that makes sense."

If he's right, and the grimoire cast its own spell, then it tore out my mother's heart and sent a shock wave through the living room and hallway, killing my father. But there was no explosion at Sylvia's.

"Magnus has called a council meeting to discuss Sylvia's death." My uncle glances sideways at me. "What happened to her was enough of a shock that I'm not going to mention the spell I felt you do. But this is the only time I can hide something that serious. If it happens again, I'll be forced to inform the council."

I shift in my seat, uncomfortably aware of Agnes the chicken hiding out somewhere, hopefully still at Sylvia's. I feel duty bound to turn her back somehow. But Uncle Ray is offering me a lifeline, and I have to take it. "It won't," I promise.

We drive in silence. This early, the streets are quiet, and my uncle doesn't bother to obey speed limits. His graying hair is neatly combed and he's wearing a suit and tie, as usual. If the suit weren't so perfectly pressed, I'd suspect he sleeps in it.

I feel numb and exhausted. My eyes are gritty and my head is throbbing. How many hours since I last slept? I'm too tired to even do the math.

"I think I felt her death," I say after a while, remembering the weird shockwave of magic I'd felt. "I was at the top of a ladder..." I trail off.

That's why my magic surged. Sylvia was part of the council and her death broke one of the bindings they created to hold my magic in check.

"I'll ask Therese to organize Sylvia's funeral," says my uncle.

Now that he's mentioned Aunt Therese, I should ask after her. His wife has been unwell for what seems like years. But I'm too weary to have that conversation now. "The police might not release Sylvia's body for a while," I say instead. "After my parents died, I had to wait for ages before I could hold the funeral."

"I can make sure they release it." He's silent for a moment, then says, "Magnus will be stepping down as head of the council soon."

I frown, not following the change of subject. "Will he?"

"This is my chance, Saffy. I know you like to think you're not one of us. You're a loner, right? Don't need anybody?" His gaze flicks to the clothes the police gave me, so different from my regular ones. "But whatever you believe, I'm here for you, and I think tonight proved it. So, can you do one thing for me? Could you keep a low profile until after the blood moon ceremony is over?"

Anger burns inside me, and I struggle to hold it in. I have to remind myself that I'm grateful to Uncle Ray; I'd still be in that interrogation room if it weren't for him.

But honestly, what the hell is wrong with him? Sylvia hasn't even been dead a full day and all he's worried about is his damn position on the council. And why does he think he has a chance at taking Magnus's job? He's not that powerful.

But I bite my lip, fighting the urge to voice my thoughts. He doesn't deserve my anger, not when he's helping me.

"The police captain that Magnus influenced will make sure nobody bothers you, at least for a while," he says. "I suggested he extend the spell to the detective, but apparently the man's new to the precinct and only has his position because of his family ties. The captain will keep him in line."

I frown, curious about the magic they'd used. "How did Magnus manipulate the captain's thoughts?"

"He didn't. The Veritas did. Magnus was the conduit. He used a rune to channel her magic."

"Can you do that too? Channel another council member's magic?"

A pained expression flickers across his face, there and gone again. "What I *can* do is use my influence to keep the press from being informed of Sylvia's death. This time, I'll make sure there's no media coverage."

"That would be a big help." When my parents were killed, reporters came around and Agnes fed them mean-spirited gossip.

Agnes.

How on earth am I going to change my neighbor back into a person now that Sylvia's not here to help? I have a feeling Uncle Ray's not going to be sympathetic if I admit how big my tiny, harmless spell really was.

As he pulls up outside my house, I see her. A small brown chicken perched on the front windowsill of the house next to mine, peering inside. Not something you see every day on a suburban street in Druid Hill.

Luckily, Uncle Ray doesn't notice her. I thank him quickly and climb out. As usual, there are some stray cats hanging around my front door, waiting to be fed. They come because my animal magic calls to them... but mostly because I buy them cat food.

Hopefully, the cats won't spot Agnes, though she's not exactly defenseless. My savagely-pecked forearms are proof of that.

Because my uncle seems to be waiting until I go inside before he drives away, I wave and let myself, and the cats, into my house. I'll go next door and get Agnes once I'm sure he's gone, and figure out how to change her back into a person when my brain doesn't feel like it's been stuffed with wool.

Inside, the cats wind around my feet, purring while they do their best to trip me. The house is quiet and still. Jess, if she's here, is sleeping.

It feels great to be home, but waves of exhaustion turn my limbs leaden. Maybe I should leave Agnes to her own devices for now. I don't even care that I'm still covered in blood, dust and dirt; I just want to sleep. If I go upstairs and collapse into bed, I can pretend the last twenty-four hours never happened.

The idea of turning back time is tantalizing. All I'd need would be one measly day.

I'd make sure Sylvia was safe, I wouldn't go up the ladder and cut myself, and I definitely wouldn't open the door to Agnes.

Problem solved.

One of the cats meows piteously at me, reminding me of my obligations. Moving like a zombie, I make my way to the kitchen. My dirt-covered work boots are by the back door. Tomorrow is Monday, and I have a rock wall to start work on. Until my overnight stay at the precinct, I'd been looking forward to the job. It'll be a good earner, especially if I can convince my rich client to do even more stone work around his new house.

I've been slowly chipping away at my debts, and for the first time since my parents died, I can see light at the end of the financial tunnel. Not to mention that after years of hard work on the house, I've almost finished repairing it.

Yeah, until yesterday, things weren't going so badly.

I'm moving on autopilot as I get out the cat food from the cupboard. Too much has happened in too short a time, and I can't think any of it through properly. I'll put out breakfast for the strays, then hit the pillow.

Only my hands aren't working as well as they should. They're trembling from exhaustion or delayed shock. When I pick up the heavy bowl I've dumped the cat food into, it slips out of my fingers and smashes on the floor.

"Shit."

With both hands on the kitchen bench, I put my head down and let out a long, tired breath. At my feet, the cats lick up the spilled food.

A door opens upstairs, then the stairs creak. "That you, Saffy?" calls Jess.

"It's me. Go back to bed."

Instead, she appears at the kitchen door. "You're up early."

She's wearing pink, puppy-printed pajamas and fluffy slippers, her long, blond hair messy from sleep. She looks like a fresh-faced college princess ready for a sorority pajama party.

Looks can be deceiving.

Her pink pajamas hide some killer tats, and while the puppies on her pajamas look cute at first glance, on closer inspection they're doing unspeakable things to each other.

Jess frowns at the spilled cat food, and the ugly pants

and gray shirt I'm wearing. When her gaze lifts to my face, her frown deepens. "You okay? You didn't just get home, did you? No offence, but you look like death warmed up." She's already coming forward to pull out one of the kitchen stools for me to sit on.

"It's nothing."

"Did you get something in your hair?" Jess clicks her tongue. "And you've cut your hand."

"It's just a scratch. Looks worse than it is."

"What happened?" she asks.

I don't want to talk about it, but I can't just brush her off. Though I swore never to depend on anybody, I owe Jess everything. Not just the money she pays to rent my spare room, but by watching her, I learned how to fit into the mundane world. She thinks my parents used to do everything for me, because it was the only way I could explain why I didn't know how to do simple things like cooking a meal that didn't taste like old car tires.

She's the one exception to my rule. The one person I like, and the only friend I need. Plus, freckles or not, my roommate just happens to be the best drummer I've ever heard, and a founding member of my favorite band, *the Flaming Buttholes.*

With a resigned sigh, I sit on the stool. "It's a long story."

"I'm awake now. I've got time to hear it."

She pulls a beer out of the fridge, pops the top and hands it to me. I doubt there's another person in the world who would have given me a beer this early on a Sunday morning. Though she's a mundane, Jess's ability to know what people need sometimes borders on magical.

I take a long, slow gulp, then close my eyes to savor the cold liquid as it slides down my throat. "Has anyone ever told you how great you are?" I ask.

She wrinkles her freckled nose. "All the time. Now, spill. Were you out all night and why do you look like that?"

I wish I could tell her. But as cool as Jess is, there's no way she'd understand the world I come from. Not to mention that telling mundanes anything about magic or witches is forbidden.

Besides, what would I say? That my cousin's heart was ripped out, I was arrested on suspicion of murder, and a couple of witches used magic to get the police to let me go?

She'd think I was crazy.

Magic needs blood because it's an inherited power that's tied to family and the life force we share through our bloodline. But if Jess saw me pull out a knife and start slicing, she'd have me committed.

Still, I have to say *something*.

"I went to my cousin's place last night," I start slowly. "You've met Sylvia. She owns Ratticus, the rat I look after sometimes. She was the smartest person I knew. A genius, really. She was kind of distant, but I don't think she meant to be. Her brain was just working on other things." I'm not sure why I want to talk about Sylvia, but it's suddenly important that Jess knows my cousin was a good person, in spite of being a member of the council. "And did I tell you about the time she brought Ratticus over and one of the cats almost ate him? Sylvia loved that rat, but she was good about it. I never saw her get angry about anything."

"What happened at your cousin's place?" Jess asks softly.

"When I got there, I found..." I swallow hard against the lump in my throat. "I found her on the floor."

"Oh no. Is Sylvia okay?"

I shake my head. My face must say it all.

"I'm sorry," says Jess. "Was it a heart attack or something?"

I shake my head again, unable to say the words. Jess squeezes my shoulder, then cleans up the broken bowl and spilled cat food without asking any more questions. I sip the beer and watch as she lures the cats back outside with more food. When she's done, I have myself back under control enough that I can look her in the eyes and lie.

"Sylvia had a chicken," I tell her. "I brought it home to look after, but it got away. It's on Agnes's front porch, and I want to bring it in before it gets hurt."

"A chicken? Really?" She frowns, but obviously thinks better of objecting to our new feathered houseguest. "Where are you going to keep it?"

"In the courtyard out back. It's not ideal, but it'll only be for a little while." At least, I hope Agnes will only have a short stay before I figure out how to turn her back. Good thing our courtyard has a high fence and chickens can't fly well.

"Help me catch it?" I ask.

"Now?" She sighs. "Okay. Let me get changed. Maybe we can lure it over with food. What do chickens eat?"

"Um." I think of Agnes. As far as I could tell, she got by on a steady diet of malice, gossip, and complaining. "I don't know about most chickens, but maybe I'll microwave a TV dinner for her. Then I'm going to sleep for a week."

SEVEN

Blearily opening my eyes, I focus on the glowing digits on my bedside table and groan. Contrary to my expectations, I didn't sleep for a week, but for an entire day. It's Sunday evening, and my stomach is rumbling.

My hand aches, and the scratches on my arms are stinging. Worst of all is the way I can't stop thinking about Sylvia. Every time I remember the way she looked, I have to fight not to break down. I wish I hadn't seen what happened to her, or smelled that horrible smell in the air. I'd give anything to forget the way her hair had clumped together and was sticking to her face, and the awful, gaping hole in her chest.

What did that to her? Could it really have been one of her grimoires?

There's only one way to keep from pulling the covers back over my head and bawling, and that's to find out what really happened.

Dragging myself out of bed, I head for the shower. Uncle Ray told me to lay low, and Detective Trent was pissed about having to let me go. That's at least two reasons to remain at home. If I were sensible, I'd stay here, out of trouble.

Who wants to be sensible?

I don't have a scrap of archivist power, but I need to take a closer look at the grimoire on the table in Sylivia's athenaeum. Dangerous or not, I need to see if it could have caused her death. While I'm at it, I'll see if I can find a way to reverse the spell I cast on Agnes, and look for Ratticus.

Decision made, I glance out the window at the setting sun. The day is over, and although Sylvia's place is a crime scene, surely the police will have finished doing all their forensic tests or whatever by now? Even if they haven't, I doubt they'd work through the night.

After washing and dressing, I go downstairs to find a note from Jess saying *The Flaming Buttholes* are playing a gig out of town tonight, and she won't be back until tomorrow. Good. I was worried she might have awkward questions about the half-accurate, incomplete story I told her last night. And I haven't thought up an explanation for what happened to the stereo.

By the time I've eaten, fed the cats, offered Agnes a microwaved meal, and been viciously pecked several times, it's dark. I leave my pickup truck at home and walk to Sylvia's.

Outside her house, I can't see any cars. Crime scene tape is stretched across the door, and the place looks dark and quiet.

I tiptoe up her front steps, alert for any sound or movement. A familiar tingling sensation tells me Sylvia's wards are active, and should have prevented anyone from the magical community getting in if they were intending to harm her. Set into the fabric of the building by someone living in the house, wards will protect the inhabitants of a place for years, especially wards that were put in place by an earth witch.

Trickier spells, like the one Magnus Fox used to influence the police captain, wear off a lot faster. I can't count on Magnus's influence holding much longer, especially if I get caught sneaking back to the scene of the crime.

The key for Sylvia's front door is still on my keyring, so I quietly let myself in and shut the door behind me, leaving the lights off. My heart beats faster as I start down the hallway. At least the smell from last time is gone. It's a different smell now, a strong chemical tang that I'd probably hate if it wasn't a million times better than the alternative.

Moonlight filters in through the windows. On the floor is a pair of latex gloves the police have left behind. I've been in this house so many times, I can't help expecting Sylvia to call from another room, or appear from around a corner. I can't believe she's not here anymore. That I'm never going to see her again.

I can feel the magic coming from her books as though they're tickling under my skin. Each has its own voice. Not that they make any kind of sound I can hear, at least not with my ears. They have the kind of voices that make my breastbone vibrate and my hairs stand on end.

Usually I can't hear them so well, but the books are loud tonight, probably because of what happened to Sylvia. I wish they could tell me how she died. It would be so much better than having to go back into the athenaeum where I found her. With every step I take, my dread grows stronger.

The living room is so dark that I need to switch on the light to find *The Lion, The Witch And The Wardrobe*. When I open it, and the portal appears, I almost lose my nerve.

But this is the only chance I have to find answers.

Sucking in a deep breath to brace myself, I push through the glowing air, into Sylvia's athenaeum.

My gaze goes straight to the blood on the floor. So much blood. One thing for sure, my uncle was wrong about Sylvia's wards. They *must* be working, or the grimoires would be bursting out of their bindings.

Apart from the blood, the small magical room looks just like it used to. The reading chair with wide arms that Sylvia liked to balance mugs of hot cocoa on is still in place, as though waiting patiently for its owner to return. Knowing she'll never sit there again makes my chest feel tight.

The only thing out of place is the grimoire on the table. Sylvia would never have left it out like that.

Stepping carefully around the blood on the floor, I creep closer. The book is completely and disconcertingly black. Like a black hole kind of black. There are no words on its cover.

Staring at it, I swallow hard. The last thing I want to do is touch it.

If my hunch is right and it's a dark magic grimoire, its power is malevolent. And even benign spells can be tricky things. When a witch casts a spell, it's the magic in their blood that powers it. The stronger a witch's magical lineage, the more potent their blood, the more spells they can perform.

Grimoires amplify magic. The instructions, the potions, the runes described in the grimoires...they're not always necessary to cast spells, but they can amp an ordinary witch up to be more powerful.

Dark magic gets its power from releasing other people's blood. Not just the blood, but the whole process of extracting it. Its power comes from pain and death. Using it is strictly forbidden.

I grit my teeth, sure that I'm not going to like whatever horrors the grimoire holds in its pages. But I need to know.

I reach out slowly toward the book. Good thing I bandaged the cuts on my hands. It's bad enough that there's so much blood in this room, but touching a grimoire with an open wound would be like climbing a lightning conductor during a thunderstorm wearing a tinfoil hat.

Moving gingerly, I brush the cover of the book with the tips of my fingers, then draw back. The book feels icy cold and sends a shiver through me. But no dark magic bursts out of it.

I drag in a breath, gather all my courage, and ease the book open.

All I see are pitch-black swirling pages. No words. No symbols. Now that the book is open, its pages lift and fall softly as though it's breathing.

A terrible sense of menace radiates from it, and it's all I can do not to close the thing.

But I've come this far. I can't back out now.

"Show me," I tell it, picturing Sylvia's hollowed-out chest.

The book sighs, and the noise sends a chill down my back. It sounds wistful. Then the pages flutter, turning themselves. They settle on what I suppose must be the right page, and the blackness swirls like smoke across the paper. From beneath the black, a few words emerge, though they're difficult to read. I sweep my hand back and forth above the surface of the book trying to wave the blackness away.

It clears slightly, showing me a single line of a spell. The words I can see on the page vibrate with so much power they're practically clawing their way off the paper. They're written in reddish-brown ink.

No, in *blood*.

It's a spell, but I can't make out what the spell's called, how to cast it, or what it does. All I can make out is the spell's first ingredient.

The beating heart of a witch.

My stomach clenches into a hard ball as realization washes over me.

Sylvia and my parents were killed because a dark witch wanted their hearts to perform this dark spell.

But what kind of spell is it?

Using dark magic comes at a high cost. It's not just that it's a crime, forbidden by the council. When a witch uses the blood of others they become much more powerful, and a lot of people are drawn to that. But the dark magic corrupts their minds. It turns them insane, and the Blood Council are forced to eradicate them.

It's basically a self-imposed death sentence.

I wave harder over the book, desperately trying to see more of the spell, but the book sighs and the blackness thickens. The page is dark again.

Maybe the wards in my cousin's athenaeum are dampening the magic, keeping the book from revealing its secrets? Perhaps outside this room, I'd be able to see the spell. Problem is, I'll never know, because only Sylvia could take any grimoire out of the—

Wait.

Didn't the detective say I'm Sylvia's sole heir? If so, these grimoires belong to me now. Does that mean I can take the book out of here?

There's only one way to find out.

But even if I can get the book out of the athenaeum, taking it out of the room's wards is so risky, it's probably the worst idea ever. But it's my only clue as to who killed three members of my family.

Too bad about the danger. I have to try.

Without letting myself think too hard in case I lose my nerve, I ease the book off the table. It weighs nothing, like it's made of air, but its icy chill seeps into my bones.

With it in my hands, I touch the wall I came in through. It dissolves for me, just as it's supposed to. Stepping out, back into the real world, I clutch the book as tightly as I can, terrified it's going to open on its own, that its dark magic is going to leech out and the spell will seep out of it like toxic black smoke to rip my heart right out of my chest.

All that happens is that a low-pitched hum emanates from the book, like it's charged with electricity. The sound makes my skin prickle. I don't like holding the book, don't want it anywhere near me. I take it into the kitchen, switch on the bright overhead fluorescent lights to banish as many shadows as possible, and dump the grimoire on the island in the middle of the room.

The last thing I want is to touch it again, but I need to read that spell.

Still, I clench and unclench my unhurt hand a few times, summoning my courage before I reach toward the book.

My fingers brush its pitch-black cover. It feels even colder out here, without Sylvia's protection spells. So cold, it bites.

My heart speeds up as I flip the grimoire open.

The pages still swirl with an inky blackness, and I lean in closer, trying to see through it. My pinky finger touches the open page. Immediately, it's like I'm attached to a vacuum cleaner that's determined to suck me up. My finger feels like it's about to have its bones pulled apart. I can't pull it back out of the book, and the suction is winning the war to drag the rest of my hand down into the page.

"Shit." Panic fills me. A burning blackness steals up my arm, and I lean back, trying to wrench my finger free. A second finger joins the pinky, and there's a moment where it seems like it could go either way. My heart pounds, and the burning sensation makes it to my eyes. As my vision starts to blur, I give one last panic-filled tug on my hand, straining with every muscle in my body. With a grinding pop, my fingers come free and I stagger backward.

I gasp in air to recover my breath. My arm feels heavy and I flick it frantically to get the feeling of darkness off me. I should know better than to be careless around a dark magic grimoire. And now the bandage is hanging off my hand, all but ripped loose by the book. One tug is all it takes to get it right off, and I shove it into my pocket.

The book is still open, humming with energy. I really don't want to touch it again, but

I can't just leave it there, especially not lying open. Who knows what could happen.

Steeling myself, I inch forward and reach for it with my uninjured hand.

Something scratches my foot.

I jump back, letting out a strangled curse as I kick out, desperate to kill the horrifying dark magic monstrosity that must be attacking me.

Ratticus squeaks and takes off toward the living room.

"Ratticus," I gasp, pressing my hand over my thumping heart. "I scared you even more than you scared me, huh?"

I drag in a breath, then quickly flip the grimoire shut. "Stay," I mutter, before turning to take care of Ratticus. The poor rat might not understand what's going on, but I'm pretty sure he's hungry.

Grabbing some rat food from the cupboard under the sink, I follow him into the room where Sylvia was killed.

"Ratticus," I call. "Come on, boy. I have food for you. I'll take you home and look after you."

I catch a movement under the couch, and bend to put my hand on the floor, palm upturned and open, some pellets temptingly displayed. Though my animal magic is bound, faint traces of it run through me, the way a strong scent will permeate everything around it, and Ratticus is scared and looking for comfort.

Moments later, I feel whiskers tickle my palm. Ratticus sniffs my hand, then cautiously emerges from under the couch to pick up and eat one of the pellets.

"Good boy, Ratticus," I whisper, reaching out my other hand to gently pat him. He jerks away, clearly still freaked out, and I make soothing noises. "It's okay, little guy. You want to come home with me? It's safe there, and there's plenty to eat."

When he moves forward again, I grab him, standing up with him in my hands. He holds completely still for a moment, then cuddles against my chest, chewing on his pellets.

"Must have been a bad day, with lots of policemen here scaring you," I murmur. "You found a hiding place though, didn't you? Shame you can't talk and tell them I didn't kill Sylvia. Let us all know what really happened."

I look over to his cage, trying to figure out what I'll need to take with me. I can't carry the whole cage, but perhaps the wheel and his food bowl? Cradling Ratticus against my chest with one hand, I drag Sylvia's backpack out of her closet and put his food into it. Oh, and I'd better take his water bottle.

Ratticus is scratching my palm with his small sharp

claws, his nose twitching as I reach for the bottle at the back of the cage with my other hand. He makes to dart out of my grasp, and I jerk to one side without thinking, trying to keep him captive.

The open wound on my palm scrapes against the wire that usually holds the cage door closed, pulling the flesh apart again.

"Ouch."

As I snatch my hand back, blood wells in the tender wound. Both types of magic surge, swift and brutal. Before I can stop them, they've forced open the gap in the council's bindings.

My mother's ring glows, suddenly bright. Its glow surrounds Ratticus, filling him with animal magic.

Suddenly I can smell dog. But not just any dog. Dead and rotting dog. The stench is so thick it makes me gag. It envelops me, closing in and suffocating me.

All I can see are blurry shapes I can't make sense of. No colors, just black and white. A couple of people, perhaps? A large animal? The shapes are too distorted to make out, as though I'm seeing them through a strange lens.

A snarl comes from the thing that stinks like decaying meat and dog hair. No, it's a voice, isn't it? But it's deep and raw, like no voice I've ever heard before.

Then I hear something else and realize with a jolt that someone's talking in a weird language. Are two people talking? Arguing? The sense of threat coming from the rotting dog is unmistakable.

Wait a minute, do I know one of the voices? Could it be Sylvia? Why does she sound so strange?

Then she screams, the shrill sound stabbing painfully into my ears. I hunch over, every hair on my body standing on end. Fear makes my throat close. I have an overwhelming urge to run, or to dig a deep burrow and curl into it...

As suddenly as it began, it's over. The world returns to normal, and I'm once again standing beside Ratticus's cage, the rat clutched in one sweaty hand.

The animal magic is spent, but my earth magic still arcs through the air, sizzling like a live electrical cable, searching for a release. When earth magic was all I had, it was far less violent, and I knew enough spells that I could focus and control it. But the animal magic has made it a lot stronger, and I'm trembling all over, about to drop. I barely make it to the nearest chair before every light fitting in the house explodes. The BANG is so loud it shakes the house. Glass showers down like rain.

Instinctively, I curl in the chair, Ratticus nestled against my chest. Sylvia's rat is shaking as hard as I am. His black eyes watch me and a strange sensation rolls up my spine.

What I saw was a vision. No, not a vision. A *memory*. And I pulled it straight from Ratticus's little rat brain.

He saw Sylvia's death. And now I've seen it too.

Only nothing was clear. Ratticus doesn't see like humans do. He can't detect colors and his vision is blurred. He doesn't understand spoken language and couldn't make out human words.

But he does have one thing. An amazing sense of smell. And the stench of rotting meat and dog hair is still lingering in my nostrils, stronger than the smell of smoldering wires from the burnt-out light fittings.

That smell belongs to whatever it was that killed Sylvia.

And that's a clue I can work with.

EIGHT

I'm still in the chair with Ratticus on my lap when I realize Uncle Ray is probably trying to get hold of me. He would have felt me use my magic again and he'll be pissed.

My legs are limp because the force of the vision sucked every bit of energy out of me. Still, I drag myself up, put Ratticus back in his cage, then go to the hallway where Sylvia's phone sits in one of her bookcases. Uncle Ray is the last person I want to talk to, but I dial anyway. Best get it over with, before he has time to get himself worked up.

He answers his phone with an exasperated sigh, not bothering with a hello. "What happened this time, Saffy?"

"I'm at Sylvia's place. Ratticus hadn't been fed since before she died. I was worried."

"Ratticus?"

"Her rat."

"Ah." He has animal magic too, so this explanation seems to satisfy him.

"I was holding Ratticus when I reopened an old cut. Then I saw something through Ratticus's eyes."

"What did you see?"

"Sylvia's murder."

"*What?*"

"It turns out that rats can't see very well," I say, not wanting to give him false hope. "The whole thing was blurry. Faint shapes with sharp smells. I heard Sylvia talking and couldn't understand a word she said. But I smelled the thing that killed her."

"A grimoire?"

"I don't think so. Whatever it was smelled horrible. Like a dead dog."

"A dog? That makes no sense."

"I know. But Uncle Ray, you didn't see Sylvia's chest. It wasn't cut open, but torn. Like with *teeth*."

"And you think a dog could have done that to her?"

"I don't know what to think." Not yet, anyway.

"You're still at Sylvia's house?" he asks. "What if the police find you there? Magnus's spell might have worn off by now, and they're probably already wondering why they ruled you out of their investigation so easily."

"I'm about to head home." Uncle Ray is right, I need to leave. I glance over my shoulder toward the kitchen, and the grimoire. I can feel its magic pulsing, even from here. What am I going to do with it?

"Good." He sighs. "I'll need to tell Magnus about what you experienced. But I'll do my best to convince him that using magic was an accident and you shouldn't be held responsible."

"Do what you have to, Uncle Ray," I say softly. *And I'll do what I have to as well.*

In Sylvia's bathroom, I find a fresh bandage for my hand, and then I look around the house, trying to see if there's anything I might need. I might not be able to come back any time soon. I'll definitely take Ratticus and his supplies with me.

And the grimoire.

The dark spell book calls to me, its magic alluring and seductive despite the danger, and I reluctantly head back to the kitchen. As much as I don't want to take it with me, it's the only choice. I'm determined to find out what that spell says, but to do that, I'll need help.

Though dark magic is forbidden, there's one man who might be able to help me. An archivist, like Sylvia, though this witch isn't part of the magical community. I've been out of the community for years, but before I left there were rumors he might be dabbling in dark magic himself.

The rumors were bad enough, I wouldn't have believed I'd ever consider willingly visiting him. But if he's still alive, maybe he can help me read the spell.

I gingerly slide the dark magic book into Sylvia's backpack along with Ratticus's food and supplies. The thing is freezing, and still giving off a low buzzing sound that makes my skin prickle. It's a relief to zip it inside the bag.

When I pick Ratticus up again, he runs up my arm onto my shoulder and curls himself into my neck. Probably a good place for him to stay, hidden by one of my thick pigtails.

The walk back to my place isn't far, but the darkness, the grimoire I'm carrying, and the stink of dead dog in my nostrils make it unnerving.

"Everything's going to be okay," I say to Ratticus as I stride along the sidewalk, trying to keep my voice at a low murmur. "We'll be home soon. I won't let any rotting killer dogs get you."

When I first catch the faint sound of dogs baying, I assume I'm hearing things. The soothing nonsense I was murmuring to Ratticus must have made me imagine the noise.

But as I round the final corner to my house, it gets louder. Somewhere in the distance, dogs are snarling, growling and barking. The sound's coming from behind me, and quickly rising in volume. As soon as I turn my head, my heart lurches into my throat.

There are lots and lots of dogs galloping toward me. They're a few blocks away, but closing in fast.

My heartbeat kicks up, and the grimoire's magic hums a little louder.

I turn and run. The thundering of paws on concrete, barking and snarling comes closer and closer. Their baying is high-pitched and excited, like they've just caught the scent of their prey.

Me.

The noise is terrifying. An image of Sylvia's torn-open chest flashes in front of me and I put my head down and sprint. Ratticus chitters in my ear and his claws scratch painfully into my skin. He's trying to burrow into me to escape our pursuers.

I race as hard as I can toward my house, which is only a couple hundred yards away. The noise is so close now that I glance back, even though it slows me down. The first of the dogs is just behind me. A huge Rottweiler with a foaming mouth and glowing eyes.

On its heels are other dogs almost as large, their powerful legs thrusting them forward. They're all focused on me and their eyes have the same chilling, magical glow. They're running so fast, they'll be on me in no time.

I piston my arms up and down, running for my life. My muscles are burning, my breath comes in painful gasps and my backpack is thumping painfully against my back, but I keep running as fast as I can.

It's going to be close.

The wards around my house are designed to stop magical threats, and magic must be what's compelling the dogs to hunt me. If I can make it onto the front step, the dogs won't be able to follow. But if the old, fading wards fail, and the dogs manage to break through, I'm dead. I'll never get my front door open before they tear me apart.

My lungs feel like they're going to explode and my vision is blurry. I'm almost there, but I can hear jaws snapping right behind me. Just three yards to my front step. Two yards...

Pain explodes in the back of my leg, just below the knee. I tumble forward and land hard on the step, twisting as I fall.

The Rottweiler's jaws dig into my calf, his fangs tearing through my jeans. Behind him, the other dogs leap forward, baying with excitement.

The other dogs hit the wards and the invisible barrier knocks them back as though they've landed against a force field. Most of my body is inside the protection, but one lower leg is still outside. And the Rottweiler still has hold of me. It's pulling me, trying to drag me back into the street.

Desperately, I grab hold of the stair rail and yank myself away from the Rottweiler, lashing out with my heavy boot. The dog doesn't even flinch when my boot slams into it. Another dog tries to latch onto my foot, but its teeth can't penetrate the thick leather of my Doc Martins. I kick it away, desperation adding weight to the blow.

With all my strength, I pull myself toward the house, trying to jerk my leg away from the enormous dog's mouth. I let out a scream of agony as the Rottweiler's teeth tear through my flesh. Blood pours from my calf and my magic almost gleefully surges free.

It's weaker than before, used up by the vision I just had at Sylvia's. But with so much of my blood flowing, it's out before I can think about trying to control the power.

My animal magic pours into the lead Rottweiler. The beast yelps. Its jaws loosen and I scramble onto the next step. Amazingly, my legs are free and my whole body is inside the protection of the wards. I gasp out a relieved breath.

And then I look up.

My magic is changing the dog.

It's making it bigger.

Before my horrified eyes, its body grows, its hair lengthening as its eyes glow even brighter. Without conscious intent to drive the magic, my fear must have powered it. Now the dog truly is a monster. It pushes against the wards and they start to bend under the strain, their magic pulsing unsteadily. The big Rottweiler's growl is loud enough to shake the ground, and its eyes glow like a hellhound from a horror movie.

My earth magic is still searching for a release. It slams into the sidewalk beneath the dogs, smashing it and throwing chunks of concrete into the air. The dogs don't so much as flinch as the stones rain down on them, but the wards shudder and spark at the unexpected burst of power.

The glowing eyes of the dogs are fixed on me, foam dripping from their mouths as they yip and snarl and bay, hurling their bodies against the invisible barrier. With a shock, I recognize one of the dogs. Mrs. Jenkin's poodle lives a few doors away, and the gentle old dog has always wagged its tail madly when I've stopped to pat it. Now it's snarling and leaping against the barrier with the rest, its eyes glowing red as it batters against the wards.

My blood is splattered everywhere, the leg of my jeans soaked with it. The denim is torn, my wounds gaping open and my flesh mangled. But even with my blood still flowing, my magic is spent.

I push myself backward up the steps until my back-pack hits the door, my breath coming in ragged gasps. The dogs won't stop. They'll throw themselves against the house's already-shaky wards until they break through. I don't know how long it will take—two minutes or two hours—but sooner or later the wards will fail under the pressure.

I need to get inside as fast as I can and call for help.

But when I drag myself up, my head swims. I've lost a lot of blood, and it's still gushing out of me. The bottom half of my leg is all chewed up and when I try to put my weight on it, searing pain screams up my leg. Balanced on one foot, I dig my key out of my pocket and force it into the lock with shaking hands. Then I stagger inside and slam the door, spattering blood as I go.

The closed door doesn't do much to muffle the sound of the dogs. They're going mad outside, fighting to get through the barrier.

Help. I need to get help.

My vision is blurry. I use the wall for support as I half-hobble, half-fall toward the living room. The pain is intense. It's dark inside, but my mother's ring is glowing so brightly it lights my way. I'm leaving blood everywhere. On the wall, on the floor. My hands are wet with it.

The living room feels a million miles away, and by the time I get there I'm sobbing with the effort. I must have blood in my eyes because I can barely see. All I can hear is my own ragged breath, and the frenzied barking from just outside.

Is it getting louder? Could the dogs have broken through the barrier? Are they about to start hurling themselves against the door?

Grabbing the phone, I peer at the numbers, blinking to clear my vision. Then I start punching in Sylvia's number before realizing what I'm doing. *Shit*. I'll have to call Uncle Ray.

My finger hovers over the buttons, but I can barely see them now. They're blurry smudges and I don't know which ones to press.

My good leg gives way and I slide down the wall and land heavily on the floor, sending a jolt of agony through my bad leg.

Dial, Saffy.

But how can I dial when I'm so dizzy, I see three phones instead of one? A wave of nausea hits me and I retch.

Something huge and heavy hits my front door with a mighty crash. The wood cracks.

The house's magical wards have given way. Now the only thing protecting me from the dogs is a door that's already breaking under the strain.

Another loud slam against the door, and it's all too easy to imagine the wood splintering. Whatever compulsion the dogs are under, it must be a strong spell.

I should shut myself in a room to put another door between the dogs and me. But every movement sends such a fire of pain up my leg, I'm afraid I'll pass out.

Blood has pooled on the floor under me and is smeared on the walls. The glow of my ring lights it up, gives a glint of red to the black liquid. So much blood. I probably would have passed out already except for the cold, stark terror that's making my heart beat like the hooves of a galloping horse.

The dogs slam against the door again and again. It's going to give way any minute. The dogs are going to come charging in here, jaws snapping and eyes glowing, set on tearing me to pieces.

I need to do something. And there's only one more thing I can think of.

With my teeth clenched, I grab the wound on my leg. My blood is hot, pulsing between my fingers. Closing my eyes, I reach deep inside myself. For the first time in years, I urge my magic to come out, coaxing every last scrap through the gap in the bindings.

The magic is all but spent. But even the small amount still inside me feels like holding twisting strands of fire.

I don't know a single spell for my animal magic, and without a rune or incantation to focus the energy, any magic is difficult to direct, especially the tangled chaos mess inside me. I picture the dogs yelping and afraid, trying to change their bloodlust to terror and drive them away. But my animal magic feeds on my fear. Instead of working on the dogs, it amplifies my panic.

Dogs appear around me, black snarling creatures with bright, glowing eyes.

My heart stutters with fear. I didn't hear the door break. How did they get inside?

They lunge at me, but their mouths go through me like ghosts. These dogs aren't real. They're just shadows, a magical manifestation of my fear. They bark and snarl and salivate, trying to tear me to pieces, and I screw my eyes shut, willing them away.

Even as the animal magic fades, my earth magic is still alive, still searching for an outlet.

With the last of my strength, I silently scream a single word, forcing it into my earth magic as it arcs toward the ground.

HELP.

Amazingly, my earth magic catches the word. It carries it into the ground, sending it out in a physical ripple. The word is a shockwave, radiating out from me, twisting rock into sound. Sending my desperate plea through dirt and stone.

The force of it empties me.

But the animal magic is empty too.

The shadow dogs are gone now, thank god. Both types of magic are exhausted and I'm as weak as a newborn. If–when–the real dogs get through the door, I won't be able to lift so much as a finger to stop them.

The best I can do is try not to pass out.

Only my best isn't quite good enough.

NINE

I'm drifting in and out of consciousness when I realize the noise has stopped. No more barking. All I hear is one of the dogs whining.

Could the spell have been broken? Or is something worse about to happen?

I hear the door handle turn. The door creaks open.

Footsteps echo from my hallway.

I want to call out, but my voice is stuck and won't come out of my throat. Who's there? Could it be whoever was controlling the dogs?

"Ms. Black?" It's Detective Trent's voice.

A surge of relief floods through me. "I'm here," I manage to say through teeth that chatter with pain.

A light clicks on in the hallway and I blink in the sudden brightness. Then Detective Trent strides into the living room. The light is behind him and my vision is blurry, so he's little more than a silhouette. Still, from my position on the floor, he looks like an enormous avenging angel.

An angel with a gun.

"Is there somebody in the house?" he hisses.

"No. Just me."

He holsters his weapon, then goes down on one knee beside me, his gaze raking over my wounds. "What happened?" Without waiting for an answer, he glances around, grabs a painting rag from next to the pile of paint tins, and binds it tightly around my thigh.

"The dogs," I say. Talking is an effort. I'm shaking, and can't get out more than a couple of words. I'm freezing too. Probably because of the blood loss.

"There's blood all over your door and front steps."

"What are you doing here?" I manage.

He frowns, tying the rag in place. "I'm not sure. Somehow, I knew you were in trouble. I guess the notification must have come over the police scanner. I must have half-heard it."

Police scanner, my ass. He felt my magic. But how on earth did he feel it? He's not a witch.

He tugs his phone out of his pocket and dials. "Send an ambulance," he says into the phone.

"I don't need—"

He's already giving them my address.

When I got hurt as a child, my mother always healed me, smoothing away scrapes or bruises with a touch of her hand. But I can't heal myself with magic, and I don't want to ask Uncle Ray for another favor. Going to a hospital might be my only option.

The detective hangs up, then disappears upstairs. He comes back with a blanket and pillow I recognize as Jess's. He must have taken them off her bed. But I don't get time to object before he's tucked the blanket around my body, leaving my chewed-up leg sticking out. And truth be told, I'm glad for the warmth. Hopefully the blood will wash out of the blanket.

"I need to elevate your leg," he says, holding up the pillow. "Okay to slide this under it?"

"Okay."

"I'll get this backpack off you first." He helps me lean forward, away from the wall I'm propped against, works the backpack over my arms and drops it by my side. "Now, can I shift you so you're lying flat?"

"I can do it." I push away from the wall to lie on my back. With my head down, I feel a little better. Not so dizzy. And my teeth don't chatter so much.

"What the—?" Detective Trent points at something. "There's a rat running toward you."

"Ratticus?" What a relief. I was afraid he might have been eaten by the dogs. I put out my hand, but Ratticus ignores it. He nestles into the blanket instead, pressing himself against me.

"You were talking about a rat when I interviewed you," the detective says. "Is that it?"

"Poor guy has had a rough day."

"The *rat's* had a bad day?" He sounds incredulous. "What happened to your leg, Ms. Black? You said there were dogs?"

"Will you find a box for Ratticus?" No doubt the ambulance will be here soon, and I want to make sure he's safe.

"A box?"

"In the laundry." I don't have the strength to argue with him, so I'm profoundly grateful when he fetches a cardboard box without insisting I answer his questions first, and follows my directions to get some food out of the backpack for Ratticus. Like a typical mundane, he doesn't give the grimoire more than a passing glance. He probably can't hear it buzzing.

"Careful," I say when he picks up Ratticus. "He's a biter."

The words are barely out of my mouth before the detective curses. "He got my finger." He drops Ratticus into the box. "The rat doesn't have rabies, does he? I'm bleeding."

"Good thing an ambulance is coming. Need to use my tourniquet?" I glance at the bloody mess that used to be my leg, then try for a sarcastic eye roll. Harder than it sounds when you're flat on your back with most of your blood soaking into the floorboards.

He shoots me a 'not funny' look. "You still haven't told me what did this to you."

"Give Ratticus some water and something to burrow into," I say, though I can already hear a siren. "And check the chicken's okay. Out the back." I motion weakly to the courtyard.

"Are you serious?"

"It's important."

"What is it with you and animals?" He walks to the back door and peers outside. "Okay, I see the chicken. It's roosting on the back of your bench seat. Looks like it's asleep."

Phew. I close my eyes and concentrate on trying to slow my breathing. When the paramedics arrive, they put me on a gurney, hook me up to an IV, and load me into the back of the ambulance. They stick sensors over my chest before leaving, and I hear the detective say he's going to follow behind in his car.

At the hospital, a doctor examines my leg. "You've lost a lot of blood," she says. "Any more and you would have needed a transfusion. The wounds are deep, but the bone isn't broken." She frowns. "What did this?"

"A dog bit me."

She blinks. "That's one heck of a dog bite. Are you up to date with your tetanus shots?"

I shake my head. I've never been in hospital before. Since my magic was bound, I guess I've been lucky.

"Do you have anyone I can call?" asks the doctor.

Jess, maybe? But she's playing a gig out of town. I shake my head again. "Nobody." Most of the time I like it that way, but right now the word sounds like an admission of failure. Like I must have screwed up my life pretty badly to have to face the cold white walls of the hospital alone.

"What are you going to do to my leg?" I ask.

"I'll have a nurse clean the wounds and give you a tetanus shot and antibiotics. Then I'll stitch you up."

"Then I can go?"

Detective Trent appears in the doorway of the small room, and the small leap my heart makes when I see him is a measure of how low I was feeling. At least he's not a complete stranger, even if he's not exactly on my side.

"I'll send the nurse in." The doctor's already turning for the door. "We'll have you out of here in no time."

"How are you feeling?" asks the detective, after the doctor leaves.

"Peachy," I say with a grimace.

"Will you tell me what happened now?"

"I was walking home when some dogs chased me. I ran for my door, but one latched onto my leg before I could get inside. I fought them off, then you arrived."

"What about the torn-up sidewalk in front of your house?"

"Maybe the dogs wrecked it."

He gives me a skeptical look. "Whose dogs were they? Have you seen them before?"

"I don't think so." I think of Mrs. Jenkin's poodle and

feel bad for lying. But the dogs were under a spell. It wasn't the poodle's fault.

"I saw some dogs at your door when I arrived. One was a real monster. Biggest dog I've ever seen."

"That's the one that got me."

"They scattered when I got close. They didn't try to bite me. So why you?"

I shrug.

"Could somebody have set them on you?"

"Maybe." Clearly somebody in the magic world was directing them. Might they be the same dogs that attacked Sylvia? But it wasn't a pack of dogs in Ratticus's memory, just one snarling shape. And it had a human voice, for all that it was deep and raw and had a definite snarl to it. Besides, the dogs that attacked me didn't smell like they were rotting.

"Who might want to hurt you?"

"I wish I knew," I say, frustrated. I shift a little, then wince.

"It hurts?" he asks.

"Like a Disney musical."

"A Disney musical?" he repeats with a puzzled frown.

"The most painful thing in the known universe."

He gives me a startled smile. A *sincere* smile. The first one I've seen him give. It changes his face, stripping away the stern detective and revealing the less-complicated man underneath. I was right about the laugh lines around his clear blue eyes: they fit him perfectly. I'm not completely sure how the deepening of laugh lines can make an already-handsome man look even more so, but it's something about the way they soften the hard, masculine angles of his face.

"Come on, everybody likes those movies. What's wrong with them?"

"The singing. And the animated princesses with the giant doll eyes and perky button noses. But mostly the songs with the relentlessly peppy lyrics that make me want to carve out my eardrums with..." The rest of the sentence fades as he cocks an eyebrow in a way that makes me wish he wasn't a homicide detective who thinks I'm a killer. That much hotness should be against police department rules. "Never mind," I say, mostly convinced the blood loss is making me hallucinate.

"Let me see what I can do. Wait here for a minute." He turns toward the door.

"Wait. Where are you going?"

"To find the nurse and ask her to give you something for your pain."

"Are you coming back?" I hate how needy that sounds, but I don't want to be by myself. He's no friend, but he's better than nothing. Talking to him distracts from the pain.

And the fact he's wearing snug blue jeans and a white T-shirt that molds to the shape of his muscles? That has absolutely nothing to do with it.

"I'm not going anywhere," he says.

"Okay. Whatever," I manage.

The look he gives me seems to say he's got me all figured out. Dammit.

After he leaves, I close my eyes, telling myself to relax. I feel simultaneously exhausted and wired. How late is it, anyway? It feels like the middle of the night.

Eventually the detective comes back in with a nurse pushing a trolley.

"I'll give you a shot first, love, then clean that up," she announces, peering at my leg.

She takes something from her trolley and holds it up.

It's a needle, only much bigger than I expected. Surely not human-sized.

"That's not really the needle, is it?" I ask. "That's a trick one you use to scare children."

"It'll be over in a second."

"Don't tell me you're afraid of needles?" asks Detective Trent.

"Ask her where she found that thing. I bet it was at the top of a magic beanstalk."

"Lift up your sleeve," says the nurse.

I do what she asks. My leg is already throbbing, so how much worse can it get?

To my surprise, Detective Trent gives me a reassuring quirk of his lips. He draws up a chair so he can sit by the bed, and I catch a hint of his aftershave over the smell of hospital antiseptic.

"Okay, all done," says the nurse after a moment. "See, that wasn't so bad, was it?" She picks up a bottle and swab. "Now I'll clean your wounds."

She bends over my leg, and I wince when the swab touches the raw cuts. Pain shoots up my leg. I feel cold and a little faint, and I'm not looking forward to having the deep cuts stitched.

The detective reaches out to rest his hand on my arm. My eyes flick up to meet his blue gaze and I breathe in oaky aftershave.

"You're a mystery, Sapphira," he says softly. "I thought you were a tough nut to crack, but look at you, scared of having your wound treated."

"I'm not scared."

"You're pale."

I don't feel pale. In fact, I'm pretty sure my cheeks are flushing.

"I was dizzy for a moment," I say. "Massive blood-loss, remember? I'm fine now."

He nods as though he believes me, but as the nurse drags her swab over my wounds, his hand stays on my arm.

And I don't ask him to remove it.

TEN

I wake up slowly the next morning. I'm in my own bed, with the sun shining in through the curtains, and I have a raging headache that's only overshadowed by the pain in my leg.

How did I get here?

I lie still for a moment, trying to remember what happened last night. After the nurse gave me something strong for the pain, my memories are hazy.

Wait a minute. Did Detective Trent drive me home?

Flashes of memory include visions of him carrying me to bed and tucking me in. I shake my head. That can't be what happened. I seem to remember running my hand over his chest, and that's clearly impossible. Must have been a dream brought on by the medication they gave me.

I want to get up, but when I move, pain shoots up my leg.

Shit. I need to pee.

Dishes clatter downstairs in the kitchen. Jess must be home. That's a relief. When she plays a gig out of town, she doesn't usually get home until late the next day.

"Jess," I call. "Can you help me get up?"

The clattering stops. "Be there in a minute," calls back a male voice. Definitely not Jess.

Surely not the detective?

No, it can't be. Maybe it's Uncle Ray? But why would my uncle be clattering around in the kitchen? And if he were here, wouldn't he have healed me by now?

Footsteps sound on the stairs and I struggle up to sitting, wincing and biting my lip.

The door opens.

It's Detective Trent. He's carrying a plate of food and a glass of water, and wearing the same jeans and white T-shirt he had on last night.

As he walks in, he glances around my bedroom. I look too, suddenly a little self-conscious about my treasures from the past. I grew up in this room, and I haven't had the heart to change everything. The desk in the corner is the one I used to do homework on. My track and field trophies are still on a shelf, and there are some old band posters on the walls. There's even a Flaming Buttholes poster I put up the year before I met Jess.

"I made toast and fried you an egg," says the detective. "There's almost nothing in your fridge except beer. How do you get by with no food?"

I blink at him. Maybe the dream I had wasn't a dream after all, and he really did carry me up the staircase and put me into bed. That would explain why I'm still wearing my bra and yesterday's T-shirt. They cut my jeans off in the ambulance, but I was in too much pain to worry about modesty. Besides, my panties are the sensible cotton boy-leg variety.

Come to think of it, I've lost two pairs of jeans in as

many days. If I lose any more I'll have to start wearing sweatpants to work.

"How are you feeling?" the detective asks, crossing to my nightstand to put down the plate.

"You brought me home?" I raise my eyebrows. "No offense, but what are you still doing here?"

"You were groggy, nobody else was home, and I didn't think it was a good idea to leave you alone. I slept on your couch."

"Thanks." It's weird that he didn't leave, but if he hadn't brought me home I'd still be in hospital. And he made me breakfast.

I reach for the plate, then frown at the fried egg which is sitting on one of the pieces of toast. "We have bread," I say. "But where did you get the egg?"

"You have a chicken."

"Um. You mean the chicken in the courtyard? Agnes? She laid an egg?" I pull my hand back from the plate, a horrible mental picture flashing through my mind. "I...uh...don't like eggs."

"You're not allowed any more painkillers on an empty stomach."

"That's okay. I'll have something later."

"Here, take the toast. That piece doesn't have any egg on it."

Seeing as he's not going to take no for an answer, I pick up the piece of toast.

"I may as well eat the egg. No sense in wasting it." He motions to the bed. "Mind if I sit?"

I shake my head and he sits on the edge of my bed, being careful of my sore leg. He puts the plate between us. He's going to eat it right here in front of me.

I swallow.

It's fine.

Agnes is a chicken now, not a person. Chickens lay eggs. People eat eggs all the time.

But when he puts a mouthful of egg between his lips, my stomach turns over. As much as I want to, I can't look away.

"Let's talk about what happened last night," he says, after swallowing.

"What happened last night?" I have a sudden, vivid image of my face nestled against his T-shirt, his scent enveloping me as he carried me up the stairs.

Oh. My. *God.*

This can't be happening. I can't have the hots for the detective who thinks I killed Sylvia, and probably my parents too. No, that's ridiculous.

"The dog attack," he says with a frown. "Now you're feeling better, let's go through it again. What happened, exactly? Because I checked, and there were no other police reports about vicious dogs. You were the only person attacked."

"That's why you stayed the night? So you could keep interrogating me?"

"I told you why."

"But you think I'm a murderer?"

He puts his knife and fork down, and licks egg yolk off his lip. "Whether you did it or not is what I'm trying to find out."

"And anything I say could be used against me?"

He tilts his head a little, studying me. "In my line of work, I see all kinds of messed-up things. Once I attended a scene where a man had beaten his mistress to death, then went home to tuck his kids into bed and read them a bedtime story. And there's been worse than that. People who do things you'd never think them capable of." He shakes his head. "But when it comes to you, I don't know. Your cousin was killed in a particularly brutal way, but last night you were scared of getting an injection. It doesn't fit. And I have a lot of other questions. Why call the police after murdering your cousin, when you were still covered with her blood? What did you do with her heart? And this morning, there were a dozen stray cats on your doorstep. There's barely anything in your fridge, but you have a cupboard full of cat food. Why is that?"

I let out a breath. "I haven't hurt anyone."

"That's what everyone says."

"What would make you believe it?"

"Tell me everything you know. Anything that might be useful."

"I already—"

"We both know there's more going on here than you're telling me. Please don't lie to me, Sapphira."

I stare into his blue eyes, the early morning sun making them seem even lighter than before. How much can I tell him? Am I really considering breaking all of my rules?

"You can trust me." His voice is soft. And dammit, those *eyes*. What am I supposed to do when he looks at me like that?

"Help me get up and I'll show you something," I say, cursing myself for being a fool even as I say the words.

"What?"

"You'll have to wait and see."

"Okay." He nods at the plate. "Finish your toast first."

"Bossy, aren't you?" Still, I want the painkillers, so I eat the toast. Then I really do have to pee, so I push back the covers. "Can you get me some sweatpants out of that drawer over there?" I ask, pointing where I want him to go.

He helps me put them on, averting his gaze while I pull them up. Then I grab some clean underwear and a faded *Public Enemy* T-Shirt, and hobble to the bathroom.

After cleaning myself as best I can with a bandage on my leg that I'm not supposed to get wet, I emerge from the bathroom feeling a little better. The restorative powers of clean clothes and brushed teeth are highly underrated.

I'm still going to have to call and postpone the masonry job I was supposed to start today, though. There's no way I'll be moving any rocks until my leg heals.

Detective Trent is downstairs in the kitchen, and I can hear him cleaning up.

"Detective," I call. "Is my backpack down there? The one from last night?"

"It's here."

"Would you please bring it upstairs? The thing I want you to see is up here."

"Xander," he says, when he joins me at the top of the stairs, backpack dangling from one of his big hands.

"Huh?"

"My name is Xander."

I raise my eyebrows. "Unusual name."

"Protector of men," he says cynically. "My mother had big plans for me."

"Okay, Xander. You can call me Saffy. Now, follow me."

I wish I'd said yes to the crutches they offered me yesterday as I hobble along the hallway to my parents' old bedroom. Xander waits patiently behind me while I use the key I keep hidden in my dresser to unlock the door.

"What's this?" he asks, stepping inside.

"My investigation room."

Actually, it was my parent's bedroom. Their bed is still

here, but I pushed it against the wall so I could move in a desk that's covered with paper. Mostly my own scribbles as I've tried to work things through.

All over the walls, I've pinned notes, pictures, newspaper articles, and anything else I could find that might help me figure out who, or what, killed my parents. Lined up on shelves are some of my mother's weird dog figures, and her old dog paintings are on the walls with everything else. Her animal affinity was strongest with dogs, and her thesis was called *Canine Art: an Examination of the Representation of Mythological Canines Throughout History*.

I used to have all this stuff hidden inside the attic, especially when I was still a suspect and the police would periodically barge their way into my house. About three years ago I decided it was safe to bring everything out and pin it where I could occasionally stare at it and try to figure out what I've missed. It doesn't prove anything other than I've been obsessively searching for answers for a long time.

I look at the clues around me, my stomach tightening with the new knowledge that some kind of dog is involved. Could it have something to do with my mother's studies? Maybe one of the canines she was researching turned out to be not so mythological after all.

Turning, I try to assess Xander's reaction. He's moving around the walls, backpack still dangling from one hand, inspecting the information I've pinned up. It's everything I thought might be relevant, including notes I've made detailing spells and magical connections.

When he stops in front of the piece of paper where I sketched out the wards around my house, my heart speeds up. The wards are broken now, thanks to last night's pack of dogs, and I have no way to repair them. They weren't designed to protect against mundanes, but only repel anyone or anything magical that intended harm. I wrote the details out on paper, trying to see any gaps. If somebody did kill my parents, how did they get into the house while leaving the wards intact?

Now the detective is studying my diagram, and I can't see his expression. I'm taking a big risk showing him all this. Nobody but me has ever seen it. All Jess knows is that this is my parent's old bedroom, and she thinks I keep it locked because their things are in here and I can't bear to go in. No mundane is supposed to know about witches, and now I'm telling Xander everything. Breaking not just my own rules, but the council's rules too.

I'm not even sure why I'm doing it. If Xander were a witch, I'd suspect he'd put me under some sort of spell. My mind just keeps jumping back to how he took me home from the hospital last night, and made sure I was safe. He took care of me, and he doesn't even know me.

It might be good to have someone like that on my side.

He studies the paper in silence for a long time. When he finally speaks, he doesn't turn toward me, so I still can't see his face.

"Those books, that occult stuff your cousin was mixed up in. Your parents were into that as well?" The question is quiet, but tension hangs in the air.

"Yes."

"And you? Are you into the occult?" Finally, he looks at me. But his expression is unreadable.

I shake my head. "They banned me."

"They?"

"The council."

He frowns. "The Baltimore City Council?"

"The Blood Council." I catch my breath, half expecting something bad to happen now that I've said the words out loud. As though Magnus might be listening, planning to strike me down with a bolt of lightning.

"Blood Council? Who are they?"

It's not until he says it that I realize how sinister it sounds. Next time I see my uncle, maybe I'll suggest the Blood Council come up with a friendlier name.

"They're the eight most powerful witches in Baltimore. They make sure nobody breaks the rules, and if there are any problems, they're supposed to solve them." I wrinkle my nose. Now's not the time to explain how badly the council let me down.

"Witches," he repeats slowly. "And you're a witch?"

He doesn't believe me, that's obvious. He's probably mentally measuring me up for a white jacket with long sleeves that buckle behind my back.

"I am." I wince. "Well, I used to be."

"You think you can do magic?"

I shake my head. "Not anymore. When my parents died, I experienced a magical overload which messed things up. The council bound my magic to keep me from accidentally blowing things up and turning people into chickens."

"The eight people on this council, can you give me their names?" His eyes are narrowed, and I can tell what he's thinking. He's so busy wondering what mischief a group of crazy people who think they're witches can cause, he totally missed my chicken confession.

"No. The council would kill me. Actually, they wouldn't kill me, but there's a living statue spell they can cast and believe me, death would be the better option."

"If these people believe they can do magic, I need to speak to them. They could be involved in your cousin's death."

"You wouldn't get close enough to them to talk. You'd

probably forget their names and what you were doing there before you even got a word out." I shrug. "Besides, I doubt the council know any more than I do. Except there is one thing I haven't told you. Sylvia was attacked by some kind of dog."

"A dog? What makes you think that?"

Ratticus's memory is vivid in my mind. My nose wrinkles as I recall that awful stench. But I'm not going to tell him I saw the murder through the eyes of a rat. He already thinks I'm delusional.

"You saw her wounds," I say. "Those were bite marks. I think a dog ate her heart right out of her chest."

His mouth tightens and I can tell he doesn't believe me.

"I have something else to show you," I say before he can argue. "There's a book in that backpack. Take out it and put it there, on the desk."

He does what I ask, moving aside my papers to clear a space for it. The grimoire is still humming, but he doesn't seem to notice.

"What do you see?" I ask.

He shrugs. "A book with a black cover. Not very informative." He reaches out and before I can stop him, flips it open. "Black pages inside. What kind of book is it?"

"Plain black pages?" I ask. "Nothing moving?"

He frowns at me, puzzled. "You see something different?"

I edge closer to it, wary of its power. "Clouds and shadows," I murmur, trying to make out what's beneath the blackness that swirls over the pages like an inky mist. "The book's hiding its spells underneath that dark layer." Not to mention that its pages are rising and falling like a sleeper's chest.

Xander shoots me look that's as clear as if he asked, '*Are you kidding me?*' out loud.

"Show me," I mutter to the book, picturing the spell I glimpsed in Sylvia's athenaeum.

The book's pages rustle, but don't turn. The blackness doesn't budge.

It wants my blood. I don't know how I know this, I just do. It's keeping itself hidden on purpose, hoping I'll give it what it wants. What would happen if I cut my hand and squeezed a drop of blood into the book's dark pages?

Nothing good, I'm sure.

"So it's a *magic* book," says Xander in a disbelieving tone. "Do you need to say Abracadabra to make the words appear?"

"You can't hear it?" I ask. "You can't see the pages move, or the mist swirl? It wasn't icy cold when you touched it?"

He gives me another one of those sideways looks, but before he can tell me how crazy I am, his cellphone rings. He tugs it out of his jeans and answers with a gruff, "Yes." He pauses to listen, then asks, "Okay. What does that mean?"

His eyes flick to mine as I watch him. Hopefully the call isn't about something that'll make me suspect number one again. I've taken enough of a risk showing him this room as it is. I don't want him to try and take it all downtown as evidence.

"Good. Do that. Bye." Xander's words are short and terse. I can't tell from his expression what he's thinking when he tucks his phone back in his pocket.

He stares at me for a moment. "They tested for foreign DNA on your cousin's wounds and found saliva that wasn't human. Matched with some distinctive tears in her flesh, they think she could have been mauled by a dog or wolf."

I let out a breath.

"How did you know that?" he demands.

"I told you. There were bite marks."

"But how did you know it was a dog and not some other animal?"

"Like what? You think Ratticus could have done that kind of damage?"

"Maybe the same dog bit you."

"No." I motion to my leg. "This is an ordinary dog bite. Whatever killed Syliva..." I can't exactly tell him about the rotting dog stench I smelled, so I change what I'm going to say mid-sentence. "The dog that killed Sylvia had to have been bigger."

"I saw the one that attacked you, remember. It was a monster."

I shake my head. "When it attacked me, I accidentally made it bigger. Okay, I know you're not going to believe me. But I'm certain it wasn't that dog."

I can tell by his expression that he thinks I'm knitting with only one needle.

"Hard to believe it was a dog attack at all," he says, mostly to himself. "An animal would usually maul a body in several places, not just the middle of the chest."

"Did they find dog saliva in my mother's wounds too?" I hold my breath for his answer. If I'd known about the dog connection years ago, maybe I'd have made more progress.

He shakes his head. "They weren't able to collect any usable DNA evidence from your mother's body. The heat from the fire..." He trails off, glancing back at the piece of paper where I've detailed the house's wards. "How many of your occult friends have dogs?"

"I know someone who might know more about what kind of dog it might have been. A lecturer who worked with my mother at the university. Mom studied dogs, so it's a big coincidence if she was killed by one. Her friend might know more about what my mother was working on when she died."

"Tell me who it is and I'll go question her."

"She won't talk to you. I'll need to go too."

The idea sends a rush of enthusiasm though me. After all these years, I'm finally making some progress. And I'm glad I have something to do other than messing with a dark magic grimoire. The thing gives me the chills, and I don't know enough about magic—my own, or any other kind—to feel safe around it, or around the man I'd thought to take it to. I'd rather lock it in here for safekeeping and follow a different lead.

He shakes his head. "You can't come with—"

"I've been looking for the answers to what happened for *years*. There's no way you're leaving me behind." I stare into his baby blues, hoping he sees how serious I am. "If you don't agree, I'll just go and talk to her on my own." Not that I can drive with my mangled leg, but I'll find a way to get there.

He sighs. "Has anyone ever told you how stubborn you are?"

"That's my best quality." Though I've been standing too long and my leg is aching, I hobble to the door. "Let me change into my last pair of jeans, then we'll take your car, okay?"

ELEVEN

"I don't see why you had to bring that damn chicken," Xander grumbles as we drive along the highway toward Maryland University with Frank Sinatra crooning about flying to the moon on the radio. I'm itching to change the station, but manage to control the urge.

Agnes is secured in a large cardboard box on the back seat. I asked Xander to find a box that was big enough, and when I went to the courtyard to get her, I discovered her busily spelling out the word HELP with pebbles. As soon as she saw me, she launched herself at my face with claws and beak outstretched.

I'm glad Xander wasn't with me to see it, because I would have had to tell him the truth about her and he'd still refuse to believe me.

Fun fact I've learned about chickens: darkness makes them go to sleep. That means she's not currently trying to kill me. I did collect plenty more scratches to add to my collection while I was getting her in the box, though.

"I'm hoping Mireya will be able to help me with

Agnes," I say, glancing over at Xander. "Not that she'll want to. But I'm hoping to convince her."

"Help you with the chicken?"

"You'll see," I tell him. At least he will if I can talk Mireya into changing Agnes back into a person again.

I shoot another sideways glance in his direction. We stopped at Xander's place so he could shower and change, and he's wearing a suit again. I much prefer him in a T-shirt and jeans, but whatever cologne he put on smells amazing. And though I'm a big fan of stubble, he looks just as good clean-shaven.

"It had better not get out and mess up my back seat," he warns.

"Don't worry." I wave my hand airily. "Your car isn't that fancy." In fact, his car is the kind of sensible, dark-colored sedan I'd expect a police detective to drive. Completely inoffensive, except for one thing.

Frank Sinatra.

Blurg. It reminds me of the kind of tedious music they play in department stores that's designed to lull people into a compliant stupor.

"Tell me about this friend we're going to see," Xander says, oblivious to my mental pain.

"Mireya's not exactly a friend." I finally give in and lean forward to change the station. There's only so long I can be trapped in a confined space with Frankie.

Nothing happens when I push the button and I realize it's a CD. Who listens to CDs these days? Especially CDs of Frank Sinatra.

"You have any other music?" I ask.

"Nope. Who's this woman if she's not a friend?"

I frown at the speaker as Frank warbles about filling his

heart with song. His clichés spew forth like diarrhea after a bad Mexican takeout.

"She was my mother's best friend, but she might not want to help us." I frown at the speakers. "Who listens to this music? Seriously, are you a hundred years old?"

He glances at me then back at the road. "Why are we going to see her if she's not going to help us?"

"I thought you might be able to use your charm."

He barks out a laugh. "My charm?"

"I'm assuming you have some, despite never having seen it myself. How else did you get to be a homicide detective so young?"

Instead of being amused by my teasing, his jaw clenches. "Through hard work and solving cases," he says through gritted teeth.

I raise my eyebrows. "Did I hit a nerve?"

"Don't be ridiculous." His voice is still tight.

"Someone tell you that you're not charming enough?"

Shaking his head, Xander keeps his eyes on the road. "Tell me about this friend of your mother's."

I watch him for a moment, wondering whether to push it. But it's not worth annoying him over, especially as he didn't want to bring me along in the first place. "She's a horticulturist, a biologist, and a historian. Lots of degrees. She lectures on the role of plants and animals in different cultures and traditions."

"I doubt your mother's research into ancient dog myths could have had anything to do with the deaths. We'd be better off talking to someone who studies animal behavior."

"Trust me," I say. "The answers we need aren't something a mundane can help with."

"A mundane?"

I motion to the stereo as another song starts, this time

with a different dude singing the same rotten elevator music. "What fresh horror is this?"

"Dean Martin." He shakes his head, frowning. "Oh, come on. Don't tell me you don't like this. Everyone likes Dean Martin."

"Everyone in the *old folk's home.* Don't you have anything *good*?"

"Like what?"

"Preferably something with guitars and drums." I tell him. "Slip Knot, or Marilyn Manson, or Eagles of Death Metal. Although anything from this century would be an improvement."

"So instead of the soothing and uplifting tones of Frank Sinatra or Dean Martin, you'd rather listen to a cacophony of discordant noise created by untalented musicians who can't sing or play an instrument?"

"Sounds perfect. Got any of that?"

We spend the rest of the way to Maryland University arguing about music. But when he finally pulls the car into the university campus, we're both laughing.

"I win," he says, a grin splitting his features. His awful music is still playing, and I've been singing along in a high falsetto, pulling exaggerated faces and clutching at my heart.

"I don't think so," I sing in the same falsetto voice, my laughter almost ruining the effect. The last few days have been full of shocks, and laughing feels strangely cathartic right now.

I'm almost sorry we've arrived.

Climbing out of the car, my leg is stiff and sore. Xander sees me wince.

"You okay?" he asks. "Need me to help you walk?"

"No, I'm good. Can you bring the chicken?"

"Bring the chicken," he repeats, shaking his head. "I don't know if you're the crazy one, or I am." But he gets the cardboard box out of the back.

I hobble next to him up the path to the main building, and ask for Dr. Mireya Oswolde. Her office is just down the hall, which is lucky because my leg is killing me. When we get to the door, I raise my hand to knock, then hesitate. Last time I saw her, Mireya said some nasty things to me. Maybe it was the shock of her best friend being killed, but there's a good chance she believes I ripped my own parents to pieces. Xander shifts the cardboard box he's carrying to one arm, then leans over and knocks for me.

I glare at him.

"You were getting cold feet," he says, unrepentant.

"I wasn't—" I cut off my reply as a tall, elegant woman opens the door. She's wearing a long black dress that looks way too somber for a sunny Monday morning. Her long, black hair hangs almost to her waist. If she were wearing a pointed hat, she would have made the cover of *Witches Today*. I have to make an effort not to roll my eyes.

She glares at me. "Sapphira Black. What corner of hell did you crawl out of?"

"Nice to see you too, Mireya." I incline my head toward Xander. "This is Detective Trent. Did you hear Sylvia was killed? The detective's investigating her death."

"I heard you were there when she died. Funny how that keeps happening. Thought you'd try your trick of stealing somebody else's gifts, did you? Taking your mother's wasn't enough for you?"

She's being coy because of the detective, saying 'gifts' instead of 'magic'. I've heard her theory before, but it still cuts me to the bone. How could she think I would kill my own parents? Especially for extra magic I never wanted, that messed up everything I had and destroyed my life as I knew it.

I'd ask how she thought I could use my mother's gifts exactly, let alone Sylvia's, but I'm so angry, I'm not sure I can form words. Besides, she's not worth it. Who cares what she thinks?

Xander steps forward, holding the cardboard box in front of him. "May we come in, Ms. Oswolde?"

She hesitates for a moment, then steps back and waves us in with ill grace.

Her office is large and filled with plants. Vines tumble from pots hanging from the ceiling, and her decorative houseplants are the size of trees. The air is heavy with the scent of the stunning flowers that probably bloom all year around, thanks to her plant magic.

Other than all the greenery, it looks like a normal mundane office. Almost. There's a small ceremonial knife on her desk posing as a letter opener.

Sitting forward in Mireya's visitor's chair is her husband, Dallas Oswolde. He's wearing a black suit, but his skin is very pale and his hair is white. He's an albino, with eyes the palest blue I've ever seen, several shades paler than Xander's. He's the strong, silent type, and he's usually lurking somewhere not far from his wife, as though he can't bear to be separated from her.

I've never much liked Dallas.

Dallas and Mireya had a whirlwind courtship and were married only weeks before my parents died, but even in that short time I saw his nasty side. I overheard him telling my uncle that he should stick to politics rather than spell casting because he was so much better at it. A statement I have to admit is probably true, but it was the way Dallas said it, with a sneer in his tone, that made me realize how arrogant he is.

He looks down on anyone who's less powerful, which is just about everybody.

I have no doubt he sees me as less than nothing now I have no magic I can use. And sure enough, his lip curls as he stands and wipes his palms on the legs of his black suit trousers. What is it with these two and the color black? Okay, so I'm wearing a black T-shirt, but at least mine has a band name on it.

"Dallas," he says, introducing himself to the detective. His eyes flick over me as though I'm not worthy of a greeting.

Xander nods back."Could I ask what your relationship was with Sylvia Black?"

"She was a friend," says Meriya.

"When was the last time you saw her?"

There's another chair beside the door, and I push a hanging tangle of honeysuckle flowers aside so I can sink into it.

Meriya glances at her husband. "A week or so ago." Dallas nods his agreement. He's never been much of a talker.

"Why?" adds Meriya. "We're not suspects, are we?"

Xander walks to her desk and puts the box down, then turns to face her. "I understand you're a biologist? What's your level of expertise when it comes to dogs?"

"Dogs?" She raises her eyebrows. "Is that what you've got in the box?"

Now I've managed to swallow my hurt, sarcasm rises in its place. "Sure," I mutter. "It's a box full of Rottweilers. How many university degrees do you have?"

Xander ignores my interruption.

"Do you mind if I speak to Ms. Oswolde alone?" he asks, looking at Dallas.

"I want my husband to stay," Meriya motions him back into his chair. "Now, what do you want, Detective?"

"What was Mom working on when she died?" I interrupt. "Was she studying a particular kind of dog? One that could have killed her?"

Mireya lets out a breath. "You're blaming her work now?"

Xander shoots me a frown. "I need to know what kind of dog might be able to tear open a person's chest."

"Tear it open how? Do you have a picture?"

He flicks through his phone to find a picture, then shows it to Mireya, holding it away from my line of sight.

Mireya shudders and her hand creeps up to cover her mouth. "That's horrible."

Dallas stands up to look over her shoulder at the phone, his mouth twisting. Then he stares at me with narrowed eyes, as though trying to decide whether I have it in me to do something like that. The pink rims of his eyes stand out against the paleness of his skin, and I find his gaze a little disconcerting.

"Is that what happened to...?" Mireya hesitates. "Was Nala killed the same way? They told me she died from a chest wound, but I never imagined anything like that."

Nala is my mother's nickname, only used by family and close friends. Hearing Mireya use it so casually makes my chest tighten painfully. She was my mother's best friend, always at our house, and more like family to me than some of my actual family. Many of my favorite memories of my childhood include Mireya as well as my mother.

And now she thinks I killed my own mother, for magic I can't even use. If my parent's death was like a knife being stabbed directly into my heart, Mireya's belief that I could have killed them is like the knife being turned in the wound.

"Yes," says Xander, his expression grave. "I can show you more photos if it'll help."

Mireya glances at me and I see a flicker of uncertainty cross her features.

Finally.

One photograph's done what all my protestations couldn't, and cast doubt in her mind about whether I'm to blame.

"It's unusual," she says. "You'd expect a dog to go for a leg or hand first."

"There were no other wounds on the body. Just the chest."

"I suppose somebody might have trained it to do that. You're sure it was a dog?"

I shake my head, recalling Ratticus's memory of Sylvia's death. "More likely they used magic to control the dog," I interrupt. "I think a witch either conjured a large dog creature or took on a dog's shape. Is that possible? I thought I heard it talk with a growly half-human voice."

Both Mireya and her husband look shocked that I'm talking about magic and witches in front of Xander. The detective doesn't look happy either. He narrows his eyes, a muscle pulsing in his jaw. Okay, so I didn't tell him about hearing the thing talk. He wouldn't have believed me anyway.

"I don't know what you're talking about," says Mireya, while Dallas sits back in his chair and folds his arms, his pale lips pressed together.

"I already told him all about us." I motion to Xander. "He knows I'm a witch and the killings had to be magical."

Mireya draws in a sharp breath. "He's mundane. It's forbidden to—"

"He's the only one interested in helping me find out what happened to Sylvia," I interrupt, my voice rising. "I don't care about the council's stupid rules. Whatever it was that did this to Sylvia killed my parents too. His help is all I've got, and he can't go stumbling about in this blind. He needs to know the truth."

She folds her arms, her posture mirroring her husband's. "Sapphira, you know we've both been appointed to the council. We'll have to tell Magnus—"

"Fine. Tell him whatever you want. Just help me work out what did this. I found a dark magic grimoire in Sylvia's athenaeum, and one of its spells uses a still-beating heart as an ingredient."

Her face pales. "A *dark magic* grimoire? Even protected in an athenaeum, that's risky. You didn't touch it without an archivist present, did you?"

"Of course not." I only just manage to control the urge to cross my fingers behind my back. I can't even imagine which particular archivist she thinks would help me. Hopefully the stupid grimoire isn't sucking my house into some horrible black magic vortex even as I lie to her. "I couldn't read what the spell did, but could somebody have used it to create a dog-creature? Maybe some kind of doggy demon?"

Her face jerks toward her husband, and they have a short, silent conversation with their eyes. They must reach an unspoken agreement, because Mireya turns to the large bookshelf that's all but hidden behind trailing flowers, and pulls out a book. "Some demons do take on dog shapes in our world. It's impossible to *create* them." She sniffs at my ignorance. "But perhaps one has been pulled onto our mortal plane."

Xander's expression gives nothing away, but I can sense a tightness about him. I don't think he believes a word of what she's saying, but maybe he's starting to wonder. The alternative is that we're all crazy, and that must be hard to believe in the gentrified surrounds of Maryland University.

"Could Mom have accidentally summoned a demon?" I ask. "And if she did, what kind of demon might it be?"

She flips though the book's pages. "The Cadejos spring to mind. They're Guatemalan spirits who take the shape of dogs. As do the Adlet, half-human half-dog creatures from Inuit mythology." She looks up at me. "Your mother had an Adlet artifact. Is it still there?"

I nod, though I'm not sure which artifact she's talking about. Mom had a lot of them, most displayed on shelves, but the most potent ones in her safe in the basement. "All her stuff is still in the house, and her safe is sealed and warded. Nobody but me can get into it."

She frowns. "You should have let Magnus—"

"She left her things to me," I interrupt. "For the last time, the council can't have them. Let's move on." It was a point of contention after my parents died, and I'm not about to let her start the argument again. A lot of my parents' stuff was destroyed in the explosion, and magical or not, I'm not handing over the rest for no good reason.

"Your mother's Adlet artifact could theoretically be used in a summoning spell. But so could many of her artifacts. And the Adlet had the hind-quarters of a dog, but a human head."

"We're looking for something that has a dog's mouth, but can still talk."

Mireya turns another page. "There's Teju Jagua, a lizard god with seven dog heads. Last recorded sighting was in Paraguay. I believe Nala had a picture of the god on her bedroom wall."

I glance at Xander. "Shouldn't you be writing this down?" I'd do it myself, only I didn't think to bring a notebook with me.

"The Yao people in China speak of a dog demon called Panhu, born from a golden worm." She inclines her head to one side. "That one hasn't been confirmed. Might just be a story."

Xander isn't looking at me, and he hasn't made a move to take out the notebook he keeps in his jacket pocket. He clears his throat. "Ah. Yes. Okay." His tone suggests he considers this a waste of time. "Going back to the theory that somebody trained an animal to do this, could it have been another type of dog? Perhaps a wolf? Or a coyote?"

"A jackal," says Dallas unexpectedly. "Mireya, what about Jeqabeel's bone?"

Mireya frowns. "Your mother kept it in her safe. Are you certain all those items are secure?"

"The wards stop anyone getting in, right? So it's secure."

She huffs. "You have to let Magnus check the wards to make sure they're still active."

"Council members don't get invited into my home. Especially not Magnus."

"We'd know if it were Jeqabeel," says Dallas. "There'd be a lot more deaths."

I raise my eyebrows at Mireya, and she puts the book she's holding onto her desk and takes another one out of her bookcase. "Jeqabeel is an ancient jackel-headed demon." She puts the open book on her desk so we can see it. "Here. This is Jeqabeel."

Xander and I stare at the picture in silence. An enormous hairy creature stands on its hind legs, big enough to hold a dead body in each hand like dolls. It has the head of a jackal but its body is human, although covered in a thick pelt of hair. It has a barrel chest and long claws coming out of hands that look more like paws.

"Your mother had a bone said to be from Jeqabeel's thigh. It was the only remaining fragment of the demon's physical form after it manifested into our dimension in the eighteen hundreds. A demon cannot die, so in theory, its essence could still be present in the bone. It was secured inside a case, and your mother was careful never to handle it."

"What's that building behind it?" asks Xander.

I peer at the smoking ruin, littered with bodies. What remains of the building looks familiar.

"The Library of Congress," says Mireya, her head cocked as she studies it. "The demon killed tens of thousands, and the Blood Council of the time blamed the deaths on a hurricane."

"But the Library of Congress can't have been destroyed," I say. "It's still there."

"They rebuilt it. It was the largest concentration of witches in history." Mireya waves a hand. "The depiction is accurate."

I wrinkle my nose at the bloody corpses lying at the demon's feet. Clearly not a live-and-let-live sort of creature. "And nobody thought to tell me a piece of this demon was in my safe?"

"Magnus said you refused to talk about your parents' possessions."

"I might have been more chatty if he hadn't bound my magic, then left me to fend for myself."

Mireya makes an impatient noise. "You must allow

Magnus to check the safe. If the bone's untouched, it wasn't involved in the killings. Let him rule it out, and check your mother's other artifacts to make sure they haven't been tampered with or used in any spells."

"Not Magnus," I say, teeth gritted. "Besides, who'd want to summon a demon? Surely nobody would do it on purpose?"

She shakes her head. "I can't begin to guess."

Xander makes a move toward the door. "Thank you for your help," he says, his voice carefully formal. "If I have any more questions, I'll be in touch."

"Wait." I step over to the cardboard box on Mireya's desk. "I need your help with something else." After unsticking the tape holding it closed, I ease the top of the box open. I'm ready in case Agnes flies at me again, but she just blinks sleepily.

"A chicken?" Mireya raises her eyebrows.

"Actually, she's my neighbor," I admit, careful not to glance at Xander. "Turning her into a chicken was an accident." Telling her what I've done is probably dumb, but I have to try to free Agnes somehow.

"That's a difficult spell." Mireya frowns. "Your magic is bound."

"Sylvia's death created a gap in the binding. When my magic escaped, it took me by surprise. I couldn't control it."

"Ah." She hesitates, looking at her husband. "Transforming flesh takes animal magic. Your uncle is better qualified to help."

"Can't you use one of your potions?" I wave my hand at her plants.

"One of my *potions*?" She repeats the word as though it's the worst insult possible.

And to a plant witch, it kind of is.

I wince. It's been too long since I was in the witching world. "An elixir. No, an essence, right? One of your concoctions, whatever you call it."

I'd forgotten how touchy witches with plant magic are about the brews they extract and mix for their spells. They're the only witches who create potions, both for their own use, and for other witches, so they're closest to the hated mundane image of a warty hag stirring a bubbling cauldron.

Bit of a sore point. Whoops.

She aims a glare at me, slipping her hands into the box to hold Agnes for a moment. "No essence can undo your spell. The transformation used both animal and earth magic, and the strands are tangled. It's too complex to unravel."

Dallas meets my gaze with his light eyes. "If that's the case, a witch would have to manipulate both earth and animal magic to undo the spell. You're the only one who can."

"But I can't undo it," I say desperately. "I have no idea how I managed to do it in the first place."

Mireya shrugs, and her husband's arrogant gaze moves back to the detective as though dismissing me.

"How am I going to make her human again?"

Xander picks up the cardboard box. "Time to go," he says.

Mireya steps in front of the door. "Sapphira, you must allow us to check your mother's safe. If you give Magnus access—"

"Magnus Fox isn't stepping a foot through my front gate." I push past her and open the door. Then turning back to face her anxious expression, I relent. "Uncle Ray can do it. I'll ask him to come over and take a look. Okay?"

"Yes," she says quickly. "Good."

"And if the wards have been deactivated? If the safe is empty? What then?"

Mireya blinks, considering the question, while Xander joins me outside her door, the box under his arm. She glances back at Dallas and her expression hardens. "If a demon has managed to enter this plane, we'll need to figure out what kind it is. Something like Jeqabeel would have the potential to kill us all."

"Great," I say brightly, starting down the hall. "At least that'll solve my chicken problem."

TWELVE

"What a waste of time," says Xander as we drive away from the university. The song torturing my eardrums is one I've heard during more than one elevator ride.

"You still don't believe any of it?" I ask, disappointed.

He shoots me a sideways look. "A dog-demon came out of a bone and killed your cousin, you turned your neighbor into a chicken, and witches built the Library of Congress. What's not to believe?"

"We're not sure about the bone part yet. Weren't you paying attention?"

"You have some kind of make-believe club. That's what this is. Like those people who dress up to re-enact the civil war, only you pretend to be witches and warlocks."

"Both men and women are called witches. Contrary to popular belief, the word isn't gender specific. And it's not like you're drowning in other leads, is it? So, what's the harm in humoring me?"

"I have real work to do. While I'm out with you, carrying chickens and chasing demons, other cases are going unsolved and a ton of paperwork is piling up on my desk."

"Will you lend me your phone?"

He shifts so he can tug it out of his pocket and hand it to me. "Who are you calling?"

"My uncle. Fair warning, there's a chance I could accidentally fry your phone. Lately I've been getting surges."

"Surges?"

"More of that stuff you don't believe." I shut off the stereo, finally getting to kill the awful music. Then I punch in my uncle's number.

He answers on the second ring. "Hello?"

"Uncle Ray, it's Saffy."

"What's wrong? Are you in trouble?"

"Everything's fine. I just need to ask you something."

"Oh." He sounds relieved it's not something more serious. "It's lucky you caught me. The blood moon ceremony is coming up, and with all that extra magical energy around, the number of disputes the council needs to deal with has exploded. I've been run off my feet." He sounds cheerful, rather than annoyed. I guess he likes dealing with all that stuff.

"We've spoken to Mireya, and—"

"We?" His tone sharpens. "Who's we?"

"Oh." I curse myself for slipping. "Well, the detective is with me. The one investigating Sylvia's death."

"You shouldn't be talking to a mundane, let alone a police officer. Get rid of him, Saffy. Tell him to leave the house."

I don't correct his assumption that I'm at home. "Would you come over and take a look at my mother's safe? I need you to make sure the protection wards haven't been tampered with."

"*What?*" His tone rises. "You think the wards have been breached?"

"No, no," I say quickly. "But I promised Mireya I'd double check."

"Oh. Well yes, I can do that. I have back-to-back meetings tomorrow, but I can spare a little time around three."

"Great. Thank you."

When I hang up, Xander shoots me a sideways look. "You don't really believe that demon stuff, do you?"

"I don't know yet. I can't see how the wards could possibly have failed, but Uncle Ray's going to check."

He shakes his head. "This is crazy. I should be following some real leads."

"Like what? Do you have any other leads?"

He presses his lips together. After a long period of silence, he reaches out and switches his music back on. It's Frank again, and now he's singing about a woman who makes him feel young. If she's to blame for this song, she has a lot to answer for.

"Hey," I protest.

"It helps me think."

I roll my eyes, but suffer the music—and his silence—without complaining, though it's a long drive back to my house.

When he finally parks the car out front to drop me and Agnes off, a strange feeling runs through my body. My magic tingles, suddenly alive inside me.

Something weird is happening.

I climb out in a daze and something slams into me on the magical plane. The strength drains from my legs and I crumple to the sidewalk.

With an exclamation, Xander runs over to me. He lifts me into his arms. Painful pins and needles run up and down my body. My magic surges, whispering to me. It wants to break free. I clamp it down hard, fighting the feeling until I have it under control.

"What's the matter, Saffy? Are you okay?"

"I...I don't know. Something happened."

"Was it your leg?"

"My magic wanted to get free. It reacted to something." I shake my head, stifling my unease. "Like when I was up the ladder and Sylvia died."

"A memory?" he asks.

"I don't think so."

He's holding me like he did last night, and the feeling adds to my disorientation. He smells so good it's overwhelming. And he's strong. Really strong. Though I'm only five foot eight, I'm mostly muscle and not exactly light. Xander's not wearing his suit jacket, and under his white shirt, his pecs are flexed and hard. So are his biceps.

I swallow, resisting the urge to run my hand over his chest. *Again*. "I'm okay now. You can put me down."

As he lowers me to the ground, I drag my mind back to the strange magical surge. What could have caused it?

"Here, let me help you inside." He puts his arm around my waist to support me, and though I don't need his help, I don't object. When I open the front door, I'm still tucked into his large frame with his arm around me.

Jess is walking through the living room, and when she looks down the hall at us, she does a double-take. Her eyes go wide and her jaw goes slack. I've never brought a man home before, and it's clear she's immediately jumped to the wrong idea about Xander.

"Hi," she says. Her voice is breathless with surprise... and if I'm not mistaken, with a large amount of delight.

I push myself away from Xander, glowering at the way

her eyes have started sparkling. "This is the detective working on Sylvia's case."

"It's *very* nice to meet you, Detective." Her smile is irritatingly large. "I didn't know homicide detectives looked like you. If I'd known, I might have been tempted to kill someone myself."

"Jess!"

She turns her wide eyes to me, putting on an innocent expression. "What, Saffy? No, don't tell me. You two want to be alone, right? That's okay, I was heading to my room anyway. Lots to do."

"Nice to meet you," says Xander to her back as she saunters up the stairs. I narrow my eyes at him, and he coughs. "I'll get the chicken out of the car," he says.

While he sets Agnes free in the courtyard, I limp into the house and open the door that leads to the basement. It smells musty because I hardly ever go down there, but when I flick the light on and head down the stairs, everything looks in its place.

The safe is big enough for me to get inside, and set into the basement wall. The way my skin tingles when I get close confirms its wards are still in place, and the thick layer of dust over everything tells me nobody's been down here for a long time.

Just like how Sylvia's deaths meant ownership of her grimoires passed to me, since my parents' death, I'm the only one who can get through the wards to open the safe.

I turn the large combination lock, dragging the code from my memory, and manage to open it. Inside, everything inside it is just as I remember. My mother stored powerful old statues and artifacts in here, and I've never been tempted to touch them. Nothing looks disturbed, including a piece of bone enclosed in a clear plastic case.

Just as I thought, this is a dead end. But I'll ask my uncle to check all this stuff just in case.

"See anything?" Xander's voice comes from behind me, near the bottom of the stairs.

"Good news and bad news," I say, pulling my head out of the safe. "The wards still feel active, which means nobody but me can open the safe, so yay for that. Bad news is, my chicken problem won't be solved by our imminent deaths."

"I told you that trip was a waste of—" He's cut off by his phone ringing, and tugs it out of his pocket while I shut and lock the safe. "Detective Trent speaking."

There's silence for a moment while he listens to whatever the other person says, then he yelps "What?" in such a shocked voice that I take a step back, wincing as my weight shifts to my injured leg.

"Okay. Yes, I'm on my way." He hangs up, and when he turns back to me, he's a little pale.

"There's been another homicide," he says. "Maryland University. A female professor killed."

"What?" I feel all my blood rush from my face. "Mireya?"

"It sounds likely." His eyes narrow at me, his expression suspicious. "What else do you know about it?"

"Me?" My brain is struggling to keep up with what he's implying.

"You take me to see someone and an hour later she's dead. That's too much of a coincidence, Saffy."

"What are you implying? That I had something to do with it?"

He turns for the stairs and takes them fast, his fists clenched. "That's exactly what I'm saying. You've been distracting me with all this nonsense, while people are dying."

"How did I hurt Mireya? We left together, remember?" I follow him up the stairs, limping after him as fast as I can. "You can't be serious?"

"You need to tell me—" His phone rings again when he gets to the top of the stairs and he curses, then answers it. "Detective Trent speaking." And a moment later, "A photo? No, I haven't seen it." Then, "But I was only—" A deep breath. "But I wouldn't... Yes, sir. No, I understand. I didn't have anything to do with... No, I won't. Yes, sir. Alright. Goodbye."

"What is it?" I demand.

He stabs at his phone's screen with one finger, then types something in with his thumb. The color drains from his face. "Shit," he says softly.

"What?"

He holds the phone out so I can see.

It's a photograph of him carrying me into my house. It's dark, so it must have been taken last night when he brought me home from the hospital. My head is nestled into his neck and I'm looking up at him. Sure enough, my hand is stroking his chest. His face is turned down to me. It looks intimate. We look like lovers.

"This was emailed to my boss," he says.

"Who sent it to him?"

Xander shakes his head. "It was sent anonymously. And in case the Captain didn't recognize you, the sender made sure to mention that you were the prime suspect in two separate murder investigations. Investigations I'm in charge of."

"Whoever sent it must have been trying to—"

"At least, you *were* the prime suspect in two murder

investigations," he cuts me off, scowling. "Until suddenly you weren't. And nobody can figure out why our focus shifted away from you." He stalks toward the front door. "The captain implied I had something to do with that, too, which is pretty damn ironic considering he ordered me to let you go, and I'm the one who argued to keep you at the top of our suspect list."

"He thinks you stopped investigating me because...?" I hesitate.

"Because, apparently, we're 'romantically involved'." He uses his hands to make air quotes, then reaches for the front door knob with a snort of derision. "Shows how much he thinks of me. As if I'd let my personal feelings get in the way of bringing a killer to justice."

My blood rises. Incensed, I hobble after him.

"You still think I murdered my own cousin? My own *parents?*"

He throws the door open. "You know what? I don't care if you did. I've worked damn hard to prove myself. I've had to do everything better, smarter, and more diligently than everyone else. And I've had to put up with a whole lot of crap. People still say I only got the job because of my mother, when I've earned it ten times over. And now, thanks to you, it's all been for nothing." His mouth twists. "I've been suspended until further notice."

"Thanks to me? That's not fair."

"Tough shit," he snarls. "Life's not fair."

The door slams shut behind him.

THIRTEEN

My leg is killing me, but I grit my teeth and drive to Uncle Ray's house anyway. Every time I need to use my pickup's ancient clutch to change gears, I let out a loud string of profanities.

But I keep going, because all I have is a head full of questions. How did Mireya die? Was her heart torn out? Where was Dallas?

Now that Xander's not talking to me, the only person who might be able to give me any answers is Uncle Ray. Mireya was on the Blood Council, so my uncle must know about her death.

I felt Mireya die.

The thought is chilling.

I even said to Xander that it felt like when Sylvia died, but it never occurred to me I was feeling another council member's death. But that magical surge had to be another of the council's bindings breaking. Another weakening in the safeguards holding my magic in check.

My parents were both council members too. Now with

Sylvia and Mireya gone, that's four council members dead. It can't be a coincidence. Somebody's targeting the council and taking them all out, one by one.

I'm sure Uncle Ray will have come to the same conclusion, but I need to make sure he and Aunt Therese are taking precautions. Especially since Aunt Therese has been so unwell.

I finally pull my truck up outside their house and kill the engine with a groan of relief. But instead of getting out right away, I sit and stare into space.

Even though I should be focusing on Mireya's death, I keep thinking about Xander.

I'd thought we had a connection. He'd seemed to relax a little around me, to open up to the idea that I wasn't a murderer. I even thought he might come around to the idea of witches and magic.

Guess not.

He was probably only spending time with me so he could figure out how to pin the deaths on me.

I growl under my breath and shove open the pickup's door, slamming it behind me with unnecessary force. Hobbling up the drive, I push up against the wards that surround Uncle Ray's house. They hold me for a moment, then release me, though my skin prickles and my next step feels like I'm walking through wet cement.

When I reach Uncle Ray's front door, I hesitate, and then decide I should knock. It's been a while since I last visited the house.

A gaunt woman answers my knock, and for a moment I think I've come to the wrong house.

"Aunt Therese?" I'm not even sure it really is her. She looks older. Much older. Her hair is gray and thin, and her back is stooped. There are bags under her eyes and pain lines etched into her face.

Though we used to be close, I haven't seen much of Aunt Therese since my parents died. My uncle said she wasn't well, but I'd assumed she was pushing me away because Mireya had convinced her I was responsible for my parents' death.

Looking at her now, I realize she must have been far sicker than I'd guessed. If she hasn't been knocking at death's door, she's definitely hanging out on his doorstep.

Now I feel terrible for not trying harder to see her. I should have insisted on visiting.

"Aunt Therese," I say. "How are you?"

She nods vaguely and motions behind her to Uncle Ray's study. "He's in there."

Though she moves behind the door, clearly expecting me to walk right past, I don't move. "You didn't say how you are," I remind her. "It's been a long time since I've seen you. Not since before..." I hesitate. "You've been unwell?"

She looks down without answering, tugging at the skirt of her dress. It's too big for her, as though she's lost a lot of weight since she got it. It's usually an easy thing for a witch to fix a dress that's too big. The fact she hasn't done it tells me an awful lot.

"I've missed you, Aunt Therese." The words slip out before I realize I'm even going to say them.

She glances up at me. It's the fastest movement I've seen her make yet. Her eyes are sunken, but something flickers in them. It's a pale shadow of the spark I remember, and I'm glad to see it. She used to be such a powerful woman, full of life and good humor. This broken woman before me is painful to see.

But as quickly as the spark appeared, it's gone again.

She shuffles backward. "I'd better go and…" She trails off, heading slowly toward the kitchen as though it hurts to walk.

"Are you okay?" I ask, though she's clearly not. "Aunt Therese? Can I do something for you?"

She mumbles something, but because she's got her back to me, I can't quite make it out. It sounds like, "I hear you." Or did she say, "I fear you"?

Maybe she really does think I'm a murderer and is worried I'll hurt her. Surely not. With my magic messed up, I'm no threat to anyone.

"Aunt Therese, won't you talk to me for a minute?" I ask, trailing after her. "I'm worried about you and Uncle Ray. I think somebody's killing council members."

She turns to me, nodding vigorously. "Killing," she repeats.

"That's right. So you need to take precautions." I hesitate because she's still nodding. "Aunt Therese? Are you okay?"

"Killing," she says, shuffling to the kitchen bench. She grabs a notepad off the table, scribbles something, then tears the page away.

"Killing," she mumbles, not looking at me. Then she comes close and her fingers press the folded page into my palm. For a split second, she looks me in the eye, and that same tiny spark is back.

"What—?" I don't understand what's happening.

"Killing," she insists. I'm not sure whether she's just repeating what she heard me say, or whether she's trying desperately to tell me something.

"Saffy?" I hear Uncle Ray's study door open. "Is that you?"

I open the piece of paper and catch a glimpse of a name,

but it's not one I recognize. Then my aunt folds her hand around mine, forcing it shut. She pushes my hand with the piece of paper into my pocket, obviously wanting me to keep it hidden. I open my mouth to ask her what it's all about, but she hustles me out of the kitchen toward my uncle's study, not giving me the chance.

With my sore leg I'm easy to corral, and when she gives me a push, I fall into the hallway. As my uncle comes out of his study, I pull my hand free of my pocket, leaving the piece of paper tucked away.

"Didn't I say I'd come by tomorrow?" my uncle says, blinking at me.

My mind is still on Aunt Therese. Does she know something about the murders? Has she given me something important? But whatever she gave me is clearly between us, so I force myself to focus on my uncle and try and act normal. "I heard about Mireya."

He nods and waves me into his study. "Come and sit down. I was taking a moment to collect myself while I feed Jemima. It's a terrible shock."

I haven't been here in years, and Uncle Ray's study is much plusher than I remember. He has golden drapes, a high-backed leather chair and an enormous wooden desk. Mahogany, perhaps? A large glass cage takes up one wall. I remember it from my childhood because I always thought it was creepy.

A quirk of the animal magic side of the family is an affinity to a certain type of creature. My mother's magic used to bring packs of stray dogs into our house, though after I absorbed her magic, I've been attracting cats instead.

Uncle Ray's glass cage holds the creatures he has an affinity with. It looks a little like a forest in there, with tree branches, fresh leaves, and a thick layer of dirt on the bottom of the tank. Even a shallow dish of water that's molded to look like a mini lake.

Inside the cage, spiders clamber everywhere. They crawl and fight, and have way too many legs for my liking. And they're big. Really big. Lots of tarantulas, and others with thinner bodies and impossibly long legs. Not as huge as the massive model spider on his desk, but still nightmare-inducing.

I try not to let him see me shudder as I slide into the guest chair that faces his desk.

He moves behind the desk to settle into his large leather chair. It looks like the kind of chair a James Bond villain would have. My nondescript uncle looks out of place as he slides into the seat made for someone with a far more menacing aspect. He leans forward, reaching out with one hand to the model spider as if he's going to pat it.

I cringe at the idea of touching it, even if isn't real.

Why would anyone want such an enormous fake spider taking up most of the room on their desk? It's really life-like. Whomever made it must really like—

The spider lifts one thick, hairy leg. I flinch backward, clutching the arms of my chair.

That monster is *alive?*

"Good girl, Jemima." Uncle Ray lets the spider walk up his arm. The thing is the size of a puppy. Its front legs are halfway to my uncle's elbow before its back legs leave the desk.

"Hungry, girl?" he murmurs. With his free hand, he takes a lizard out of a little box on his desk and feeds it to the spider.

I look away, swallowing. The lizard is alive, and

watching it squirm in the spider's mandibles isn't my idea of a bag of chuckles.

"Did I see you limping, Saffy?" asks Uncle Ray. "Are you okay?"

"I was attacked by a pack of dogs." Shifting in my seat, I keep my gaze averted from the lizard bloodbath.

Is it my imagination or can I hear chomping?

"One of the dogs tore up my leg. And their eyes were glowing, like they were under a spell."

"Under a spell?" He frowns. "Somebody sent them to attack you?"

I nod, but I have other things on my mind. "Do you know what happened to Mireya? I mean, how it happened? Was her chest...?"

"Like Sylvia's?" He nods. "Apparently so. Her heart was missing."

I close my eyes. Mireya and I might not have been besties, but she didn't deserve to die that way. Nobody does.

Maybe Uncle Ray realizes I don't want to watch Jemima having lunch, because he gets up and starts coaxing the spider off his arm and into the cage.

"Is Dallas okay?" I ask. "He was with Mireya when I saw her."

"He wasn't there when it happened, but he's the one who found her."

"That's rough." I don't like the guy, but he and Mireya seemed close, and I know how devastating it is to find the body of someone you love.

"Is that why you came?" asks my Uncle, sliding the lid of the spider cage back into place. When he turns, I see he's swapped the monster spider for a smaller one. Smaller in comparison, that is. Although it's not *Jurassic Park* sized like the first one, its fat body still takes up his entire palm and its back legs are on his wrist.

"I came to ask what you think is happening," I say. "Everyone who's died has been a council member. That must be why they're being targeted. And you and Aunt Therese are on the council, which means you're both in danger."

My uncle nods. "I've already discussed that possibility with the other council members. We're taking precautions." He leans against his desk. "It's you I'm concerned about. You're not spending time with that detective, are you? It never pays to get too close to a mundane. He's not part of our world."

"It's your world, not mine." The words come out sharper than I intended. "Besides, the detective's okay. He took me to hospital to get patched up."

He clicks his tongue and comes over to me. "Which leg was hurt?"

"This one."

He moves next to my chair. There's a thick coating of blood on his palm, though I didn't see him cut himself. He sweeps his middle finger through the blood and uses it to draw a rune on the leg of my jeans.

Wait a minute. What happened to the spider? Is that where the blood came from?

"Uncle Ray did you just kill—?" The question flies out of my mind when his eyes light with a soft glow and he hovers his hand over the rune. A tingling sensation spreads down my leg and the pain dissipates into nothing.

"That's so much better," I say with relief. "Thank you."

"I know it doesn't feel like it, but it's your world too." His voice is soft. "If you get hurt again, come to me. Stay away from mundanes."

"I doubt I'll see the detective again. He's off the case and he blames me for it." Standing up, I try walking on my wounded leg. It feels normal; the dog bite has completely healed.

"Did you kill that spider and use its blood?" I ask. "Isn't killing a creature to use its blood against the rules?" Harming a *person* to use their blood is the realm of dark magic and strictly forbidden. But a spider's blood? I've never heard of a witch doing that. It hadn't occurred to me that it might be possible.

"There's no law against it," he huffs. "Do you think I'd break the rules?"

"No," I say honestly. "I think you're the last person who'd break them." It sounds like I've upset him, so I search for a change of subject. There's a picture of Aunt Therese on his desk. She's dressed to play tennis, and has a racket over her shoulder and a huge smile on her face. I try to match the image in the photo with the woman who opened the door to me earlier, and it's almost impossible.

"Is Aunt Therese going to be okay?" I ask. "I didn't realize how sick she was." I finger the piece of paper in my pocket, wondering whether to ask my uncle about it.

Before I can decide, the phone on his desk rings and he picks it up. "Yes," he says, glancing at me. Then, "Alright, fine." He hangs up abruptly, wearing a sour look as though the call wasn't a pleasant one.

"Who was that?" I ask.

"More blood ceremony madness. The moon's proximity is disturbing everyone. I'll be glad when it's over." He stands up, frowning. "I need something to drink, don't you? Wait here and I'll get us both something."

"You're busy, and I have things to do."

"No, wait. Please don't go yet, I enjoy your company. Sit for a few minutes." He waves at a chair. "You'd like some hot cocoa, yes? I'll get us a drink, then you must tell me about your visit with Mireya. You and Dallas were probably the last people to see her alive."

He bustles out. When the door shuts behind him, I test my leg by rubbing the place where the wound used to be and stretching my muscles. Then, drawn by morbid fascination, I drift over to watch the spiders in the cage fight with each other.

But my mind is on Aunt Therese.

I didn't even ask what's wrong with her. Something psychological? Alzheimers, perhaps? Whatever it is, it must be impossible to heal through magical means.

I should spend some time with her. Perhaps I could offer to help Uncle Ray caring for her. It's not too late to make up for my long absence.

I've just glanced at the clock on the wall, wondering where Uncle Ray is, when he comes in carrying two cups of steaming cocoa. Though it hasn't been my drink of choice for a dozen years, it smells good.

"Here." He hands one to me. "Now, tell me what you and Mireya spoke about."

The cocoa is surprisingly delicious, far better than I remember. I sit in the big armchair and sip it while I tell him about my visit to Mireya. I'm going to tell him about Agnes too, and ask for his help to change her back into a human. But first, I relate everything Mireya and I talked about, including what I can remember about all the different types of dog demons she mentioned.

My uncle watches me intently, nodding at parts of my story. Then he murmurs something I don't catch.

"Excuse me?" I try to ask, but what comes out sounds like, "'Sckusmm?"

My uncle doesn't seem to notice my inarticulate question, because though his gaze stays on me, his mouth is still moving. I can't make out the words he's murmuring.

My toes are tingling, but when I try to wriggle them, nothing happens. I can't move my legs. They feel dead. Or paralyzed.

Uncle Ray puts his cup on the desk. Blood is smeared on its side.

Shit.

The mug of cocoa slips from my fingers and lands in my lap, before my hands fall by my sides. I can't say anything. Can't cry out. My head lolls forward, then the floor rushes toward me. Every muscle in my body fights for a way to protect my head as I fall. It's no use. The side of my head hits Uncle Ray's plush rug hard enough that stars fill my vision.

"Are you alright, Saffy?" My uncle kneels by my side to turn me over. "I had no choice."

My mind screams profanities, but my mouth won't form the words. Hell, I can't even blink angrily at him. All I can do is stare up at my uncle's traitorous face.

"Was this really necessary?" he asks. But he's not speaking to me now. Somebody else steps into my view. A tall man with a long gray beard. *Magnus Fox.* I should have known.

"She wouldn't have come willingly," says Magnus. "And the Veritas needs to see her to determine the truth."

My chest feels like iron bands have tightened around it. Whatever spell Uncle Ray cast has paralyzed me so completely that it's hard to breathe.

The Veritas is the witch with the ability to create living statues.

And now, as I lie on his plush rug, unable to move or even scream, I realize my uncle has given me a taste of the horror of that punishment.

FOURTEEN

The council is headquartered in a huge mansion in the forested area of Druid Hill Park. It's hidden from the city's mundanes using a complex spell that's been in place for hundreds of years. When they look in the direction of the council chambers, they see a part of the forest too thick and dark to penetrate, and if they try to get close, they don't even feel the magical nudge that steers them right past it.

Though my parents came here all the time for council meetings and ceremonies, I've never been here. The wards that surround the place are so strong that nobody can get near the place without an invitation.

Mostly frozen in the back seat of Uncle Ray's car, I'm not exactly in a mood to appreciate my first visit.

My uncle's spell is wearing off, and I'm finally getting enough movement back that when we pull up to the front doors, I can get out of the car by myself. But my legs are weak and I can only move slowly. Somewhere in the distance an elephant trumpets. The Maryland Zoo is just down the hill, and I can feel how unsettled the animals are, even from here.

Aunt Therese gets out of the passenger seat and stands with her back to me, looking out over the gardens. I'm thankful Magnus Fox drove here in his own car so I didn't have to endure his company.

Uncle Ray tries to take my arm to help me walk up the steps leading up to the building's impressive entrance, but I manage to shake him off.

"I trusted you, Uncle Ray," I snarl. And while I haul myself up the steps, I inform him about the exact characteristics of the foul stream of fecal discharge he resembles. I count it as a small win when I manage to stagger unaided through the building's front doors and see that his face has flushed a deep shade of red.

The lobby is enormous, with a gold and marble theme that makes it feel both opulent and cold. Two statues stand guard beside a grand staircase. They're made of stone, but intricately carved. A man and a woman. Both have wild, unseeing eyes. The woman has her arms flung up and her mouth open in terror, as though the sculptor captured her mid-scream. The man has his hands up too, but in a defiant, attacking posture, though he looks just as terrified.

My throat closes and I stop dead.

They're not statues. They're witches who've been judged by the Veritas. They're still alive, unable to move or speak for the duration of their sentence, however long that may be.

That's what could happen to me.

"Come on," says Uncle Ray. "This way."

Aunt Therese walks slowly but purposefully through the lobby, as though she's being drawn forward on a string. She was silent in the car, and now I wonder if she even knows I've been brought here against my will. Ignoring me and Uncle Ray completely, she turns down a long corridor.

It takes a while for me to convince my legs to move again. Only the knowledge that my uncle could just restrain me with another spell gets me to follow him. Last thing I want is for him to use that paralyzing spell again now that I've seen the real living statues. I'll never have another nightmare-free night as it is.

He leads me down the corridor after Aunt Therese, and through a set of big double doors into a circular room. Though the room itself isn't large, I need to crane my neck back to see the ceiling. It extends up the full three stories of the building, and there's an enormous round skylight set into the roof that shows a wide expanse of sky.

This must be the room where the council conducts its ceremonies, because there are circles carved into the floor, all connected to make one large ring. The circles are a dark blackish-red. The deep grooves in the floor must have had so much blood running inside them that it's stained the marble.

The council members are all there, staring as Uncle Ray leads me in.

Magnus Fox stands tall in the first circle, his expression stern. His long gray beard hangs to the top button of his wrinkled gray shirt. Next to him is Dallas, his pale face filled with grief and rage. Dallas's eyes are bloodshot and his clothes askew, his shirt buttons in the wrong holes. He looks like a man on the edge.

Next to Dallas is Amber, another friend of my parents' who turned her back on me after they died. Then there's Aunt Therese, picking at a thread in her dress. Uncle Ray is next, then a young girl who looks totally out of place. She's around twelve or thirteen, I guess, and wearing white while most of the others are in black. Her dress is long and made of satin, and her long hair is as white as Dallas's.

The six of them aren't just in random places. Each stands in one of the circles carved into the floor. There is one circle for each council member, with two empty ones where Mireya and Sylvia must have stood.

Only there aren't eight circles. There are nine. One isn't stained with blood, which is why it's harder to see. But yeah, definitely nine circles, with three of them empty. It's a weird thing to notice at a time like this, but why is there an extra circle on the floor?

My gaze flicks back to the young girl. Her hands are smeared with blood, and when she turns her face to me, her eyes are completely white.

The Veritas.

"Sapphira Black, you are here to answer two charges of murder," says Magnus in his deep, booming voice. "You're accused of killing Sylvia Black and Mireya Oswalde."

"I didn't have anything to do with their deaths. I'm innocent."

"You must have had something to do with it," snarls Dallas. He glares at me with pure hatred in his eyes. He's just looking for someone to blame for the death of his beloved wife, I get that. And if he hadn't put me in the firing line, I'd feel a lot sorrier for him.

"The Veritas will determine whether you speak the truth. Come forward."

It's clear he wants me to move inside the large ring, but I can't force my feet to move. My heart is pounding so hard it hurts. This is it. If the Veritas decides I'm guilty, I'll become another statue decorating their lobby.

"You are here to be judged," says the girl. Though her voice is soft, with a lisp that would have been cute on a normal kid, it still echoes around the room.

"You're a little girl." I cast an accusing look at my aunt

and uncle. I'm facing the most horrible future imaginable, and it'll be in the hands of a child to decide?

"I am everyone and everything. I seek the truth. Come before me."

Her words take on a deeper tone, and suddenly my feet are moving without my consent. I let out a growl of anger and dismay, unable to stop myself walking toward her.

Her white eyes glow. When she catches my gaze, I can't look away. The room dims, and in the dark, her features take on a sharper quality. Shadows highlight the lines of her face and she seems more like a devil than a young girl.

I stop directly in front of her. Her eyes dominate her face. She reaches out with one bloody hand and drags her finger across my forehead, drawing a rune on my skin. Though I'm innocent, I feel the urge to blurt out a confession. The Veritas's white eyes glow brighter. They're all I can see.

I open my mouth, the urge to confess growing stronger by the second. The words "*I did it*" are clambering up my throat, crawling toward my mouth. My hands itch to cover my lips, to stop the words bursting out. But I can't move, I can't do anything other than fight the compulsion to admit guilt for a crime that's not mine.

The words are too strong to hold in. I *need* to speak them.

My body shakes violently and I pant for breath. Sweat drips into my eyes, stinging them, and I can't blink it away.

I won't let the Veritas win. I refuse to say the words.

Pain rises out of my soul, deep and excruciating, until it takes over my whole body. Ribbons of agony roll over my skin, dig into my muscles and send needle-like jabs through my body.

Is this how the desperate, frozen people in the lobby

were convicted? Were they forced to say the words, whether they were true or not?

Are they even now feeling this level of torture?

I'm not going to bend. I did not kill my parents. I did not kill Sylvia. I did not kill Mireya. No one can make me say I did.

I clench my fists, feeling my muscles tighten. My arms are strong and I focus all my attention on squeezing my fists as hard as I can. Anchoring my body. Anchoring my mind.

I am tough.

You cannot crush me.

I'm made from the same rock as the walls I build. I'm solid. Unbreakable. Stone.

A sound forces its way out from my lips, but it's not words. It's a scream. A long, lung-burning scream that tears at my throat and adds another level of pain to my already suffering body.

I don't know how much longer I can take this. I can't see the girl in front of me, she's disappeared behind the black dots and tears in my eyes. But I can feel the pressure of her magic on me, squeezing me until I feel like I'm going to burst open like a piece of ripe fruit.

And then it stops.

I collapse to the floor, gasping for breath. I can't do anything other than lie flat for a long time. When I finally lift my head, the girl's eyes aren't glowing anymore.

Did I pass the test? What happens now?

I push myself up to sitting, though my body feels boneless, like I've been fed through a pasta maker and turned into noodles. I'm not sure I'll be able to stand up.

"You're free to go," says the Veritas.

"What?" yells Dallas. "No, you can't let her go." His fists are clenched and he starts forward as though to attack me. "Death follows her. Wherever she goes, witches are murdered. She must know *something*."

I flinch as he looms over me, but he freezes in the act of reaching for me, as though he's hit an invisible wall.

"I passed?" My voice comes out as a croak. "You believe I'm innocent?"

"You're free to go. That is all." The Veritas is holding Dallas back with her mind, but there's no trace of effort on her young face.

The other witches in the circle murmur, as though they're not entirely convinced I didn't pull some sort of trick. But Magnus speaks up. "Only the innocent can withstand the compulsion to admit guilt."

"The Veritas is too young," snaps Dallas. "She's not powerful enough."

Though my throat's bone dry, I can still give a derisive snort.

"Can you stand, Saffy?" asks Uncle Ray, coming forward to help me to my feet. "I'll take you home."

But I yank my arm out of his grip and shoot a glare around the room that I hope is full of the contempt and anger I feel for them all.

"I'd rather walk." And as weak as I am, I manage to storm out without falling over my own feet.

FIFTEEN

It's been four days since my enforced visit to the Veritas. I've finished the job I was supposed to start on Monday, building a small block wall. The work took three days, though if I hadn't been so strung out and distracted, I'd have finished it in two.

Now Agnes and I are in my backyard, glaring at each other like we're two prizefighters before a match. The last few days haven't made her any fonder of me. Though I've tried to explain what I'm doing, she won't listen. We circle each other warily, facing off, assessing who's going to be the first to make a move.

We've been at this for what feels like forever.

I've sliced shallow cuts in both my palms, and I can feel my magic pressing against its bonds. With two council members dead, the bonds are weaker now, and it takes all my strength to restrain my magic. I've never held it in like this before, and I'm starting to shake with the effort. I have no idea what effect being in this state is having, but it feels like my magic is building up, getting stronger and stronger.

Pretty soon, I'll have to let it escape, and I'm more than

a little afraid of what might happen, like when a river is dammed but about to burst. But if I'm going to change Agnes back I have to attempt it.

Agnes has her wings spread. She struts stiff-legged, using her wings to help her move, watching for an opportunity to carve a chunk out of me. Behind her, an egg sits in a makeshift nest she's fashioned out of grass and torn paper. The worst part was when I heard her clucking as she laid it. It sounded painful.

"I'm trying to help you," I tell her for the hundredth time. "Let me touch you and maybe I can change you back the way you used to be."

She feints at me, but when I reach for her, she jumps away and all I get is handfuls of feathers. My magic almost escapes and I just manage to haul it back, but now my hands are coated with feathers attached to my now-sticky blood. When I shake them, the feathers don't come loose. "Damn feathers," I mutter, wiping my hands on my jeans. "Damn stupid chicken."

But I should know better than to let myself get distracted.

With a loud *cluck-cluck-claar*, Agnes leaps for my face. I jerk my hands up, trying to grab her out of the air. My bloody hands brush her body and my magic bursts free.

The animal magic explodes out of me. Literally.

It feels like a bomb detonating. The force rocks me back, and hundreds of feathers rain down over me. Heart racing, I stare up at where they're coming from. Feathers fall into my mouth and land in my eyes.

What the hell just happened? Have I killed Agnes? Did I tear her to pieces?

Before I can see more than feathers, I feel my earth magic launching itself into the courtyard's paving stones.

They fly up like missiles and I stagger back, throwing my arms over my head to protect it.

My knees give way, and I sag to the ground, sputtering feathers out of my mouth. There's now a crater in the courtyard. Broken paving stones are scattered everywhere, and a layer of feathers coats everything like fluffy snow.

In the middle, seemingly unharmed, stands Agnes. *Chicken* Agnes. Her brown feathers are intact, so my animal magic must have conjured the feather storm out of thin air.

At least one question is answered. Chickens *can* blink. Agnes blinks very slowly, and the eyelid that comes from the front of her eye is milky and semi-transparent.

"Are you okay, Agnes?" I ask.

She blinks again, a little faster. Then she flaps her wings, sending up a cloud of feathers. She looks as shocked as I am by the mess I've made of the courtyard.

"Saffy? Was that you?" Jess's voice comes from inside the house, making me jerk with surprise.

I leap for the back door, just getting through and closing it before my roommate appears.

"Saffy?" She stops when she sees me. "Did you hear that noise?"

"Oh yeah. Neighbor was making a racket." I ran my hand over the top of my hair and pull out several feathers. "Agnes complains about our music all the time, but I think she must be giving a drum lesson to an orangutan. Nothing else can explain a crash that loud."

Jess frowns. "You're covered in feathers. Did something happen to the chicken?"

"The chicken's fine. It just laid an egg. What are you doing home? I thought you had band practice?"

"Your cousin Sylvia's funeral is today, isn't it? I'm going with you."

"You don't need to—"

"I'm going with you," she repeats, and I recognize the set of her lips. No use arguing., and I don't protest too hard, even though she's a mundane, and therefore won't be welcome. I need all the support I can get.

When we walk through the doors of the old chapel in the far corner of Druid Hill Park, and all I get are glares from the other mourners, I glare back. If they don't like a mundane being here, tough.

It's not until the service starts that it occurs to me they could be glaring because they think I'm the one who's killing witches.

Good thing my response works either way.

"Tough crowd," murmurs Jess in my ear after the service is over and everyone's filing out of the chapel, giving us a wide berth as they head toward the refreshments that are being served in the lobby. "I feel like a slab of steak at a vegan buffet."

Dressed up for the funeral, Jess looks like a totally different person from the one I'm used to. Her normally wild blonde hair is swept into a tidy bun, and she's wearing a black dress and high heels instead of her normal jeans. She even has a little black veil, like widows wear to funerals in movies. It partly covers her eyes, and I was hoping she wouldn't be able to see all the glowers we've been getting.

"They're just upset about Sylvia," I lie. "It's not personal."

"You sure?" Through her veil, I see an eyebrow arch. "Because I know you well enough to be sure you've done something to upset them."

I have a wad of tissues balled in my hand, still soggy

from the service, but Jess's certainty makes my lips twich. She's kinda right.

Magnus Fox and Uncle Ray walk by, heading out of the chapel. My nostrils flare as Magnus brushes past. He definitely has a scent that reminds me of dogs.

Uncle Ray doesn't stop to speak to me, probably because Magnus is murmuring something to him in a low voice. Didn't Uncle Ray mention that Magnus was going to step down from the council soon? My uncle's probably doing some political maneuvering and that's why he doesn't want to be seen talking to his misfit niece. Not that I'd talk to him anyway. I'm still mad over the whole drugging me and handing me over to the Blood Council thing.

Aunt Therese is still sitting in the back row of the chapel though everyone else is filing out. Her head is low and her face deathly pale. I was hoping to have a chance to talk to her about the piece of paper she stuffed into my pocket, but she looks even sicker than when I saw her a few days ago. Her eyes droop like she's fighting to stay conscious. I'm afraid talking to her would only upset her.

Afternoon tea is being served in the lobby outside the chapel. Not that I want to stay for it.

"Let's go," I say to Jess. "I want to get home, change out of this dress, toast Sylvia with a cold beer, then put something on the stereo that's loud enough to guarantee we'll need hearing aids by the time we're thirty."

Jess tucks her arm into mine. "Sounds like a plan. My feet are killing me. I remember now why I never wear heels this high."

"The last time I wore a dress was to my parent's funeral," I say with a sigh. "Pretty soon I'll start having a nervous reaction every time I *see* a dress."

"At least you got all the feathers out of your hair." She

hesitates. "Seriously, Saff, what's the deal with the chicken? Yesterday I saw it pecking at the fence with its beak. It was scratching out *words*."

I blink and silently swear at Agnes. "You know, I read something the other day about how our brains are wired to look for patterns. We're always looking for meaning in simple co-incidences. Like calling a certain coin lucky if it happens to be the one that wins a prize. Amazing, really, how you could have seen letters in random chicken scratchings."

She narrows her eyes and her tone turns dry. "The chicken had written, *Help, I'm a person*. If that's a trick my brain was playing, I'd better see a doctor." She looks at me like she knows more than she's letting on, but there's no way she knows the truth.

"Wha—?" I manage to turn my shock into a cough. "Oh, sure. I think Sylvia taught the chicken how to do that as a joke. Crazy, right?" I force a laugh. "My cousin might have been bookish, but she had a wild side."

"Smart chicken. Could be a judge on *America's Got Talent*." Jess's bone-dry tone makes it clear she doesn't believe a word that's coming out of my mouth.

Actually, I'm amazed at how well she's taking this. If I were her, I'd probably have booked both the chicken and myself into therapy.

I'm searching for a change of subject when I spot a tall figure in a corner of the lobby, his gaze roving over all the mourners as though he's taking mental notes about each of them.

Xander.

I haven't seen him for days. What's he doing here?

He's wearing a much nicer suit than the one he was wearing when I met him, so he's either being respectful or he's making an effort to blend in. I don't normally go for men in suits, but he looks good. Very James Bond. Especially with his square jaw, chiseled features, and the secret-agent way he's scanning the room. His icy blue eyes seem to miss nothing.

When those eyes land on me and widen, I feel myself flush. His gaze goes from my toes to the top of my head before they settle on my face. There's appreciation in his expression, and I have to fight the urge to reach up and brush back my hair. Though I usually keep it tied back in pigtails, today I'm wearing it loose, falling down my back. I don't often leave it free because the last thing a stonemason needs is hair falling in her face and getting in the way.

"Don't look now, but Detective Hotpants is over there," whispers Jess. "He's looking at you. And check out those *shoulders*."

"His name's Xander." I've given her an abridged version of the things that have happened since Sylvia's death, leaving out any mention of magic. Or about the connection I thought I had with Xander, seeing as I was wrong about that anyway.

"He's obviously into you, so why are you standing all the way over here?" She clicks her tongue. "Let's go say hi."

Before I can object, she drags me over to him. "Nice to see you again," she says with a smile. "We almost met the other day. I'm Jess."

"Saffy's roommate." He nods. "I remember. You're the drummer, right?"

"Is there a big police file on me?" Jess sounds only mildly curious. "Lots of pages?"

Xander shrugs. I bet there *is* a thick file about Jess, and he's read it. First time Jess and I met, there was a fight in the club her band was playing in and she got arrested. And that wasn't her first brush with the law. Drumming in a band that's still up-and-coming doesn't pay well, and she occasionally disassembles cars for a less-than-savory mechanic to make ends meet.

"What are you doing here?" I ask Xander. The last time I saw him, he was hurling nasty accusations at me. He'd better not be stalking me at my cousin's funeral.

He hesitates. "Just seeing who came to the funeral."

The way his gaze was searching the mourners as though cataloguing their faces fills in the rest for me. He's definitely on the case. With all the suspects in one room, no wonder he's here.

"They've lifted your suspension?" I'm relieved despite myself. It wouldn't have been fair if he'd lost his job because he was helping me.

He shakes his head. "I'm still suspended. But nobody else from the department is here. I had to come."

Crap. "Oh," I say stupidly.

"Look, Saffy, about what I said..." he says.

"Yes?"

"I'm sorry. It's not your fault. I was taking it out on you."

"A common theme," I say drily, but my heart is thumping. I'm not used to people apologizing.

"I was upset. I hope you can forgive me."

The relief I feel makes me a little edgy. I shouldn't be this happy about Xander saying sorry. But he's the only person who's prepared to help me investigate what happened to my parents, and that's important to me.

"I forgive you," I say quietly. Beside me, Jess pinches my arm. That's our code for something exciting, when we don't want anyone else to know about it.

"So maybe—"

"I need to talk to you," I blurt over top of his words.

"About what?"

Now it's my turn to hesitate. I glance at Jess, then at the lobby full of witches. They're mobbing the table of food set up in the corner, though I'm still catching some glares. This isn't the time or place to ask for his help with secret clues.

"Well," says Jess after a long, awkward silence. "I have… a phone call to make. In my car." She gives me a raised-eyebrow look that's easy to read, even with half her face covered by the veil. Xander can probably read it too. Jess isn't known for her subtlety. "You should take your time, Saffy. The call I need to make will be a long one."

As she walks out of the lobby, Xander hunches his shoulders. From his expression, I get the impression he's uncomfortable with Jess's too-obvious matchmaking. And no wonder, after the photograph somebody sent to his boss.

"I'm sorry they haven't reinstated you," I say.

"It's not your fault. My boss has been gunning for me for a while."

"Why? What did you do?"

"Not me. My mother. She's Anna Trent." When I look at him blankly, he says, "Come on, Saffy. Surely you've heard of Baltimore's mayor?"

I blink. "Your mother's the mayor? Wow. Okay. But why would that turn your boss against you?"

"Everyone at the station is convinced it's thanks to my mother's influence that I'm the youngest detective on the force." Xander runs a hand through his hair, making it stick up on one side in a way that's kind of adorable.

Not that I want to notice things like that, dammit.

"That sucks," I say.

Xander shoves both hands into his pockets and sighs. "What do you want to talk to me about?"

Before I can answer, a harsh male voice comes from

behind me. "What are you doing here?" When I turn around, Dallas is looming over me. His fists are balled by his sides and his white face is blotched red with rage. He's in the same stage of dishevelment as he was at the council chambers, with his pale white hair sticking out in all directions like a demented halo and his suit rumpled.

"Come to gloat over what you did?" he demands.

I shake my head. "Sylvia was my cousin. I have a right to be here."

"You know more than you're saying about the killings," he snarls, his eyes almost fully white in the light shining down on us from the chapel windows. "Are you practising dark magic?"

"I had nothing to do with Sylvia's death. Or Mireya's." It's like I'm a broken record.

His lip curls. "The Veritas was soft on you. Wherever you go, people die. Tell me why, or I'll kill you myself."

Then he mutters something I can't hear. It must be an incantation, because a cold breeze gusts across my face and my hair lifts. The space between me and Dallas is suddenly alive with power. My skin tingles with it. I glance down and see blood oozing from his palm where his fingernails have dug into his flesh. Dallas's threat isn't an idle one.

His air magic is incredibly strong.

I reach out and grab his arms above the elbow. He's taller than me, but like most witches, he doesn't bother to work out. His arms are scrawny compared to mine. When I squeeze, there's surprise in his expression. But he mutters something else, and the breeze that's lifting my hair turns into a wind that flicks it back and forth.

"Go on then," I say in a low, angry voice, leaning forward into the gale that's started whistling in my ears.

"Kill me here, in front of all these witnesses. See what happens to you."

Xander puts his hand on Dallas's shoulder. "You'd better go."

Dallas looks at him, the mutter dying on his lips. The wind around me slackens, becoming a breeze again.

"The mundane policeman," he spits. "Somebody to clean up the mess."

"I'm not the janitorial type," Xander says through clenched teeth. "Never was much good at cleaning."

I give Dallas a shove and he staggers backward. Xander steps between us, his bulk as impressive as ever. "Go," he orders.

To one side, I see Magnus frowning in our direction.

Dallas sees him too, and he takes a step backward, his mouth twisted in a bitter snarl. "This isn't over," he hisses at me.

I have a smart-mouthed response ready to let fly, but I manage to hold it back. Just. Dallas could slam me against the ceiling with his magic, and despite my bravado, he looks close enough to the edge to actually do it.

As Dallas vanishes through the door, Xander turns back to me. "There's something wrong with that guy," he mutters, almost to himself.

I shrug. "He's grieving and angry." Some people react badly to the way Dallas looks, but I wouldn't have thought Xander would make that mistake. "He just wants someone to blame."

"Not just that," says Xander slowly, like he's still thinking it through. "In my job, I see a lot of people who've done terrible things. You develop a kind of sixth sense for who's guilty when you're interviewing people, I guess. It's not infallible, but I can generally tell when someone's involved in the crime."

His words make me blink. "You think Dallas...?"

Xander lets out a breath. "There's definitely something off about him. I noticed it when we interviewed them at the university. It's only become worse since then."

Could *Dallas* be the murderer? The idea is shocking. Dallas is on the *Blood Council,* for crying out loud. The ramifications of that are more than I can even think through right now. "Why would he kill his own wife and then act crazy about it?" I ask.

"People do it all the time. The husband or wife is the first suspect in any murder case, and the number of times I've seen a guilty husband play the part of the grieving widower... let's just say it's not new."

Staring at the doors that Dallas just stormed through, I think about what he's saying. He's seen something in Dallas's face, a hint of a murderer.

"Hey," I say indignantly, realizing what else this means. "Did you look at me and see a murderer?"

Xander shakes his head. "You didn't seem like a murderer. But you were at the scene of the crime, covered in blood, and in shock. It looked like you'd lifted the body, and why would you do that? The other rule in detective work is that the simplest answer is often the right one."

At least he didn't think I was crazy just by looking at me. "So what do we do now?" What I'm really asking is how we find out if Dallas is involved.

Xander doesn't answer. Probably because there are no answers. Seems all we have are too many questions and nothing else.

Almost nothing else.

"I've been given some information," I murmur. "But I

can't tell you about it here." Our argument with Dallas didn't go unnoticed and it feels like the entire funeral party is staring at us. I can't pull out the note Aunt Therese gave me in front of them all. The words she wrote unsteadily on the piece of paper have been going around and around inside my head since I first read them. I don't know what the hell they mean. But now I've got the chance to ask an actual detective to decipher it for me.

"Then where?" he asks.

"Can you come to my place tomorrow morning? Around eleven. By then Jess will be at band practice and we can talk in private."

I'm relying on his curiosity to make him want to help me, and I'm not disappointed. I can see it in his expression. Xander has a hunger for the chase. The same hunger that made him come here even when he's suspended, and to keep after me when his boss told him I shouldn't be a suspect.

If the others at the station think he needed to rely on a hand up from his mother to get him to the top, they're blind and stupid. It's obvious Xander will do whatever it takes to get to the truth.

"Okay, fine," he says. "Tomorrow at eleven."

I start to move toward the door, not wanting to keep Jess waiting too long, but he stops me with a sound. "Saffy," he says, then hesitates.

"Yes?"

"You look nice."

I open my mouth and close it again. My cheeks heat as different responses run through my mind. Should I tell him he looks nice, too? Should I ask him to join Jess and me for a beer and some loud music?

Or should I fire back a snarky remark?

Dammit, I'm so bad at this. Jess is good at flirting. She has a different boyfriend every other week. I've always liked being alone so I never bothered to learn how to play the game.

After a moment, Xander's gaze flicks back to the witches. He's in detective mode again, assessing the suspects. And the silence has gone on too long. If I say anything now, it'll sound awkward.

"Thanks," I manage, one hundred percent sure it's the dumbest response I could have given. Then I turn and walk away.

SIXTEEN

The next morning, Xander turns up with his chin dark with stubble, wearing an old, faded T-shirt and jeans. His unemployed clothes, I guess.

The rough look suits him a little too much. Today he's more James Dean than James Bond. More *Rebel Without a Cause* than *Licensed To Kill*. Of all the Xander looks I've seen so far, it's definitely my favorite.

"Come in," I say, opening the door wide. His shoulders are so broad, he makes my hallway look smaller.

"You've still got scratches and gouges in your front door," he tells me. "Those dogs made a mess of the wood."

"I'll add it to the list of jobs I need to do," I say, waving a hand at the paint tins in the living room. "You want a coffee?"

"Thanks." When he sits at the kitchen counter, I pour us both a cup. Then I take the stool next to him and tug the piece of paper Aunt Therese gave me out of my pocket, smoothing it out so he can see the name scrawled across it in barely-legible writing.

"Demarcus Devlin," he reads. "Who's that?"

"Nobody. At least, not according to the Internet. I'm not even sure it's a person. It could be a spell name, or a place, or the name someone gave to their car." I rub the back of my neck with frustration. "I've searched as hard as I can, and I can't find anyone or anything called Demarcus Devlin."

"And you want me to...?"

I shoot him a hopeful look. "You must have access to police databases and things, right? If it is a person, you might be able to find him. Or her."

"Why would I want to? Who is he?"

"Maybe nobody," I admit.

It's likely the name is straight out of a delusion Aunt Therese was having. She probably made it up. It might not even have anything to do with the killings. She might have been trying to set me up on a blind date.

But there's something in my gut that's telling me this is important. Something about the way Aunt Therese squeezed the paper into my hands poked at my long-dead intuition. "If we can find out what it means, it could give us vital information about the case," I add, trying to sound more hopeful than I feel.

"Where did the name come from?"

I take a gulp of my coffee to buy time, because I don't want to answer. When she gave me the name, Aunt Therese acted like she was passing on a huge secret.

But how would she know anything Uncle Ray didn't? Unless there's something going on at the council she doesn't want to tell him. Or maybe she can't tell him. Perhaps she's been spelled to stop her revealing the secret to anyone important, and writing down this name for me was the only way she could pass on the information.

"I'd prefer not to say," I tell him finally, putting my cup

down. "But if you help me check it out, we could find something that'll help the case. Catch the murderer and they'll probably lift your suspension, right?"

"I could pull in a favor, but I want to know why. It's not a game, Saffy. I won't use police resources lightly."

"I keep being accused of murder," I say, with more bite in my voice than I'd intended. "That's not a game either. And I refuse to sit around and wait to be accused again. For all I know, this Demarcus Devlin might be the one who killed my family. Are you going to help me find him or not?"

He hesitates, running one hand through his hair. I glare back, arms folded, until he sighs. "Just tell me this name didn't appear in a puff of smoke from a magical spell."

"You'll just have to trust me," I say impatiently, uncrossing my arms. "If you can't bring yourself to accept magic is real, then at least believe me when I say this is important."

He shoots me a narrow-eyed look. "If magic were real, wouldn't you be able to wiggle your nose and conjure your cousin's murderer?"

"Wiggle my nose? Like the genie in *I Dream of Jeannie*?" I huff out a loud, disgusted breath. "Way to insult me."

"Well, what can you do? What can you show me?"

My indignation falls away. "Nothing," I admit.

"Yeah, you conveniently can't use the magic you claim to have, except to turn people into chickens." He shakes his head, but he's also tugging out his phone. He dials a number. "Hey, it's me. I need a favor. Can you run this name for me? Demarcus Devlin. Yeah, that's right."

He spells out the name for the person on the other end, then hangs up.

"Now what?" I ask.

"Now we wait."

"I have donuts from the place down the road. You want one?"

"Sure."

As I put a donut onto a plate for him, I catch movement from the corner of my eye.

Agnes.

Somehow she's managed to climb up to the kitchen window and she's sitting on the sill, peering at the detective. She flaps her wings, trying to get his attention though he's facing the other way. Then she taps her beak against the glass.

Xander frowns, glancing around, but Agnes is just out of sight.

Before Agnes can rap on the window again, I cross to the brand new stereo I've just had to pay a small fortune for. "You want to hear some real music?"

"Do I have a choice?" he asks around a mouthful of doughnut.

"Nope." I flick the switch and the opening notes from *Thrill Me* start playing. I love this intro. It's like the calm before the storm.

"What's this?" he asks, already wincing though the loud part hasn't started yet.

"*The Flaming Buttholes.* Jess's band. They're going to be huge."

"Huge what?" His shoulders hunch. "Do they have the market for hearing aids cornered? If so, they'll be millionaires."

"The really good part is coming up." I twist the volume knob higher.

His phone rings and he makes a cutting off motion with one hand. "Got to answer this," he shouts over the music.

When I turn it off, he pretends to wipe perspiration off his forehead. "Saved by the bell."

I shake my head sadly at his lack of musical taste as he puts his phone to his ear.

"Trent speaking."

While his attention is focused on his call, I cross to the window and open it, pushing Agnes off the sill. She flaps to the ground and glares up at me while I close and latch the window.

The detective has tugged a worn notepad and pen from his pocket and is scribbling an address. "Thanks. Yeah, yeah, I owe you." He hangs up and taps the address with the pen. "That Devlin guy owns a thrift store on a street I know all too well. It's a bad area."

Aunt Therese didn't make the name up after all. "Let's go," I say, my excitement rising.

He insists on finishing his coffee and donut before we go out and get into his car. And instead of starting the engine right away, he pauses with his hand on the key, giving me a half-smiling look.

"I think you'll like this," he says. "It's a lot better than those Fiery Bottoms, or whatever they're called."

"What?"

He starts the engine. A song blares out of the stereo, the sound turned up loud.

"This." He shouts over it, grinning at me. "Michael Bublé. He's contemporary. Hugely popular. Millions of fans can't be wrong."

With a groan of pain, I clap my hands over my ears. Overly dramatic, maybe. But the song is so sweet and syrupy, I can feel my brain liquefying. And not in a good way.

"I'm sorry for whatever I've done to deserve this torture," I shout. "Please turn it off."

Xander cranks the sound louder and as he pulls out from the curb, he starts singing along to the song with so much enthusiasm I can only laugh. He has a nice baritone. If only he'd sing along with something *good*, I'd be able to enjoy it.

Three dreadful songs later, I've worn out my entire repertoire of groans and pained expressions and I'm almost ready to give up all semblance of dignity and good taste, and start singing along with him.

Almost.

Thankfully, before I can, he parks across the road from a dingy-looking store and switches the car off. I stare through the dirty window at the piles of junk inside the store. Used furniture, mostly, although I can see a bookcase full of what looks like old car parts.

It's a funny place for a store, because the street is mostly lined with boarded-up houses and there's a couple of shifty-looking guys hanging out on the corner who may as well be wearing name tags that say, 'Hello, I'll be your drug dealer today.' This isn't a place I'd come alone.

"You wait here. I'll go in and ask some questions," says Xander.

"I'm coming too." I get out before he can object and jog across the road in front of him. No way I'm waiting in the car by myself.

When I open the shop's door, a little bell jingles merrily into the gloom.

Junk is piled high in stacks, with chairs teetering on top of tables. The walls are covered with pictures, signs, and hanging ornaments. A large tin chicken sitting on an armchair sends a pang of guilt through me. I've been reasoning with Agnes every day, trying to convince her to let me try again. But she keeps well clear of me, and I haven't been able to get close. I'm still not talking to my uncle, but I suppose I'll have to swallow my pride and call him for help to change her back.

The bell jingles again when Xander comes in, and he looks around before picking a path through the junk to the counter in the back. A middle-aged man sits behind it, reading a book about card tricks. In contrast with the layer of grime in the store, he wears a neatly-pressed white shirt. His long, blonde hair is tied back from his face and he has long, elegant fingers that probably come in useful for hiding aces in his sleeve. I can't sense any real magic, though. This guy isn't a witch.

"Can I help you?" he asks, not looking up from his book.

"I'm Detective Trent from the Baltimore Police. I have a few questions to ask."

The guy's eyes jerk up and his gaze narrows on Xander. "What kind of questions?"

"Are you Demarcus Devlin?"

The man gives the tiniest of nods, his expression suspicious. "Why are you asking?"

"Do you know a woman called Sylvia Black?"

"Never heard of her." One of his hands disappears in his pocket and Xander tenses. But surely Devlin's pants are too tight for him to have hidden a gun or knife in there.

"Interesting book." Xander leans closer, his eyes sharp. "You like doing magic?"

"A hobby, that's all. Card tricks at parties. That kind of stuff."

The man pulls his hand out of his pocket and pops the top off a small vial. The smell of burnt matches lingers in the air, and all my hairs stand on end. *Magic.*

Xander straightens, his expression going bland. "Okay. Thanks for your time." He turns and walks to the door.

I'm opening my mouth to protest when I realize Demarcus Devlin must have cast a spell that only worked on Xander. I don't want to give myself away, so I follow the detective out.

"That was a dead end," says Xander as he gets back in the car.

"Not even close," I tell him, frowning. "That guy is a mundane, but somehow he used magic to get you to walk away. What the hell is going on?"

SEVENTEEN

"I'm telling you, you got spelled," I repeat. I had to pull Xander's keys out of the ignition to stop him driving away and we've been sitting in the car arguing ever since.

"I didn't get 'spelled'." Mouth pulled down with annoyance, Xander makes quote marks with his fingers.

"Then why'd you leave that store so quickly?"

"Because your lead was a dead end, and it was clear that man had nothing to do with my case."

"You didn't even ask him any questions."

"Yes I did."

"What's your name, and did you know Sylvia? They don't count."

He holds out his hand. "Give me the keys, Saffy."

"He spelled you. There must have been blood in the vial he opened, and a witch must have given it to him. Still, he shouldn't have been able to use a spell like that, even if somebody cast it for him in advance. I've never heard of a mundane being able to do that."

"That's ridiculous. You expect me to believe—?"

I grab his arm, cutting him off. The thrift store's door

has opened and Demarcus Devlin is shiftily lurking at the entrance. He switches the sign on the door from Open to Closed, then locks it before walking to a van that's parked at the side of the building.

"Quick. He's leaving. Follow him." I shove Xander's keys back into the ignition.

"There's no point—"

"Just do it. Trust me, Xander, you won't regret it. We're onto something."

"Fine." He turns the key and when the Bublé song resumes, he switches the stereo off mid-warble. "But only to prove he's going for a burger at McDonald's."

The van pulls out and Xander lets a couple of cars get between us before following.

"We're going to lose him," I protest, watching the van turn down a side street. I'm on the edge of my seat, leaning to the side as if I'm going to be able to see around the corner more easily.

"Relax. I know what I'm doing."

I hope so. This is the closest I've been to finding out something useful.

Xander keeps the van in sight until we get to an industrial area, with fewer people and cars. Then he hangs back even more. Somehow, I manage not to criticize his tailing skills despite the tension running through me.

Up ahead, the van turns into a pot-holed, overgrown parking lot. There's a brick building at the rear of the lot with a decrepit railway car on one side of it.

"What is this place?" I ask as Xander slows.

"It's an abandoned train station. The train line used to run through here. In fact, the tracks are probably still over there, hidden in all that grass."

I watch the van park in front of the building, while Xander pulls over a little way up the road.

"What's he doing here?" I ask.

Xander shrugs. "Visiting an old train station isn't a crime."

"Pretty sure here's not here for a burger." I fling the car door open. "I'm going to find out what he's up to."

"Saffy, what are you doing?" He gets out too. "You can't chase after him. He could be dangerous."

"I thought you were sure he's innocent?" I hurry toward the lot. The van looks empty now. I didn't see where Devlin went, but it had to be into the brick building.

With his long legs, Xander has no trouble keeping up. "Are you hoping for trouble?" Then he frowns. "Doesn't your leg hurt, walking this fast? Come to think of it, why haven't I seen you limp today?"

"I got better."

I'm about to head through the gate when Xander pulls me back.

"We need to be a little more stealthy than that, Saffy. Let's find a way in through here." He motions me to follow him onto the neighboring property, past a derelict-looking house.

We creep along the rotting fence until we find a place where the boards have fallen in. After pulling away the vines that have grown over it, we find a gap big enough to squeeze through.

Once through, we use the old railway carriage for cover so nobody will be able to see us approach. When we're as close to the building as we can get, we both peer around the edge of the carriage.

The brick building has arched windows that might have

been beautiful once, before they were boarded up. Graffiti is scrawled along one side.

"What's that sign about?" I ask, pointing at a neon sign over the door. It's switched off, and in the bright daylight it's hard to read. "Does it say *Trainwreck'd*?"

"I think this might be an underground nightclub. Probably doesn't have a liquor license and opens illegally. Places like this tend to move around."

Xander crouches low and stays bent over as he jogs to the door. I follow his lead, feeling like an FBI agent in a movie. Hopefully not a movie where the good guys get killed.

Xander reaches the door and tries the handle, but it's locked. Devlin must have gone in and locked it behind him.

"What do we do now?" I whisper, peering around to make sure nobody's watching us.

"We come back later when it's open."

"What? No. Let's break in now." I can barely hold myself still, I'm so sure there's something inside this building.

He gives me a sharp look. "Breaking in would be illegal. Better to walk through the front door later, without calling attention to ourselves."

"Devlin will probably be gone by then."

Xander shrugs. "We might be able to figure out what he was doing here. It's probably something perfectly innocent."

"What if it's not? What if we spooked him by showing up in his store, and he's here to get rid of some vital evidence that could prove he's in league with the witch who killed Sylvia?"

"And what if he's here getting lunch? I don't have a warrant. Not to mention, I've already been suspended." He takes my arm and tugs me away with him. "Coming back tonight is all we can do."

I protest all the way back to the car, but Xander's mind is made up and I have no idea how I'd break in through a locked door without his help. It looked too thick and sturdy to force open.

"Let's stake out the place to see if anyone else shows up." I slide into the passenger seat. "And when he leaves, we can follow him. See where he goes."

"I'm not sitting out here to wait for an innocent man." Xander slides the keys into the ignition, but doesn't start the engine. His gaze drops to my jeans. "What happened to your leg?" he asks again. "What did you mean when you said you got better?"

"My uncle healed it."

He sighs, closing his eyes for a moment in a weary gesture. "Of course he did. He waved his fingers over it and said the magic words?"

"More or less." I'm tempted to show him where the wound used to be, but I'm wearing jeans. To prove I'm not lying, I'd have to peel them off.

Xander lifts his eyes skyward. "Why am I listening?" he asks the roof of the car. "It's clear you need help. Why don't I drop you off at the nearest psychiatric hospital and stop chasing leads that don't go anywhere?"

"This case has magic written all over it. You'll have to figure out a way to come to terms with that, or we'll never get anywhere." Saying that reminds me of the dark magic grimoire. I've been putting off trying to read it again because it gives me the creeps. But there's somebody who might be able to help. A witch who's even more of an outcast than I am, and rumored to dabble in the darker side of life. Like Voldemort, nobody wants to say his name.

I've never met him, but I know where to find him.

"I have one more lead," I say slowly, wondering if I'm making a huge mistake. "There's a man who might be able to shed light on some of this. Only I think he might be dangerous."

"Dangerous how?"

"I don't know, exactly." I shoot Xander a sideways look. "He has a bad reputation."

"Another in your circle of witch-believers?"

"Not in the circle. Outside the circle. Way out."

"Are you going to tell me any more than that?"

"I'll do better. I'll take you to see him."

"Saffy—"

"Do you have any other ideas?" I ask. "If so, I'd love to hear them."

He sighs. Then he starts the car engine. "Address?" he says wearily.

EIGHTEEN

"You're seriously telling me this man's name is *the Unseen*?" asks Xander, switching off the car engine.

"That's what everyone calls him. I don't know his real name."

"And this dangerous, evil man lives here?" I follow Xander's skeptical gaze to the Unseen's house. It's a freshly-painted wooden bungalow in suburban Baltimore, with a white picket fence and colorful rose bushes under the windows. A pair of garden gnomes are fishing in a pond filled with goldfish, surrounded by lawn that's perfectly green. The place looks sweet enough to make my back teeth ache.

"That's right." I shift the backpack on my lap. We stopped at my place on the way, so I could pick up Sylvia's bag with the grimoire inside. For the last few days, I've kept it shut in the furthest corner of the darkest cupboard of my locked investigation room. The grimoire's low-level hum sets my teeth on edge, and I have no safeguards against its power. Holding it feels like fondling a grenade that's lost its pin.

"Why did you bring that?" he asks, nodding to it. "And how exactly do you think this Unseen guy can help us?" Xander frowns. "He's not invisible, is he? Please tell me I'm not going to end up talking to empty air, because I really will drop you at a psychiatric—"

"I need to know why witches are losing their hearts," I cut him off. "There has to be a reason, and it's to do with a spell that's in this book. I found it at Sylvia's place, in her secret room."

"Secret room?" His voice rises in outrage. "You stole evidence from an active crime scene? And didn't tell the police about a hidden room containing that evidence?"

I nod impatiently. "Point is, the book won't let me read it unless I give it blood, and there's no way in hell I'm going to do that. Rumor is that the Unseen deals in the same dark magic as the book. We're here because he might be able to tell us what the spell does."

"You think you have to give the book *blood*?"

"That's what it wants, but giving in would be way too dangerous. I'm not even supposed to have the book. Only archivists handle the more powerful grimoires, let alone black magic ones."

"The book is dangerous." He repeats it flatly. Then, to my surprise, he laughs. He has a nice laugh. It's rich and deep. "It's too much. I give up. I'm going to surrender to your madness and ride the crazy train to Magic Land. Tell me, Saffy, why is the book dangerous? Will opening it cover you in paper cuts?"

I should be annoyed at his stubborn refusal to believe anything I say, but even as I roll my eyes, I find my lips twitching. His laughter is contagious.

"The grimoire has power and purpose of its own," I tell him. "Magic isn't like in the movies. You don't just recite special words to cast spells. You have to learn how to use your power in a certain way to get the result you want." I shake my head. "It's hard to explain. But one way for a witch to share knowledge of how to cast a spell is to imprint that spell into a book. To give the book power."

"The book can think for itself?" He eyes my backpack. "Should we have offered it lunch?"

Shaking my head with mock disgust, I get out of the car and sling the pack over my back. I take a deep breath and brace myself before opening the gate. Then the magical wards that surround the house catch me, holding me like a fly in a web. My skin itches and burns. I'm trapped, and I can't move. Can't scratch or run or even cry out. On my finger, my mother's ring flares into life, her blood glowing from within the red stone.

"You coming?" asks Xander, walking past me as though the Unseen's barrier doesn't exist.

The pain intensifies for a moment, then lets me go. The wards withdraw and my skin stops burning. I hesitate, not wanting to go further. But Xander's already knocking on the front door, so I rub my arms and join him.

An older man with silver hair and friendly eyes answers the door. He's wearing a brown knitted cardigan with leather patches on the elbows, saggy brown trousers, and fluffy slippers. When he smiles, he looks like a kindly grandfather.

"Hello," he says. "What can I do for you?"

Xander glances at me, and I can tell he's wondering if we've come to the right house. But there's a buzzing in my ears like I'm standing next to an electric power station, and the back of my neck is prickling.

"I'm Sapphira Black. I need your help." I turn a little so the Unseen can see the backpack I'm wearing. "With this."

The Unseen's expression changes as he looks at the backpack and I know he can feel the magic coming off it. "A grimoire?" he asks. "Where did you get it?"

This is the first time I've ever seen him in the flesh, and it feels a little like meeting the bad guy from a scary story. I swallow hard. "From my cousin. Sylvia's dead and her heart was taken."

His eyes widen. From his expression, this is news he didn't know. Now that I think about it, I doubt he hears about much that happens inside the witch community. Though I've heard him spoken about, nobody I know will have anything to do with him.

"And the mundane?" the Unseen asks, his gaze flicking to Xander.

"A friend."

The Unseen hesitates for a moment, then opens the door a little wider. "Come in. But be prepared to pay the price."

I glance at Xander, uneasy as to what price the old man might demand. But we need the information he can provide, so I step over the threshold.

Everything changes.

The bright, white hallway shimmers and becomes dark and forbidding. The taint of unpleasant magic crawls over every surface, setting my teeth on edge.

Worst of all is the Unseen. The kindly grandfather is gone. Now he's bent and wizened. His gray skin is covered in scars and scabs. His rotten teeth are sharpened to points, and when he leers at me, I see a few gaps where teeth are missing.

Beside me, Xander draws in a sharp breath. He gapes at the man. "H-how?" he stutters. "But you looked...?"

When his shocked stare falls on me, my own discomfort

isn't so bad that I can resist murmuring, "Want me to book you the room next to mine in the psychiatric ward?"

But the Unseen's expression makes my flash of satisfaction disappear fast. The old man's bloodshot eyes are still on my backpack, and the avarice in them makes me feel like hugging it to my chest. *The grimoire.* I silently curse myself for not foreseeing the problem in bringing such a powerful, dangerous book to a dark witch.

I edge back toward the door. "Actually, I've changed my—"

"You've crossed my threshold. You must finish what you started."

Taking another step back, I crash into Xander. His hands grip my upper arms and I stop, dragging in a breath. First things first. We need answers, and I'll figure out a way to pay for them later.

"This way." The Unseen opens a door at the end of the hall. Stairs lead down into darkness.

The old man sweeps his hand toward the stairs. "After you."

Hell, no. I shake my head. "You first."

With a creepy grin, he disappears into the blackness. Xander and I exchange glances. If things get nasty, I'm going to regret bringing Xander along. But for now, I'm glad he's here.

"Hasn't he ever heard of lights?" Xander asks, peering into the black. "This whole place is a series of safety and health violations. He causes trouble, we could threaten to call an inspector."

His tone is light, but he still looks pale. Discovering that magic really does exist must have shaken his whole view of the world. The fact he's still willing to follow the Unseen down a dark staircase into who-knows-what says a lot about his character.

"Stick close," I say, then give him a half-smile I hope looks reassuring. But when I ease down the first few steps, apprehension makes my chest tight. A sense of *wrongness* bears down on me, heavy around my shoulders, and my breath gets stuck in my throat.

Xander is right behind me. "Can't you turn on a light?" he yells into the darkness.

An unpleasant laugh is all the reply he gets. There's no hand rail, and when I grope to find the wall, my fingers encounter something warm and wet. I pull my hand back in and keep it close to my chest as my foot searches for the next step.

"It's like walking into ink," Xander murmurs from behind me. "Are you still there? I can't see you."

"I'm here. I'm going to grab your hand." I reach behind me and Xander's solid fingers slide into mine. I can pretend all I like that I'm the one who's reassuring *him*, but the truth is I feel steadier knowing he's close behind me. He has an inbuilt confidence, probably something he developed while working his way up through the police force.

His touch helps me take another step into the darkness as the sense of wrongness gets stronger. When I swallow, the taste of blood makes me gag. The air is thick with it. Is it seeping from the walls? It's all I can smell and taste. My lungs are filling with it.

I freeze, fighting panic.

The Unseen's basement is full of blood. We're going to drown in it.

"You okay?" Xander squeezes my hand. "Why'd you stop?"

"You don't feel that?" I ask hoarsely, already knowing the answer from his tone.

"Feel what?"

I drag in a breath, forcing more blood-tainted air into my lungs. I'm not going to drown. Whatever the Unseen is making me feel, it's not real.

In my mind, I concentrate on building a stone wall. Rock by rock, I piece the imaginary wall together, building a barrier between me and the spells that swirl around us. The wall protects me from the suffocating feeling of wrongness, of blood and death that must come from the Unseen's dark magic. After a minute, I take another step. Then another.

I lose count of how many steps there are until my foot finally lands on concrete instead of wood. The end of the staircase. A dim light flickers, brightening when I step toward it.

The room I'm walking into slowly illuminates, though mist hangs in the air, making it difficult to see much more than I could when it was pitch black.

We're in a basement. Peering around, I can make out shelves lining the walls. It smells damp and rancid, but the feeling that I'm choking on blood has gone.

Still, it's shaken me. For a moment I consider not letting Xander's hand go, but how would that look?

"You coming?" The old man's voice comes from near the light source. He sounds amused.

"If you make it easier to see," I snap.

A moment later, the mist clears. The Unseen is standing by a long wooden bench at the end of the room. A lamp beside him is the source of the light. Some of the book-shelves lining the room are filled with statues, bottles, jars, and trinkets. Most hold books. They must be dark magic books, because I'm fairly sure the unsettling energy that's raising the hairs on the back of my neck is coming from them. Although I'd bet that none has as much power as the grimoire in my backpack.

In one corner an enormous stone statue looms. It's a horned creature with a hideously deformed head and a sinuous, eight-legged body. The stuff of nightmares.

Somewhere in the corner, liquid is dripping. The sound reminds me of the drowning feeling, and I suppress a shiver.

The old man motions me closer, his small eyes gleaming. "Bring the grimoire here."

Reluctantly, I pull it from my backpack. I don't want to give it to the old man, but I need answers.

"Some kind of dog has ripped out three peoples' hearts with its teeth," I tell him. "There's a spell in here that uses the beating heart of a witch as an ingredient. It won't let me read the whole spell to find out what it does, so I need you to take a look."

The Unseen takes the book eagerly, tugging it from my hands, and puts it on the table. Instead of opening it, he dips his fingers into a small, dark bowl full of ink. When he draws them out, his fingertips have turned red.

The substance in the bowl isn't ink. It's blood.

The book opens on its own and the pages rise to stroke the Unseen's fingers, to lick the blood from his hand.

A chill crawls unpleasantly across my skin. Beside me, Xander draws in a sharp breath.

The Unseen turns his hand over to let the book lap every last drop of blood from his fingers. The slow, sensual way the pages move makes the act obscene. It's hard to watch, especially when I notice the Unseen is missing the tip of his little finger. That makes it worse somehow, because with blood slicked over his stump, it looks as though the grimoire might have bitten his finger right off.

But when the book is done drinking, it opens for the Unseen like it's offering itself to him, pages spread wide. The black mist rolls away and writing appears.

I crane my neck to read it, but the old man's hand is in the way. He's stroking the page as though he's feeling the spell rather than reading it. And the book is responding, the paper lifting to meet his touch.

Xander moves his lips close to my ear. "Wish they'd get a room," he mutters.

I hadn't realized how on edge I am, but the joke makes the tightness in my muscles ease a little. "You can see that?" I whisper back, unnecessarily. Then I lean closer to the Unseen. "What does it say?" I ask him. A putrid smell comes from the old man's body, like rotting fish.

"Consuming a living, beating heart can transfer the witch's magic." He murmurs the words as though talking to the book as much as to me.

"Eating the heart while it's still beating?" I shudder.

"Yes."

Grimacing, I peer at the spidery writing. There are tiny pictures among the words. Pictures that move, demonstrating things I don't want to see.

"Somebody got a dog to eat people's hearts so they could steal the soon-to-be-dead witch's power?" I want to make sure I understand what he's telling me. "But what use would that be? Nobody can control two different types of magic at once. They get tangled."

Then it hits me.

The spell he's describing must be what whoever murdered my mother was attempting to use. But it only half worked. He released my mother's magic when he killed her, but I'm the one who absorbed her magic, not him.

Why did the spell go wrong? Perhaps because I was nearby at the time?

"It's possible to utilize different types of magic at once." The Unseen's breathing has quickened, like he's excited. "But it takes great strength."

"Who'd have that kind of strength?"

The old man gives me a horrible gap-toothed, yellow smile. "A practitioner," he says with relish. The word is a euphemism for a witch who practices dark magic.

"I only know one of those," I say, giving him a meaningful look.

His smile grows wider. "An unproven allegation."

Beside me, Xander stiffens. He may not understand everything we're talking about, but he's obviously figured out that I've just accused the Unseen of killing my parents, Sylvia, and Mireya.

Not that I seriously think it was the Unseen who killed them. If it were, I doubt he'd be standing here, answering my questions about the grimoire.

The Unseen's hand stills on the book's page, and he cocks his head as though listening to something I can't hear. When he speaks, there's a longing in his voice that makes me deeply regret coming here. "If a practitioner absorbed every type of magic and was strong enough to control them, he'd become more powerful than you can imagine."

The implication dawns on me right away. I'd assumed the killer was targeting council members because of their position, but that may not be the reason. Each of the eight types of magic has a representative on the council.

"That's what the killer's doing? Going after each type of magic?" I frown, my mind spinning. "The first witch he killed was my mother, but he didn't get her magic. Something went wrong and it created an explosion that killed my father and knocked me out." I'm thinking it through as I speak. "But the killer did nothing after that for several years. Why not?"

Xander speaks up for the first time, nodding toward the grimoire. "Perhaps he couldn't do anything until he found that book at your cousin's house. It showed him how to get the spell right."

"Maybe. Nobody but me could have taken the grimoire out of her athenaeum, but I've been wondering how the spell could have been cast in there with Sylvia's wards active."

"Cast by a dark witch with great power," suggests the Unseen.

"Whoever it was took Sylvia's archival magic. And Mireya's plant magic."

"How many types of magic are there?" Xander asks. Seems he really has accepted that magic exists, and all it took was watching a horrible grimoire sucking the blood off a creepy practitioner's fingers. Go figure.

"Eight." I count them off on my fingers. "Earth. Air. Fire. Water. Animal. Plant. Truth. And the archivists. That's why there are eight council members. They're the strongest witches with each kind of magic."

With his head down, fondling the grimoire's pages, the Unseen looks like he's talking to the book. "There are nine types of magic."

"What?" I frown. Surely I didn't hear that right.

"Once enough hearts have been consumed, the practitioner's power will be immense," says the Unseen. "But to gain that power, the witch must perform the spell themselves. They must consume the heart. Not a dog."

"But there was dog DNA on the wound," says Xander, before I can circle the conversation back to check that I didn't really hear the Unseen say there were nine types of magic. "And Saffy, didn't you mention something about a rotting dog smell?"

"A rotting dog?" The Unseen's face jerks up, his gaze sharpening. "There's a demon that's said to have that smell. If a demon possessed a witch, that witch would have great power."

"Not the hairy demon that Mireya showed us?" asks Xander. "What was its name? Something to do with jackals."

The Unseen lets out a loud breath and the stench of week-old fish fills my nose. "Jeqabeel," he breathes. The word sounds reverent. Then his eyes widen and his gaze jerks back down to the grimoire. "Could it be?" He dips his hand back into his bowl of blood. This time, when he strokes the pages they turn themselves to the flyleaf at the very front of the book. The name of the witch who wrote the grimoire is inscribed in letters that have an ominous red glow. The Unseen lets out a long sigh, his face going slack. He looks awed. "I didn't dare to hope," he whispers. "A treasure beyond imagining."

"Who is that?" I ask, tilting my head to try to read the name. "Does it say Zavier Cross? No, that's a G. Zavier Gross?"

"One of the greatest witches who ever lived." The Unseen runs his fingers reverently over the name. "He found a way to drop the veil and bring one of the most powerful demons into this world."

"He's the one who let Jeqabeel loose?" My voice rises with horror. "And he wrote this book?"

"I was told the Council had destroyed this grimoire." The Unseen's face twists, somehow becoming even more ugly, though I'd have bet everything I owned that wasn't possible. "After they trapped Jeqabeel, they executed Zavier Gross and his entire family, and burned his house to the ground."

"Why would this Gross guy want to set a dangerous demon free in the first place?" asks Xander.

"Power has rewards, mundane, but it's something you could never understand. You could no more imagine that type of power than a cockroach can understand how it feels for an eagle to fly."

"But Jeqabeel's essence is trapped in his bone. The bone is still in Mom's safe. Her wards are secure..." The Unseen's gleeful stare makes my voice trail away.

Shit. After drugging me and dragging me in front of the Veritas, I told my uncle he wasn't welcome in my home. He hasn't checked the safe, or any of Mom's artifacts.

"I saw the bone in the safe," I say stubbornly. "And I'm sure the wards are intact."

The old man shakes his head, his eyes gleaming. "Poor little broken witch, so easily deceived. With a little power and cunning, a thief could replace the bone with another. How would the broken witch know, when her magic is chained?"

I hate to admit it, but he has a point.

NINETEEN

"Aren't we jumping to conclusions?" Xander scowls at the Unseen, probably still sore from being called a cockroach. "Just because this book was written by that Gross guy, doesn't mean for sure that we're dealing with Jeqabeel. Didn't Mireya suggest other possibilities? There was one with a golden worm, I remember that much. I like the sound of a worm demon better."

"Jeqabeel has a stench like you described," says the Unseen. "It can possess and control the minds of witches. It will compel a witch to do whatever it takes to bring the demon fully into our world."

"It can control people from inside the bone?" I shake my head. "That can't be right. The bone was in my basement. In a locked and warded safe, but still. Not exactly the safest place for an evil killing machine with mind control powers."

"To influence a mind, the vessel needs to be touched. And it feeds off magic. In a mundane's hands, the bone would be powerless."

"The bone's in a protective casing, so nobody can touch it."

Xander shakes his head. "I don't believe that ugly demon from Mireya's drawing could be walking around free."

"Not walking. Not yet." The Unseen licks his lips, but it looks like an eager gesture rather than a nervous one. "Not enough death for the demon to be free. Not even close."

"Okay," says Xander. "That's good then, right?"

"Someone's trying to set it free?" I swallow. "If one of my parents accidentally touched the bone, could the demon have killed them?"

"If one of them touched the bone, the demon would have possessed their mind. It needs a conduit. A slave to do its work."

"So this witch-slave, whoever it is, killed my parents and the others in order to steal their magic and get strong enough to release the demon into our world."

"I don't get it," says Xander. "If the demon is eating hearts with its own jackal teeth, it must already be here."

"If it were free on this plane you'd be dead." The Unseen's voice is sharp. Certain. "When Jeqabeel achieves its corporeal form, it will be unstoppable. All will pay homage, or die." The Unseen's lips curl back, revealing his horrible sharpened teeth. Is the old man smiling? Surely not. It must be a grimace.

"Tell us how to stop it," Xander demands.

The Unseen stares at him a moment, then gives a sneering laugh. "You wish to stop it, mundane? You have as much chance of stopping the moon from rising." His gaze goes to me. "And you, little broken witch. Jeqabeel will turn you into dust."

I'm over the whole 'broken witch' label, but I grit my teeth. "Just tell us what we need to do."

He's still stroking the pages of Sylvia's book and when

he glances down at it, his eyes glint with avarice. "You ask for more help? It's time to make payment."

"What do you want?" I ask, though I already know.

"The grimoire."

I shake my head. "No. Never. What else?"

"The grimoire," he repeats more insistently.

"Forget it. The book is warded. Now Sylvia's dead, it belongs to me, and if you try to take it by force, Sylvia's wards will activate and blow your house up." I have no idea whether that's true, but my cousin was a powerful archivist and she'd be sure to cover a grimoire like this with protection spells. It's likely something bad would happen to anyone who tried to steal it.

"You must pay what you owe." The Unseen's jaw tightens and his hand goes to the bowl of blood on his desk, as though he's itching to cast a spell. His longing for the grimoire is written in every line of his face.

My fists clench and I raise them in front of me as though I'm ready to fight him for the book. If only it were that easy. Physically, he's no match for either Xander or me, but his magic could flatten us both.

His gaze flicks down to my fists. His eyes widen and he stares at my hands. No, at my mother's ring. his expression changes to one of speculation. Then he gets a calculating look I don't like at all.

"I'll take your ring as payment," he says.

I drop my fists, and my other hand reaches to cover my ring. "You can't have that either."

"The grimoire or the ring." His expression is set and his tone final. "You must choose, or I'll take the mundane instead."

Xander steps forward, his back stiff. "You think you can threaten me?"

"You're not having the mundane," I keep my tone even.

"And you're not giving him the book." Xander states flatly.

I have to agree. I've been wondering what other terrible spells are detailed in the grimoire, and how bad it would be if the Unseen got his hands on them.

Xander knows the ring I wear is my mother's and I'm sure he guesses how much it means to me. He doesn't know it contains my mother's blood, and even if he did, he wouldn't understand why that's a big deal.

Every choice the Unseen has given me is unthinkable. But after watching him stroke the book's pages and seeing the mist-shrouded paper respond like a fawning puppy, I can't stomach letting him have the grimoire. Whatever secrets it holds are too dangerous to leave in his hands.

"What do you want with my mother's ring?" I demand.

"That's none of your business."

Even knowing I'll have to give it to him, I still hesitate. Blood is power. Once he has my mother's blood, he may be able to use it to gain some power over me.

But what choice do I have?

Reluctantly, I pull the ring off my finger, squeezing it over my knuckle. I place it in the disgusting yellowed palm of the Unseen, regretting it even as his fingers close over it. His triumphant expression makes me want to wrestle it straight back from him.

"Tell us how to stop the demon," demands Xander, his voice rough.

"Jeqabeel's essence is trapped in the bone. The power it requires to escape it and regain its own form is immense. It must absorb more magic than you can imagine, and bathe in a river of blood."

"How do we stop it *before* it gets that much blood?" I ask.

"Find Jeqabeel's disciple."

"You mean the witch that's doing the killing for it?" asks Xander.

"It needs magic," says the Unseen. "It has already feasted and will be eager for more."

"Maybe we can catch the killer in the act." Xander tugs his notebook and pen out of his pocket. Probably his police notebook, because as he flips to a clean page, I glimpse other notes describing cases. "It's targeting council members because they have the strongest magic, right? Who are they?"

"The remaining magic types are air, fire, earth, water, and the Veritas," I say. "And animal magic, seeing as he didn't manage to get that from my mother."

"The Veritas are few," says the Unseen. "Their line is dying."

"I met a Veritas the other day. A young girl. I didn't like her."

"You were tested? And you survived?" The Unseen narrows his bloodshot eyes at me. "But your magic is bound, correct?"

"That's right."

"And you defeated a Veritas?"

I shake my head. "I didn't defeat her. She wanted me to admit to the murders, but I'm innocent. I wouldn't confess to something I didn't do."

He studies me without speaking, a frown creasing his pock-marked brow. I must have been right that the Veritas can make innocent people confess anything. So much for truth. She's clearly the council's tool to get rid of people they deem inconvenient.

"What about the other council members?" asks Xander.

"I've already warned my uncle. He said the council were taking precautions."

He taps his pen on the page. "Who do you think is most vulnerable?"

"Dallas is a mess right now, and probably not being careful. But I'm the last person he'd want to see or listen too. Magnus Fox is head of the council, but he won't help us either. The Veritas is sheltered in the council chambers." I snap my fingers. "Amber's the earth witch who replaced my father on the council. Sylvia mentioned she was spending all her time in the library, working with the archivists to record some new spells. I bet we could find her there."

"Which library?" asks Xander.

"Yes," I say, unable to resist. "Exactly."

He gets it right away and his eyes light up. "There's a witch library? Can't wait to see it."

He flips his notebook closed and tucks it in his pocket as though it's a done deal. He must think visiting her there will be an easy thing to do.

Little does he know.

TWENTY

"This is just the George Peabody Library," says Xander as we walk up the stone steps to the historic library for the John's Hopkins University. He sounds disappointed.

The whole way here, he asked a million questions about witches. Now he's decided to include magic in his world view, he's trying to fill his detective brain up with all the facts. I have to hand it to him, he's taking the whole thing well.

"Not exactly," I tell him. "Where we're going, there are a few differences." I'm feeling grim, but determined. This is going to be difficult without magic. Maybe impossible. But we need to try.

Our footsteps are loud as we cross the lobby, then we cross through the exhibition gallery and go into the spectacular reading room. No matter how many times I see it, the interior of the library always takes my breath away. Five levels of books, all visible from the ground floor as you look up through nineteenth century railings and architecture. It's beautiful.

A few students are studying at the desks in the center of

the atrium, and a small group of tourists are taking photos, but the library is relatively quiet. I head to the back, into the far corner of the lower floor. Usually, witches use magic to cover their tracks and make sure no mundane sees where they go. I don't have that luxury. I'm going to have to be stealthy.

Finding the right set of book stacks is easy. The next bit I'm less certain about. I used to come here with my mother, but she was the one who always got us in and I'm not exactly sure how.

My heart contracts at a sudden, vivid picture of my mother bringing me here when I was young. Once I asked how long it would take to read all the books in the library. She laughed and told me I should let her know how long it took after I'd done it.

I miss her so much, and I hate not wearing her ring. My hand feels naked and I'm more vulnerable without my mother's talisman. I wish she were here now. She had such powerful magic that with a little blood, it seemed she could solve any problem.

All I have is the stubbornness I was born with.

Browsing my way along the shelves, I take a deep breath and close my eyes.

"What are you doing?" asks Xander. "Maybe I can help?"

I shake my head, concentrating. Searching with my mind for the tingle of magic. It's harder because of the grimoire I'm still carrying in my backpack. Its terrible dark magic hums at the edge of my perception, clouding everything else.

Squeezing my eyes tighter, I concentrate harder. It must be here somewhere.

There.

A faint tickle in my brain. An awareness of power, coming from a little way ahead.

With my eyes still closed, I let that tickle guide me forward. It grows into the uncomfortable sensation of pushing through a powerful protection ward, before my outstretched fingers brush the spine of a book. The source of the power.

On the shelf, the book looks like all the other hard-cover historical reference books around it, except older, more worn, and less appealing. The words have faded on its cracked spine, so its title is illegible. "This is it." I pull the book out of the shelf. "This'll get us where we need to go. I hope."

The front cover of the book is nothing like its spine. It's bright and modern, with a familiar face on the cover. Xander eyes its title. "*Harry Potter and the Chamber of Secrets?*"

"It was Roald Dahl's *The Witches* when I used to come here with my mother."

"That doesn't look like it belongs here. What's to stop an unsuspecting member of the public finding it? Or one of the staff?"

"Here." I hold the book out, offering it to him.

He reaches for it, but his hand only gets halfway to the book before it moves sideways.

"I can't touch it," he says, trying again. "The air around it is slippery. My hand slides right past it." His eyes are wide. "This is weird. How is it doing that?"

I glance around to make sure we're alone. The tourists are still near the entrance, and we're tucked far enough into the corner that none of the students can see us.

"You think that's impressive? Watch this." I flip the

book open and a portion of the bookcase behind it shimmers and fades into nothing.

"What the—?" Xander reaches toward it and his fingers disappear into the hole. "Oh shit," he whispers.

Unlike Sylvia's athenaeum, the secret basement room the portal leads to does actually exist in this time and space continuum, so it doesn't feel like walking through jello.

"Come on." I put the book back before stepping through the shimmering black hole into the space beyond.

So far, so good.

The doorway closes behind us and dim lighting shows us the way down the metal spiral staircase. The rail gives us something to hold onto as we descend round and round. The difference between this stairwell and the last one we went down together isn't lost on me.

"How far does this go down?" asks Xander.

"Several floors. I remember feeling like the stairs would never end when I came here with my mother."

"Was that the last time you were here?"

I nod. "Not much need for magical books when my magic is all messed up."

"You said the problem is that you have two types of magic now, right?"

"I used to just have earth magic, and was learning lots of spells to use it for different things. But adding animal magic made both types a lot stronger. They get tangled together and normal spells aren't powerful enough to control them."

"But the Unseen said there was a way to control them both?"

"Dark magic," I mutter, grimacing.

"What's—?"

I cut him off, not wanting to explain about dark magic. "I'm not supposed to use my magic and I haven't had access to them for a long time. The council bound them to keep any accidents from happening." I think of Agnes and flush.

"What was it like, having magic?"

A question like that deserves a proper answer. I stop. "Everything was easier. I didn't have to fight to get by."

He stops on the step below mine, turning to face me. "Has it been hard? Living without it?"

In the dim light, his eyes are in shadow. There's nobody else to hear. No reason not to answer honestly, with a simple 'Yes'. But my throat closes on the word, so I just nod.

The last few years, I haven't even admitted to myself how hard it's been. I always tell myself I don't miss it, but Xander can probably see the truth in my expression.

"I'm sorry." He's on the step below me, so he doesn't look as tall as usual, but his bulk is still comforting. I like having him with me. All these years I've had to be strong and get on with things. I'm glad I don't have to do this alone.

"It's fine," I say, taking a deep breath. "I'm used to it now. I've got a good life. And the truth is, I don't think I'd want my magic back even if I could control it. Having power made me soft. Learning to do without it was difficult, but I'm stronger now. It was a crutch, and now I don't need it." I smile at myself and shake my head. "Does that make any sense at all?"

He puts one hand on my arm and suddenly I'm very aware of how close he is, and how we're alone in the semi-darkness. The shadowy stairwell accentuates the masculine angles of Xander's face and the hard line of his jaw. When he leans closer, I breathe in his scent. He has a fresh, slightly woody smell, like he's been out chopping firewood in a field of long grass.

His hand tightens on my arm to draw me even closer. "Since I've met you, my world's been turned upside down."

His voice is low. Intimate.

"In a bad way?" I ask.

"Nothing's the way I thought it was." His gaze drops to my lips and his thumb skims across the flesh of my arm.

"That didn't answer my question."

"Saffy." His voice has a rough edge now. "I want you to know I—"

The lights flicker off, plunging us into darkness. Metal groans and the ground shudders. I clutch the stair rail to keep my balance, my heart pounding.

Then the lights come back on.

"What was that?" demands Xander.

"I don't know. But I think we'd better hurry."

We take the rest of the stairs at a run. The bottom of the staircase looks like a dead end. There's just a wall with a large statue of a gargoyle in front of it.

The gargoyle is carved from stone. Its eyes are stone too, though its pupils are black obsidian.

"Let us through," I tell it. "It feels like something bad might be happening."

"Who seeks entry?" the gargoyle asks. Its stone jaw moves as though it's alive. When I was young, I was fascinated by it, trying to work out how stone could move like that. Now it reminds me of the living statues in the council lobby and looking at it makes my bile rise.

"Sapphira Black and Xander Trent."

Its cold stone pupils move slowly from me to Xander and back again. "Prove your magic."

"I can't. My magic is messed up."

"Then you cannot pass."

"I have magic, I just can't use it."

The gargoyle is silent.

"What does it want?" Xander frowns. "And where would we go? There's nothing down here."

"My great grandfather created you," I tell the gargoyle, my voice rising. "He was a powerful earth witch, and I'm his descendant. You really want me to let my power go when I can't control it? Anything could happen. Chaos and mayhem. It could turn you into a hamster. You want to spend the next hundred years squeaking at everyone who comes down here?"

The statue doesn't respond. It's as quiet and still as a... well, you know.

The floor shudders again, and I grab Xander's arm to keep my balance.

"What's going on?" he demands, and I'm not sure whether he's talking to me or the gargoyle.

"Nothing good," I say grimly. "An earthquake, maybe. Or explosions. The way things have been going, it wouldn't surprise me if the entire building falls down."

Xander glares at the gargoyle. "I'm a police officer. Let us in *now*."

I bet that commanding tone works a treat on subordinates. But as far as the gargoyle is concerned, he may as well be talking to himself.

Dammit, I'm going to have to cut myself and let my magic out. It could bring the building down on our heads, but without being able to prove I'm not mundane, we're not going anywhere. I just wish I wasn't carrying the grimoire in my backpack, because the low, unpleasant buzz of power it emits sets my teeth on edge and makes it hard to...

Wait a minute.

Gritting my teeth against the icy-cold, nasty feel of the thing, I pull out the grimoire and present it to the gargoyle as though inviting it to choose a meal from an all-black menu.

"Here's magic."

Made of stone or not, the gargoyle flinches.

The wall behind the gargoyle shimmers and dissolves, granting us access to the library. When I shove the grimoire back in my backpack and step past the gargoyle, I find shelves full of books. The most powerful grimoires are held in secret athenaeums like Sylivia's, but there are still hundreds of magical books here. They make my skin tingle.

Wait, I can smell something. Is that smoke?

"Stay close," says Xander. "A fire may have started. In a library, that can't be good."

The acrid smell of smoke gets stronger as we weave our way through the shelves, heading toward where I remember Amber's office was, at the back of the building. I can't see or hear anyone.

"The place shouldn't be empty." I speed up. "It's the middle of the day. There should be people here. And if there's a fire, shouldn't the alarms and sprinklers have gone off?"

Then something powerful stops me dead. A shock of power makes my hair stand on end. My nostrils fill with the stench of rotting meat and dog hair, and with it comes a wave of nausea. My stomach roils and I bend over and gag. The magic feels dark and old and dangerous.

"Are you okay?" Xander puts his hand on my back. "What's that smell?"

With my hands on my knees, I lift my head. "Something's happening. Not far ahead." Not just *something*. I know exactly what it is. It feels exactly like when Sylvia and Mireya died, only worse.

Much, much worse.

The floor shakes again, sending books tumbling to the floor.

"Can you walk?" asks Xander. "I can carry you if—"

"I'm okay." I move forward, clenching my jaw and forcing myself toward the terrible thing I can still feel. The books vibrate with power that's far stronger than I would have expected to feel from them. The dark magic has awakened them. The air is awash with so much energy, I'm amazed Xander can't feel it.

"What's that?" Xander's voice is sharp. "Something moved up there." He points, and we round the corner together.

Blood spatters the books around us. Blood is everywhere.

A person stands over a body on the floor. No, it's not a person. It's a demon. It has a jackal's head and a man's body, and is wearing a cloak that hides its clothes, with only its hands uncovered. Human hands, covered in blood. More blood cakes the jackal's muzzle. Its stench is overpowering.

The demon snarls at us. At its feet is Amber. But there's a hole in her chest where her heart used to be. We're too late.

"Get back." Xander shoves me behind him, then tugs out a gun I didn't know he was carrying. "Police," he yells. "Get—"

The jackal creature launches itself at us.

A gunshot almost deafens me. The demon flies backward, its body toppling the shelf behind it. All the books crash to the floor.

The demon pulls itself up to standing. Blood leaks from below its shoulder where Xander shot it, and even from where I am, I can feel the dark power that surges through the blood, making it glow.

The beast charges again. It hurls me into Xander and we hit the shelves hard, going over with them.

I lie sprawled awkwardly amongst shelves and books, expecting the monster to attack before I can scramble to my feet. A drop or two of its blood must have landed on me because my magic is surging.

"Are you alright?" demands Xander as I pull myself out of the downed shelves.

"I'm not bleeding," I say curtly. It's a relief, because if I were, there'd be no way I could keep my magic contained. "Where'd the demon go?"

"Up the stairs."

"We can't let it get away."

Xander nods and races after it. I follow, a little slower because the sheer amount of magic in the air is making my head swim.

A gunshot blasts from in front of me. Xander must have the demon in sight. I want to warn him that it seems immune to bullets and could probably kill him without too much trouble, but it takes all my energy just to keep up, especially racing back up the stairs we came down.

At the top, the doorway shimmers. Xander leaps through it after the demon as though he's been travelling through magical doorways his entire life.

When I burst through after him, back into the regular mundane library, the demon has Xander by the throat. Xander scrabbles at its hands, trying to get free, but the demon is too strong. It lifts him off his feet. Its muzzle opens, horrible tongue lolling.

It's squeezing the life out of Xander.

Tearing at the skin on one wrist with my fingernails is an instinctive reaction. So is reaching for the forces inside me. As my blood oozes, I pull my magic free of what remains of the council bindings. Struggling for control, I manage to picture the demon being flattened, trying to focus the energies on it as they tear out of me.

My animal magic hits it so hard, the demon staggers and drops Xander, who scrambles backward. The animal magic pours into the demon, while I collapse to my knees in shock.

It worked. I can't believe it. My magic did what I wanted.

My moment of amazed celebration is cut off as my earth magic hits the ornate marble column behind the creature, creating an explosion that sends chunks of marble flying. A moment later, I feel the animal magic dissipate. I didn't draw enough blood.

The demon turns on me, snarling. It looks unharmed.

Shit.

I brace myself as the demon charges.

There's nowhere to go, nowhere to escape. The creature slams into me, sending me flying into the column behind me. Pain explodes through my body and the column crumbles, pieces of stone raining down. Part of the second level of the building collapses, and big chunks smash into the marble floor, narrowly missing me.

With my hands around my head to protect it, I curl up to try to avoid as many falling rocks as I can. One bounces off my shoulder. Another smashes on my leg.

The demon looms over me, coming to finish me off.

Gunshots boom, deafening me. The demon recoils. It wheels around to face Xander. I think the bullets are only pissing it off.

Xander squeezes off another shot. The creature claps its hands over the wound and for a moment I dare to hope it's actually been hurt. Then it stalks toward Xander, its blood-slicked palms extended.

Xander levitates off the ground as though snatched up by an invisible hand. He kicks and thrashes, but the demon's magic holds him up, lifting him high into the library's central atrium.

Then his legs and arms jerk out. They splay wide and he lets out a shocked yelp. It looks like the demon's power has hold of each hand and foot, and is going to tear Xander apart. To rip him into four pieces.

"No!" I try to scream the word, but it comes out a croak.

Scrambling to my feet, I grab the closest thing to a weapon, one of the rocks that fell. I hurl it at the creature with all the strength and power gained from years of hard physical labor. The rock flies straight and true, with all the force of my fury and fear behind it. It slams hard into the beast's cloaked back.

The demon doesn't seem to notice.

Xander cries out in pain. His T-shirt rips at the seams, stretched too far. His muscles will tear next.

The demon's too strong. It's going to kill us both, and there's nothing I can do to stop it.

TWENTY-ONE

Blind panic fills me. I can't let the demon kill Xander.

Launching myself forward, I stumble across a pile of fallen books and slash my arm against the splintered edge of a toppled bookcase. The skin rips open. My blood flows.

My magic surges again, and this time I use my rage and terror to grab hold of it, gripping both strands of magic as hard as I can. I don't care if they're tangled and I can't control them. It's my only chance.

The picture in my head is one of pure desperation. Saving Xander and killing the demon. Nothing else matters.

With a scream of anger, I let the magic go.

My earth magic roars in my senses. It's wild and unbelievably strong. I've always thought the animal magic was the strongest, but now my earth magic's intensity is shocking. The two types of magic somehow feed and intensify each other. Their power is all I can feel.

The rubble of broken marble pieces littering the floor all lift together, flying into the air. They swirl around me, forming a tornado of missiles. There's no wind, just a chaotic, violent mess of rocks, spiraling and crashing against each other. The rock tornado builds until it's roaring through the library's central atrium, straight for the beast. When the rocks slam into the demon, Xander drops to the ground.

The demon is swallowed, hidden from view inside the swirling debris. Then it's launched out of the tornado. It flies like a missile and slams into shelving on the far side of the library. The demon scrambles unsteadily to its feet and lurches for the door. Staggering and bleeding, it disappears outside.

For a moment, all I feel is relief. And then a pebble hits me in the face and I yelp in pain, holding my hand to my cheek. Blood pools in the wound and the whirling rocks surge faster.

Books and bits of broken desks and shelving join the tornado, making it bigger and more violent. Instead of calming down, it's gathering momentum. I've lost all control of it. Small stones fly out and continue to pelt me. One slices a hot gash into my arm, feeding the magic even more. Another hits my leg so hard I cry out and almost fall.

The tornado moves closer to Xander and I try desperately to pull back the power, to stop it. I've never been able to see the magical energy like I can now. I can trace the bright strands with my eyes as well as feeling them. I try to pull on the strands, but my animal magic is in the way. It's tangled in the earth magic, twisting in the stone tornado, yet it's not being discharged the way my earth magic is, making it impossible to reign in.

Its rocks spiral around the library's atrium, slamming into everything in its path. Xander covers his head, but the maelstrom is on him now. Rocks and books pelt him. Instead of being saved, he'll be beaten to death.

I take a sobbing breath, my arms covering my head to

protect against flying missiles, and strain with every ounce of energy left inside me, trying to harness the windless tornado. The stones keep flying.

In the distance, sirens wail.

Right in front of me, Xander's completely hidden by a swirling wall of rocks. I have to stop them before he's beaten to a bloody pulp.

If he isn't already.

Straightening my shaking, swaying body, I reach out again and try to grasp the glowing tangled strands of animal magic. At first, they slip away from me, stinging my fingers. But I grit my teeth and take a step further into the maelstrom of magic. Stones are hitting my arms, but I ignore them, and use my brute strength to grasp hold of a strand of animal magic. I will not fail Xander.

My hands are clenched tight around the animal magic, and I yank it back toward me. The magic digs into my skin, distorting my flesh, and the pain is more than I can bear. But I don't stop. I can't stop. I drag the animal magic back inside me, inch by inch, never stopping, whimpering with the pain as I do it.

My hands mutate, my skin hardening and my nails becoming claws. My face burns as it twists and deforms. But the ragged wound on my arm has stopped bleeding, and the tornado of rocks is slowing.

With a last, raw scream, I yank the last of the animal magic out of the tornado, forcing it back inside what's left of the council's bindings.

The rocks fall to the ground. In the middle of the debris, Xander lies motionless.

I hobble over to him, almost falling on him in my desperate rush to see if he's okay. He's covered with cuts and welts. Every bit of skin I can see is either flayed open, or black and swollen. What if he's dead? I grab his arm with hands that have recovered their normal shape, praying he still has a pulse.

When my blood-covered hands land on his skin, a shock jolts through me. The council's bindings are too weak to restrain the animal magic I dragged back inside me. Before I can stop it, the magic pours into Xander.

His wounds heal in front of my eyes. The bruises, cuts, and welts vanish, leaving his skin smooth. He groans and rolls over.

"You're o-okay?" I demand. "I th-thought you were d-dead." My teeth chatter, a reaction from unleashing so much power.

"I thought I was, too." He pushes himself up to sitting and I try to help, but I'm so weak I hardly have the strength to hold myself up. All I can do is flop down next to him.

"Where is it?" asks Xander, looking around but not making any move to stand up. "What happened to the demon?"

"It g-got away."

"Shit."

I swallow. Now I know Xander's safe, frustration creeps in. The creature that killed my family is still out there. That thing ate my mother's heart.

And it's a lot stronger than we are.

Xander reaches out with both hands to take my upper arms. "You look like you've been through a war." He checks me over, his brow pulled down in concern. Then he pulls me closer. "You're shaking," he murmurs. "You're cold?"

I drag in a deep breath and focus on calming my heart's wild beating. "The effect of the magic. I'll be alright in a minute." At least this time my teeth don't chatter.

Xander tucks me against him and wraps an arm around

me. Considering he was all but dead a minute ago, he seems remarkably alive now. Not just alive, but warm and strong. I like the way it feels as I mold myself against his chest.

The siren is getting louder really fast, and I consider suggesting we make ourselves scarce so we don't have to answer any difficult questions. But it's probably too late now anyway, and I don't think I have the strength to move.

We're totally alone in here, for now at least. Everyone must have evacuated the building when the demon's dark spell made it start shaking.

"I don't get it," says Xander thoughtfully. With my ear against his neck, the words rumble in an appealing way. "The old man said the demon's essence was trapped in the bone. He said it was using a witch to do its work. He didn't say anything about a jackal-headed thing walking around with an actual, physical body."

"That can't be Jeqabeel's corporeal form. A man with a jackal's head isn't the monster we saw in the drawing." I shudder. "Maybe that's what happens when you let a demon control you. The demon must have lent the witch its face to eat hearts. That has to be the way it absorbs the power."

"It was strong, whatever it was," says Xander. "We're looking for a powerful, evil witch. Any spring to mind?"

"Magnus Fox." The name tastes bitter in my mouth. "In the months before my mother died, there were murmurs that she should became head of the council instead of him. Maybe the position meant so much to him, he was willing to kill for it." It's been a pet theory of mine for years, but one that no one else is willing to consider.

And now he smells of dog. Suspicious much?

Suddenly I remember the grimoire. My backpack is gone. It must have been torn off when the demon threw me into the library stacks. "Xander," I say urgently. "We need to find—"

"Freeze!" shouts a voice from the door. "Police!"

Xander lets go of me and puts his hands up, then slowly turns toward the policemen storming in. I follow his lead, getting to my feet when they order me to. I let them pat me down, glad they haven't handcuffed me. Maybe I'm too sorry a sight, covered with cuts and bruises, and probably deathly pale.

I'm worried about the grimoire, but it must be down in the lower levels, where the mundanes can't go, at least. And with the mess down there, hopefully nobody will stumble across it.

The policemen lead us outside, past firemen who are running in. Several police cars are parked in front of the building, but they take us to an ambulance. The medics check us for injuries and one asks me to sit on a gurney while she starts bandaging the worst of my cuts.

When Xander discovers he doesn't have any cuts to bandage, his wide-eyed gaze jerks to me. He must have felt that final discharge of my magic, but probably hadn't realized what it did.

If only I could heal people intentionally, it would be a handy skill to have. My animal magic must have responded to my fear for him. If it weren't so difficult to control, I might try to do it again. I'd love to heal my own aches and pains.

More police cars arrive while I'm arguing with the medic over whether she can take a pair of scissors to my last pair of jeans to clean a gash on my leg. I insist on yanking the denim up as far as I can instead, refusing to wince at the pain.

Then a large black sedan pulls slowly to the curb. The

back door of the car opens and a tall woman steps out, dressed in a neat black skirt and white blouse. I recognize her as Baltimore's outspoken mayor, Anna Trent.

Beside me, Xander curses.

"Your mother?" I ask unnecessarily. She has eyes just like Xander's, only hers are glacial. There are lines of strain around her mouth, but no laugh lines that I can see. Her brow creases in what looks like anger as she stares at the library. Smoke billows out some of the lower floor windows and there's a large crack in the library's outside wall. I wince. That was probably my tornado.

The mayor stalks over to Xander, taking in his disheveled state. Both his jeans and T-shirt are torn, and he's covered with dirt and blood. His hair is so thick with stone dust and fragments, it's standing on end. But there's no worry for him in her expression.

"What are you doing here?" she demands. "With *her*?" Lip curled, she motions at me. "A suspect in at least one murder case."

"I didn't kill anyone," I say.

Ignoring me, she leans closer to Xander. "What happened to the library?"

"You wouldn't believe me if I told you." His voice has gone flat and his face is expressionless. A different person to the man who hugged me just a little while ago.

His mother makes an impatient sound. "Vandalism? Destruction of public property? Arson? They're just minor charges to add to her rap sheet, Xander, but I expected better from you."

His eyes jerk to hers. "You think we did all that damage? Nobody saw... anyone else coming out?"

"Was somebody else there?"

"Of course there was. Another woman's been killed."

"Another murder?" demands his mother. "In there?"

Xander hesitates, glancing at me. I know what he's thinking. They'll never find Amber, because her body is hidden in the depths of the library, shielded by magic in an area that mundanes can't get to.

"Ma'am," interrupts a policeman who's been hovering. "I'm sorry, Mayor. We'd prefer if you don't talk about what's happened until we've questioned them and taken statements."

Xander turns to him. "Am I under arrest, Harry?" He nods to me. "Is she?"

I wince. Not at the question, but because the medic is washing grit out of the wound on my shoulder and her touch isn't gentle.

"We need to find out what happened, Detective Trent. I can't say more than that until you've spoken to the leads on this case and given a statement."

"I'm trying to protect you," hisses his mother. "You're making it impossible. She'll have a very public trial, then they'll throw away the key. Do you really want to get caught up in it? To throw away all your hard work?"

I swallow hard as the reality of our situation sinks in. What if I end up in jail?

And if Xander's charged with a crime, he'll never get his job back.

"Saffy's innocent, Mother."

"Don't be naïve. You've been suspended, your career is in tatters, and now this? If you don't care about your reputation, what about mine?"

The policeman turns to the young medic who's probing the cut on my arm. "How long to bandage her up? I need to take them in."

"You're going to charge us?" asks Xander. When the policeman hesitates, he adds, "Come on, Harry. It's me."

Harry stares at him for a moment. Maybe he gives a small nod, because Xander's lips flatten into a tight line.

I sag back on the stretcher. What are we going to do now? There's no way I'll be able to stop the demon from inside a jail cell. And the possibility of being locked away for weeks or months, let alone years, isn't one I want to think about.

"I'll speak to the captain," says Xander's mother. "There's probably nothing I can do to save your career now, but at least one of us needs to try." She stalks back to her car.

"We'll take you both into the station now for formal interviews," says Harry with an apologetic look.

"You'll have to wait," says the medic, not looking up as she concentrates on searching the cut on my leg for stone fragments. "She has another wound I'll need to take care of before you take her away."

"Finish up inside the ambulance," says Harry. "I want her kept secure."

The medic makes me lie flat on the gurney, then loads it into the ambulance. I get one last look at Xander's stony expression before the doors close. Harry stands behind the ambulance's rear window, as though he's standing guard.

The medic feels the flesh around the gash on my forearm while I look around, scanning for a phone. Uncle Ray might be used to doing Magnus's bidding, but I need to find a way to call him and warn him about his boss. If Magnus is under the demon's control, my aunt and uncle aren't safe.

The medic is wrapping gauze around the cut when the

ambulance's engine starts. I frown at her. "Where are we going?"

She doesn't answer, but moves to look through the window that separates us from the driver. Before she can get there, the ambulance takes off violently, sending her crashing against the vehicle's back doors. I clutch the sides of the stretcher to keep from falling off.

Outside the window I can see policemen running after us, their guns drawn.

TWENTY-TWO

The ambulance careens wildly and it's all I can do to hold on.

"What's going on?" yells the medic. "Who's driving?"

"I can't see."

Could the demon have possessed the ambulance driver?

Sirens start up behind us, but they don't sound close. Whoever our kidnapper is, he has a reasonable head start on the police.

The vehicle tears around a corner at top speed, and we're thrown against the side of the ambulance. I land hard on the medic's leg and she grunts with pain.

"Sorry," I tell her, gripping onto the ambulance's side cabinets so it doesn't happen again. Then I raise my voice and shout toward whoever's driving. "Who are you? What's happening?"

The ambulance turns a corner so sharply, it rocks onto two wheels. The medic yelps and I grip the cabinets more tightly. If the driver answers my question, I don't hear it over the clanging of medical equipment bouncing around on the metal floor.

When the van lands hard on all four wheels, the medic and I share a wide-eyed look. We both concentrate on hanging on as the ambulance weaves around more bends at top speed.

Then the ambulance brakes hard, and the medic and I both fall forward. The engine cuts out and the driver's door slams. We barely have time to haul ourselves to our feet before the back door of the ambulance opens.

For a moment, all I can see is a big man, silhouetted against the brightness of the day.

Then Xander steps forward, his expression grim. "You okay?" he demands. "Come on, we need to keep moving."

"You stole the ambulance? And you outran all those police?" I jump out. We're behind an industrial building in a small, potholed parking area that's out of sight from the road. I can't hear any sirens. In fact, I can't hear anything. The place is deserted, the windows boarded up. There's nobody in sight.

"I've lost them for now, but the ambulance is too visible to stay lost for long. They'll be looking for us." He turns to the medic. "Sorry about the wild ride. You're not hurt? I'm afraid I can't leave you the keys to the ambulance. You'll need to walk back to the main road."

The medic doesn't say anything. Her expression is wary and her face pale, but she doesn't look injured.

Xander takes my hand and tugs me away. "Come on, Saffy."

He was healed while my body is still aching and exhausted, but adrenaline is pumping through me, so when he starts to run, I manage to keep up.

We race down the street, then duck through a narrow alleyway and take a short cut through an abandoned lot. "Where are we going?" I pant.

Xander slows. "Away from here. We need to find somewhere to plan our next move and figure out how to stop the demon."

He helps me over the wire fence at the back of the lot, and we jog along somebody's driveway before emerging onto another quiet industrial street, then turn onto a narrow one-way alley that runs behind a large brick building. It has cars parked tightly down one side.

"Stop," I gasp, pressing my side where a stitch is starting. "I think I know where we should go."

"We can't go back to either of our homes." Xander is breathing almost as hard as I am. When he stops, I lean against the side of the nearest car to catch my breath. I'm beat. Using that much magic really took it out of me.

"I know a quiet place where they won't find us." I hold out one unsteady hand. "Give me your phone and I'll call Jess. She'll drive us there." I really wanted to keep my roommate out of all this, but it's gone too far for that. For all I know, the police will question her. If she's going to find out I'm on the run, I'd rather tell her myself.

He tugs his phone out and gives it to me, but Jess's phone goes straight to voicemail. "She must be at band practice." I hand his phone back with a curse. "She never hears her phone when she's drumming, and their practice sessions go for hours."

Xander eyes the car I'm leaning against. "We'll have to take a car, but let's find one that's been left unlocked. Smashing a window to get in will make too much noise and call attention to us."

I raise my eyebrows as he walks to the next car and tries the handle. "I didn't figure you for a law breaker."

"I'll do just about anything if there's a chance we can keep that jackal-headed demon from killing again." His voice is grim, his expression determined. It's easy to see why he's the youngest detective on the force. He's like Eliot Ness bringing down Al Capone. Or like a pit bull with its teeth sunk into flesh. At the thought, the skin on my leg prickles where the Rottweiler got me and I wince in remembered pain. I definitely prefer thinking of him as Eliot Ness.

"Besides, we'll just borrow the car," adds Xander. "The owner will get it back undamaged."

"You already convinced me." I keep pace with him and try the passenger-side doors while he tests the ones on the driver's side. The door of a beaten-up Ford opens, and I grin. "Bingo."

Xander pulls the wires out of the dashboard like a pro, and within a minute or two he gets the car started.

While he drives, I keep my ears peeled for sirens. I've never been on the run from the law before. There must be a warrant out for our arrest, and now we've stolen a car as well. Just another crime to add to my rap sheet, as Xander's mother would say.

"Turn right here," I direct him, pretending confidence. Meanwhile, I'm trying to figure out where we are and how to get onto the freeway.

"Where are we going?" he asks.

"Turkey Point. Near the water."

"What's there?"

"A house that'll be deserted." I shoot him a glance. "You ready to add a little B and E to your list of crimes?"

He shrugs, but his expression is stony and I immediately regret joking about it. He's got a lot to lose. Though, come to think of it, he's already lost everything. Stealing the ambulance and evading capture will have sealed his fate, career-wise.

"Whose place is it?" he asks.

"A client of mine. And we don't have to break into his home. He has a boat house out the back we can stay in. This time of year, he won't be there."

We drive in silence while my adrenaline fades and exhaustion takes its place. I keep seeing Amber, limp and bloody on the floor, with a terrible beast standing over her.

"If that thing didn't have a jackal's head, it could have almost been a regular man," Xandar says in a musing tone. His mind is obviously going to the same place mine is. In fact, I'm not sure I'm ever going to be able to think of anything other than our experiences today.

"I guess this is all in a day's work for you?" I ask. "You must see horrible things on the job all the time. And you're probably used to being in mortal danger."

"Oh yeah." He shoots me a sideways glance. "I can't count the number of times I've seen a jackal-headed demon eating a person's heart. Or been beaten by levitating rocks. All in a day's work for sure. I could barely hold in my yawns."

"But you must have dealt with grisly deaths before. And serial killers? Criminals shooting at you?"

He sucks in a breath, lifting one hand from the wheel to drag it through his hair. "Sure, I've seen some bad things. But never anything like this."

I close my eyes. What little strength I had left has drained away, leaving me limp. Exhaustion has settled into my bones, so I'm relieved when we arrive at Turkey Point.

I give Xander directions to the large house by the water where I worked last summer. The sun is setting as we park the car out of sight from the road, then walk cautiously around the back of my client's palatial house. The curtains are drawn and the one window we can see through shows no vehicles in the four-car garage.

"Looks empty," I say with a relieved sigh. "The boat house is this way." I limp toward the two-storied cedar and steel building. It extends over the lapping water, with a boat ramp leading down from the big double doors right into the sea. I search for the fake rock near the door of the boat house, and slide it open to find the key.

"Not smart leaving the key in something obvious like that," says Xander, shaking his head.

"Lucky for us. I didn't want to have to break in."

"You said this pace belongs to your client?"

"See that rock wall?" I point to the high wall that runs the entire length of the long driveway. "That's my work. Took me a few weeks to build it, and he let me sleep in the boat house so I didn't have to commute."

"You did that?" He lets out a low whistle. "I had no idea. It looks like it'd take a lot of hard work and a whole lot of skill."

"Like a giant, 3-D jigsaw puzzle."

"More like a work of art."

I shoot him a pleased look as I unlock the boat house door. It opens onto a storage area where a sleek, expensive black jet boat takes pride of place. A couple of kayaks are attached to racks on the far wall, and a wind surfer leans in the corner. Water skis are stored ready for use, along with lifejackets and everything else a rich thrill-seeker might need.

"Nice," says Xander, running his hand along the side of the jet boat. "Your client must have quite a bit of money. What does he do?"

"Drug dealer."

"What?"

I manage a tired grin. "Or maybe a banker. I never asked him. Living quarters are upstairs." I lead the way up to the living space with a double bed and couch, a bathroom, and small kitchen. A balcony on one side has a stunning view over the water, and the windows at the other side look back to the main house. It's pretty and full of light, and I hope the bed is as comfortable as I remember.

"The bathroom's through there," I tell Xander. "I can't wait to take a shower." I desperately need to get the grime off, but instead of heading for the bathroom, I collapse onto the bed, too tired to worry about getting it dirty. Everything hurts. This must be what cheese feels like once it's been through a grater.

Xander prowls around the small room, peering out the windows, opening the fridge to check its contents, looking in cupboards and generally taking stock.

"Find anything interesting?" I ask, working the elastic hair bands out of my hair before lying with only my still-booted feet off the edge of the bed.

"There's enough canned food for us to make a meal." He shakes his head, his lips pressed together. "But I don't like staying in someone's house or taking their food. It feels wrong."

"It's not his main house. And if I'd had a chance to ask him, I'm sure Malcolm would let us stay. He's a nice guy. Generous."

"How close a friend is he?" asks Xander, the question a little too casual.

I throw one arm across my eyes, enjoying the thought that Xander might be a little jealous.

"As well as that stone wall down the driveway, he wanted lots of stonework in the main house. I worked here on and off for about three months."

The bed moves and I peek out from under my arm to

see Xander sitting next to me. "That doesn't answer my question."

"Just moved rocks for him. Never saw him naked. Does that about cover it?"

Instead of answering, he unlaces my boots and works them off my feet for me. As comfortable as they are, after all the running around we've done today, it's a relief when they come off.

"Thanks," I say, hoping my socks don't smell. I really should get up and have a shower.

Xander kicks off his own shoes and lies beside me with a sigh. "I'll just lie here for a minute before I go and wash up. You can take the bed tonight, and I'll sleep on the couch."

I wave a hand, my eyes closing. They feel like they're made of lead. "The couch is tiny. You can sleep here. I'm too exhausted to stay awake a second longer."

"I'm tired too. It's an after-effect of shock. Exhaustion is normal."

"We'll probably both have horrible demon nightmares." I'm already almost asleep, so the words come out in a mumble.

Xander rolls onto his side. My hand is resting on my stomach, and he covers it with his own. "If you have a bad dream, I'll wake you. You do the same."

Something about the gentle tone of his voice makes my throat feel tight. I lie still with his hand on mine until his breathing becomes deep and even. He takes up more than his share of the bed, but I don't complain. There's something about having his bulk next to me, especially after a day like today, that makes me want to move closer to his warmth.

I fall asleep listening to the sound of his breathing.

TWENTY-THREE

I wake slowly, warm and comfortable, snuggled into Xander's side. My face is pressed into his shoulder, and his breath is on my forehead. The grittiness on my skin reminds me I didn't get around to taking a shower last night. Somehow, even after all the dirt, sweat, and blood of yesterday, Xander still smells good.

A blanket is over us and I'm fully dressed. Xander isn't. At some point in the night, he must have taken off his torn T-shirt. The blanket is pulled up to his torso, but his shoulders are bare.

My gaze lingers on the arm that's on top of the blanket, admiring the defined sections of muscle and the ridges between them. Not much of his chest is visible, but what I can see is just as impressive. I lick my lips. It's been a long, *long* time since I woke up next to anyone. And never anyone with a body like Xander's.

His face isn't bad either. I lift my eyes to admire his chiseled features, only to find him gazing at me with amused eyes.

"Seen enough?" he asks with laughter in his voice.

My face warms, but I keep my gaze steady. "I can't be certain," I muse softly. "There's a lot of you I haven't seen yet."

Heat flashes in his eyes and he leans into me. His lips find mine, searching and soft.

As soon as our lips touch, the events of the last few days drop away.

It feels incredible. Not just the fact that I'm able to push all the worry and pain away, but *he* feels incredible. The way his lips move against mine, the way his hand runs up my arm. He's real, and warm, and hard in all the right places. Life instead of death. Pleasure instead of pain. He's everything I've been craving. Exactly what I need.

His mouth explores mine, gently at first, then our kiss becomes deeper. My body reacts with an intensity that shocks me. Pure lust pools inside me. And when I run my hand over his muscles, relishing their bulk, it only gets stronger.

He runs one hand into my hair and down my neck. Everywhere he touches, I want more. I need his hands on me. His mouth to taste me. I want him to touch me everywhere.

But when Xander knocks his hand against one of the cuts on my arm, I draw in a sharp breath.

He pulls away, frowning at my gauze-covered wound. "I'm sorry."

"That's okay." I swallow, trying to calm the wild beating of my heart. Common sense is fighting its way through the blind lust I'd all but given in to. I wish I could lose myself in his arms and forget about everything. But I can't. Not when that *thing* is out there killing people and we're the only people who've seen it.

Xander is watching my face and my change of mood

must be obvious, because he pulls back a little more and sits up. When the blanket falls right off, the sight of his entire torso makes me wish harder than ever that we could stay in bed.

"We should come up with a plan." His voice is rough.

I drag in a breath, forcing myself to sit up too, rather than reach for him again. "The list of witches the demon will target next is getting smaller. It has archivist magic, plant magic, and earth magic. If I'm right and Magnus is the witch under Jeqabeel's control, it has his water magic too."

"We'll ask your uncle to warn everyone in your community. Not just the people we're assuming will be targeted, but everyone with magic. In case the council members are too well protected now, and the demon switches to an easier target."

"There's one other lead to follow up," I add. "*Train-wreck'd*. The nightclub where that mundane went who was doing magic. That's too suspicious to ignore."

He nods. "Let's talk to your uncle today, then head to the nightclub tonight, when it opens."

"Sounds like a plan." I give a soft sigh, hating to close the door on what we started. But what else can I do? "You want to have the first shower, or shall I?"

He puts his hand on the blanket over my leg. "Saffy." His expression is serious but his eyes are soft. "I want to tell you that I—"

His phone rings, cutting him off. He gets up to grab it from the bedside table, checks the screen, scowls, then hits the button to send it straight to voicemail.

"I'll have first shower, seeing as I'm up," he says. "But I'll be quick."

He stretches, and the fact that he's only wearing jeans makes the action difficult to look away from. He really is a work of art. I curse under my breath. What had he been about to say before the call interrupted him? That he wanted to pick up where we left off when all this was over? Or that he was already regretting kissing me?

Instead of asking what I really want to know I ask, "Who was calling you?"

"My mother."

"You two don't get on?" It's a silly question. That much was obvious when she turned up outside the library.

"She's ambitious. I am too, in my own way, but nothing's ever enough for her. She's relentless."

"She didn't seem to like me much." I comb my fingers through my hair, as though that's going to make the slightest difference to my disheveled state. "Not happy about you spending time with a fugitive, huh?"

"Not overjoyed." He heads to the bathroom.

"Can I use your phone to call my uncle?" I ask as the door shuts.

"Sure."

Uncle Ray doesn't answer, but I leave a long message on his voicemail, relating all we've learned and asking him to pass the information on to the other council members. I also tell him to be careful about who he trusts.

I don't come right out and name Magnus, not in so many words, but I'm sure he'll figure out who I mean. My uncle's pretty smart.

Getting up is difficult, because all my cuts and bruises hurt like hell. My muscles protest, and my bones ache. Shame my animal magic didn't heal both of us.

When it's my turn for a shower, the hot water stings, but it feels good too. Less good is putting my filthy jeans and T-shirt back on. If I'd had a crystal ball, I would have left myself some clean clothes last time I stayed here.

"Breakfast?" asks Xander, when I'm out of the shower, my hair back in its usual pigtails. "There are two delicious options on today's menu. Either dry cornflakes, or canned spaghetti. Which takes your fancy?"

"Tough choice." My stomach rumbles so loudly, we both laugh. We fell asleep without eating last night, and I'm suddenly starving. "If we're going to visit my uncle, I vote we stop for coffee and bagels on the way. But in the meantime, dry cereal might fill the gap."

He pours us a couple of glasses of water to go with our breakfast, and we sit down at the little table to eat.

"Did you always want to be a detective?" I ask, swallowing a mouthful of cornflakes with an effort.

"When I was a kid, I wanted to be a musician. My dad loved music and he taught me to play guitar. We used to make up our own songs. But then he started going deaf. Brain tumor. Not being able to hear music was the toughest part for him."

"He was a Frank Sinatra fan?" I ask, connecting the dots.

"The biggest."

So *that's* why Xander likes old music. Suddenly I feel bad for hassling him so much about it. "I guess he died?"

He nods. "I was thirteen."

"That's tough."

"Not as tough as having both your parents killed and then being accused of their murder," he says softly.

I look up from my corn flakes and my eyes lock with Xander's. "Death is always tough." Suddenly the cornflakes are even harder to swallow. Too many people have been killed by the demon. I can't bear the thought it might kill again.

"After my father died, my mother threw herself into

work. Now she's obsessed with her job. It's all that matters to her."

I take a big gulp of water to help the cornflakes go down. "I'm sure you matter too."

"She likes the fact I'm a detective. It's good for her career to have a son who's on the force."

"Do you like being a detective?" I ask. But I already know what his answer will be. The determination in his face when he talked about stopping the demon told me all I needed to know. That, and the fact he was promoted to the rank of detective so young. If the only reason he was on the police force was because his mother had pushed him into it, I doubt he'd have been so successful.

His phone rings again, and he glances at it. "If I don't answer, she'll just keep ringing. May as well get this over with." His mouth flattens as he brings the phone to his ear. "Hello, Mom."

"Xander? Are you okay?" Her voice is so shrill, he winces and pulls the phone away from his ear. She's loud enough that I can hear every word.

"I'm fine."

"The entire police force is out searching for you and that... *woman*."

"Her name's Saffy."

"She murdered at least two people that we know of. Probably her parents, too."

"No, she didn't."

"Listen, Xander, if you bring her in, you won't be charged with anything. I've made arrangements. You won't get your job back, but you'll be able to walk away from this. You can still have your life back."

"I'm not doing that. She's innocent."

"Don't be naïve, Xander. They have proof. There's no

doubt she killed her cousin in the most gruesome way possible."

Xander raises his eyebrows at me. I put my spoon down and shake my head. What kind of proof could they have? Did someone plant false evidence? My stomach clenches. What if I end up convicted on a murder charge? It doesn't matter that I'm innocent, I could still get a life sentence.

"She didn't kill anyone. I'm trying to find the person who did."

"She's going to drag you down. Don't let her ruin your life."

"I've got to go, Mom."

"Xander, wait. Tell me where you are. I'll come and get you. We can sort this out together."

"I'm fine. I'll talk to you later." Xander hangs up with a sigh. "She wasn't like this before my father died," he says. "At least, I don't remember her being this intense. She was more relaxed back then."

"I'm sure she just wants what's best for you."

"People assume my mother pulled strings to get me promoted." His mouth presses into a bitter line. "Thing is, I'm not entirely sure she didn't. She denies it, but having a successful son is just so damn important to her. I think she'd do anything to get what she wants."

"You're good at what you do."

He pours more cornflakes into his bowl. "She said they have proof you killed Sylvia. Any idea what that could be?"

I shake my head. "We've seen what really did it, but who's going to believe us?"

"After your parents' murder, it took several years for the demon to kill again. Now it's killed three people in quick succession. Why?"

"Like you said, it needed the spell from Sylvia's grimoire."

He nods slowly. "Maybe. Could there be another reason? When the first spell went wrong, perhaps it got injured. It could have been waiting all these years for its injury to heal, or to get stronger. The Unseen said the demon would need a lot of magic to be able to escape from the bone. Perhaps the witch it's got working for it wasn't powerful enough until now."

I tap my lip, considering. "There are certain times when there's more magic around. Uncle Ray was complaining just the other day..." I stop and slap my forehead. "I'm an idiot. Why didn't I think of it sooner? I bet it has something to do with the blood moon celebration."

"Blood moon?"

"In a total lunar eclipse, the moon turns red and magic gets stronger. This year is special, because the moon is closer to the earth than normal, so it's a super blood moon. Uncle Ray has been complaining about all the mystical energy making witches edgy."

"Stronger magic?" He raises his eyebrows. "Thereby making it easier for the demon to get the power it needs?"

"I've barely had anything to do with the witch community for so long that if Uncle Ray hadn't mentioned it, I wouldn't even know it was happening. But of course, you're right." I stand up, the realization sending a surge of nervous energy through me. "The council are planning a special ceremony this year, to renew the bonds which unite all the members." My voice rises. "Magnus runs the ceremony. If he's under the control of the demon it'll have all the power it needs."

"When is it?"

"Not sure. Tomorrow, I think." I pick up my bowl and

dump it in the sink. "Can I use your phone to try and get hold of my uncle again? He needs to call off the ceremony in case the demon is—"

The window over the sink looks out to the main house, and I'm distracted by a flash of movement in the yard. Craning my neck, I see two men dressed head-to-toe in black creeping to the back door of the main house, their guns drawn.

"They're here." I drop the bowl and spin to Xander, grabbing his T-shirt to pull him to his feet. "The police have found us."

TWENTY-FOUR

We bolt for the stairs.

"How are we going to get out of here?" I demand as we rush to the bottom.

"We'll take that." Xander points at the sleek jet boat. "Get in." While I clamber into the boat, he sprints for the big double door, unlatches it and swings it open. Then he goes to the winch. The boat sits on the top half of a steeply-sloping track that disappears into the water. The winch lets Malcolm gently lower his expensive boat down the ramp. Only Xander doesn't have time to be gentle. I grab both sides of the boat and hang on tight.

Xander spins the winch handle as fast as he can. The boat flies down the ramp and carves into the water, throwing up a wave that drenches Xander, who's already running to jump in.

The craft rocks violently as he leaps on board. I unhook the cable while Xander starts the engine. It roars into life.

I imagine all the policemen freezing in the act of searching the main house and sprinting toward the boat house. But Xander's already twisting the throttle and the boat takes off fast enough that I'm thrown against the stern.

We speed down the inlet, leaving the boat house behind. Policemen run to the shore.

"Duck," I yell at Xander urgently, terrified they're about to start shooting. He hunches down with me as a loud noise cracks over the water.

"Shit." His wide eyes meet mine. "I didn't think they'd fire."

I flatten myself against the back of the boat, then realize a bullet might be able to punch right though the hull and pull my limbs in as tight as I can. Xander has his head up so he can see to steer. My heart is racing. At least when the demon attacked us we could see it coming. If a bullet hits either of us, we could be dead in an instant.

Xander keeps the throttle wound tight, and as we roar across the water the seconds stretch out into minutes. No more gunshots ring out. Have they decided not to shoot us after all?

Xander glances back. "We might be out of range," he says loudly enough to be heard over the engine noise. "And we're not a very big target. Hard to hit."

I force my body to uncurl so I can glance back. The shore is disappearing fast.

"They're probably on their radios, calling for reinforcements," he says.

"Coastguard?" I ask.

"Maybe."

I scan ahead, trying to make sense of the land in front of us. I know this area reasonably well, but everything looks different from out here.

"Where are you heading?" I ask.

"We'll ditch the boat somewhere on the other side." He gestures to a long stretch of land in front of us.

I squint to where he's pointing. "I think that's Wilson Point Road."

"Having to cross the inlet should slow down anyone chasing us."

Wilson Point bristles with dozens of jetties. Almost every house has one. "Over there." I point.

He shakes his head. "Further in. If we land at the public boat ramp, there'll be other boats coming and going. We won't stand out so much."

I peer ahead, searching for a place to pull in. "There," I say finally. Not only is there a ramp, but a jetty to tie up to. A couple of fishermen are launching a boat that bristles with fishing rods, and there's a teenager on a jet ski. No police that I can see.

When we careen up to the jetty, Xander kills the engine while I stop us from slamming into the posts. There's a rope attached to the front of the boat, and I scramble with it onto the jetty, then tie the boat up so it doesn't go drifting out to sea. At least Malcolm will get it back.

"We need to get out of here," says Xander. "Find a car, if we can."

"You don't think they'll have closed the road?" I ask, as we run toward it.

"Not yet, I hope."

There's a parking lot next to the public boat ramp, but there are too many people around to risk stealing a car here. The houses are few and far between, but after running for long enough to put the boat ramp well behind us, Xander motions toward one with a detached garage. We jog over and peer through the dusty garage window. At first glance, it looks empty. Then I spot a couple of mountain bikes.

"Look." I tap the window. "If we take the bikes, we could cycle through the trees. Get away, even if they've closed the road."

"Good idea." Xander examines the padlock on the garage door. He picks up a rock from the collection that decorates the edge of the garage, then lifts it to smash the padlock.

"Wait." My earth magic gives me extra sensitivity, and one of the rocks in the display doesn't feel right. I grab it. Yup, it's plastic. Sliding open the base, I pluck out the key and hand it to him.

"I told you putting a key in an obvious place was a bad idea," He unlocks the padlock and pulls the door open. "You never know who's going to break in."

I take one of the bikes. When I turn, Xander's holding out a helmet.

"Safety first?" I cram it on over my pigtails.

"We'll be less conspicuous if we're wearing them. Hopefully anyone who sees us will think we're just out for a ride, having some fun."

He puts his own helmet on, then takes the time to lock the garage door behind us and put the rock back where we found it. "No sense in advertising the fact we were here," he says to my impatient look. "We'll have to head down the road for a while, then find another path."

My bike is a little too tall for me, but we don't have time to mess around with the seat, so I balance on the pedals without using it. With his longer legs, Xander's faster than I am. I cycle as hard as I can while watching for any sign of the police.

We pass the Martin State Airport, and then come to a busy road. I ride across with my head down. The police have already fired at us once. If they catch sight of us, will they shoot again? Do they want to kill us?

On the other side of the road is a forested area. I'm relieved to reach the cover of the trees, but I can't celebrate for long. I'm too busy guiding my bike over mounds of dirt and across tree roots. There's no real trail here, so we have to find our own path through the trees, dragging our bikes through bits that are impossible to ride though, and going as fast as we can where the ground isn't totally overgrown. I'm not used to mountain biking, and riding over this kind of terrain takes all my concentration. Not to mention that my legs are burning. Even after I take the time to adjust my seat, it's still hard going.

"You okay?" Xander calls over his shoulder.

I don't have enough breath left to answer. He's bigger than I am, and as unfair as it is, his gender gives him an edge. Keeping up isn't easy.

After riding through trees, up slopes and down gullies for what feels like hours, we arrive in a residential area where there's no forest to hide in. We put our heads down and ride quickly past the houses, though I'm already exhausted.

By the time we find another place where we can drop off the road and into more trees, I'm just about beat. The only reason I make it any further is that there's a long down-hill stretch that lets me rest my aching legs for a few precious minutes.

My breath is coming in gasps by the time Xander finally stops ahead of me. My legs are on fire and my lungs feel like they've been turned inside out. Before he can even suggest we take a break, I've dropped my bike and collapsed onto the ground next to it.

He drops to the ground too and takes his helmet off.

"Let's rest." He sounds breathless and he's flushed with exhaustion. At least it's not just me.

"Good idea." I lie full length on the ground, not caring that twigs and stones are poking into me. "We must be far enough away now. They won't find us."

A sound starts up in the distance. A siren. It gets louder and louder, until it sounds like it's about to burst through the trees. I jerk up to sitting, my blood pumping again. Ready to grab the bike and pedal for my life.

Then the siren starts to quieten. The police car's gone past. But the road can't be as far away as I thought.

Xander meets my gaze. "They won't expect us to have gotten this far so quickly. They don't know we have bikes." His tone is reassuring.

"How long have we been riding?"

He glances up, as though to judge the time from the position of the sun. "It must be close to lunchtime. Let's get our breath back, then keep moving. Though it'd be safest if we can find somewhere to hole up until dark."

"What about warning my uncle to call off the ceremony?"

"My phone is back at the boat house."

I let out a long breath that's halfway to a groan.

Xander picks up a twig and snaps it in half, then throws the pieces away. "Maybe we can steal another car," he says. "But it'll be dangerous in broad daylight."

I take my helmet off, then lie back down, my face turned so I can see him. "I'd give my right arm for a drink of water."

"Me too." He licks his lips. "Maybe we can find a house that's unoccupied and let ourselves in. Get a drink and something to eat, and call your uncle from there."

"Okay." A thought occurs to me, and I frown. "How do you think the police found us at the boat house?"

"The phone call from my mother." His tone is harsh.

"What, they traced the call, like in the movies? You think she's working with the police and that's why she rang you?"

He doesn't answer. He doesn't need to. His expression tells me enough.

TWENTY-FIVE

In the house we break into, we drink several glasses of water and eat a loaf of bread we find in the fridge, spread with butter and jam. But as hard as we search, we can't find a telephone.

"What now?" I ask, when we've given up the search and regrouped in the kitchen.

I keep glancing at the front door, certain that at any moment the owner will burst in. Today I've learned that being a burglar is not a viable career path for me. I don't have the right temperament for crime.

Xander glances at the clock on the kitchen wall. "It's almost five o'clock. It'll be dark soon." He pulls out his wallet and puts a ten dollar note onto the kitchen counter.

"What's that for?"

"Payment for the food we ate."

I smirk at him. "You're not exactly a bad ass."

"Yeah? Well, I'm not the one who washed the glasses and plates we used and put them away."

"Let's get out of here." I turn and limp toward the door. "But we should ditch the bikes. Now I know why cyclists wear padded shorts. I may never walk normally again."

"You think you had it tough?" He grimaces. "I think certain parts of my body have swollen to twice their normal size."

"Then it's unanimous. No more bikes. Let's steal another car."

He nods. "I guess we'll have to."

We sneak out the back of the house, then creep around to the street. This is a quiet residential area, and most people must be still at work. There are almost no cars around, only a few in driveways. All are locked.

"We'll need to break a window to get into one," I say after we've walked for an hour or so.

"It's too quiet around here. Someone will hear." He glances at the setting sun. "At least once it's dark, we'll have some cover."

I suck in a frustrated breath. "The whole day has gone and we haven't managed to warn anyone about the ceremony. And I still can't believe the police shot at us. Are they going to kill us on sight now? Shoot first and ask questions later?"

"There was only one shot. It was probably some rookie letting loose without permission."

"I hope you're right."

"I am." He lets out a loud breath. "We're both exhausted. There's a park over there. Let's find a quiet spot to sit and rest. When it gets fully dark I'll break a car window and we can get out of here."

We find a group of trees near the back of the park that hides us from the road. When I sit down, Xander lowers himself next to me and puts his arm around me.

The feel of his warm body is so good, it makes me want

to bury my face in his neck. What have we gotten ourselves into? Wanted by the police. On the run. And for all we know, the demon has already killed enough witches to get the magic it needs. It could have gained enough power to get free of the bone, and be about to burst forth and reign terror on us.

"I want to close my eyes," murmurs Xander. "But if I do, I'll fall asleep."

"I'll wake you if you do. I'm tired, but I can't sleep. There's too much going on in my head."

He lies down on the grass and I lie with him, his big arm over my body. For years I've been fending for myself, determined to get by without the community or magic I used to take for granted. I took pride in developing my strength and independence. I told myself I didn't need anyone.

But Xander has pushed through all my defences. Though I haven't known him long, I've come to depend on him. And if I lost him now, it would hurt.

So much for being strong. Where Xander's involved, I'm becoming weak and vulnerable.

The thought terrifies me. But at the same time, I close my eyes and feel my muscles relax. In spite of the hard ground and the fact the entire police force is after us, I feel my breathing slow. And though my brain is still in turmoil, my thoughts slip away into blackness.

I WAKE with a jolt in the darkness. Xander is snoring softly in my ear, his arm heavy on my side. I can feel every twig and stone underneath me, digging into my already battered and aching body. How on earth did I manage to fall asleep? And how long did I sleep for?

"Wake up," I say, struggling out from under Xander's arm.

"What time is it?" asks Xander, sitting up and yawning.

"I don't know, I feel asleep too. But the moon's not that high. It's probably about nine or ten."

"After all that cycling, we both needed a rest." He gets to his feet and winces. "I haven't done that much exercise in a while."

When I push myself up to standing, my entire body hurts. "I wish I knew my aunt and uncle were okay. But Uncle Ray should have picked up my message. And he did say he was taking precautions."

"Maybe we should go to the nightclub first," Xander rubs his eyes and yawns again. "It's a good time to go and we may not get another chance."

We hobble out of our hiding place and back to the road. Xander picks a car that's not too close to a house and uses a rock to break one of its back windows. We drive slowly out of the area, keeping our eyes peeled for police cars.

We make it to the nightclub without trouble, and park our stolen car in the darkest corner of the rutted, overgrown parking lot. There are plenty of other cars here, and the neon sign is lit up. A loud bass beat thumps out of the rundown old train station.

Trainwreck'd is pumping.

Amazingly enough, the bouncer doesn't so much as blink at us when we walk in, even though our clothes are sweaty and torn, with an assortment of bloodstains providing the finishing touches. All I've done to get ready for the club is pull the hairbands out of my hair and comb it out with my fingers. Xander brushed a few twigs off his filthy jeans. Other than that, we look exactly like we've spent the last couple of days getting beaten up by a demon, running from the police, and sleeping in a park.

Could the desperate fugitive look be in fashion? Maybe the bouncer thinks we spent hours making ourselves look this way.

Nope, the bouncer doesn't care. He's letting everyone in, though the place is already full. Despite its middle-of-nowhere location, this must be the most popular nightclub in Baltimore.

As we head down the stairs into the basement club, the heavy beat of the music rises to meet us. A bar stretches along one end of the large room and the massive crowd of partygoers is thronged against it. The DJ has a booth beside the heaving dance floor.

"See anything suspicious?" asks Xander in my ear.

I shake my head. Maybe this is going to turn out to be a waste of time, but at least we can grab a drink before we leave. And for some reason I feel less conspicuous in this crowd than I did roaming the streets. Perhaps because it's dark in here and the strobe lights make it hard to see anything in much detail. Or because we're underground, among people who are too absorbed with each other to bother with us.

"Let's head that way," he says, pointing to the other side of the club.

Then I feel it. A tingle of magic. There's something—or someone—magical here. It makes the hairs on the back of my neck stand up.

Xander leads us into the far corner, where the crowd is a little thinner. I scan the room, looking for where the magic might be coming from. The prickling on my skin gets stronger. Somebody's performing a spell.

Is it hot in here?

I feel flushed, mostly because Xander's so close. Suddenly, his muscled body is all I can think about. He's got to be the best-looking guy here.

Xander's hand snakes around my waist. He pulls me against his chest and puts his arms around me, holding me against him. "Saffy," he says, his voice hoarse. "I want you."

My body responds instantly. My face lifts to his and our lips crush together, my urgency matched by his.

Our kiss is even more amazing than the one in the boat house. This time, I give myself over to the sensation completely. My hands slide over his chest and then up around his neck, against his bare skin. He takes the kiss deeper, his tongue dancing with mine, creating butterflies inside me that travel into my core.

He pulls me tighter against him and his body feels so good against mine that I moan against his lips. I forget about everything but him. His mouth, his hands, his body are all I need.

With a low growl he slips his hand under my T-shirt. He strokes his way up to my breast. His touch lights fires on my skin. I want him more than I've ever wanted anything, and I don't care where we are or who might be watching. Nothing matters but the need burning inside me.

Dimly, I realize the DJ has started playing a different kind of music. It's a hypnotic, swaying beat that has me sliding my hips against Xander in an unconscious response.

I force my eyes open. The people next to us are necking just as passionately. The woman's top is lifted, exposing her breasts.

"Xander." I try to push him away.

"Mmm?" His lips are on my neck.

"Xander, stop. Now." I push hard and manage to make a little space between us, though he lets out a frustrated sound. "Look." I sweep one hand around the club, that just a few minutes ago seemed so normal. Now it's become a writhing mass of sexual energy. Everyone in here has paired up. Some are in three-and-foursomes. And there's a group in the corner I give only a single, horrified glance.

"Look what's happening. This isn't normal. Someone's cast a spell."

Xander doesn't look where I'm indicating. Instead he pushes one hand into my hair and gazes into my eyes. He's so handsome, it almost stops my heart.

"A spell?" His voice is low and hoarse with need. "I don't think so. I've wanted you since the moment I met you. And you want me too, don't you? So why fight it?"

"Look around, Xander. Something's making you feel this way."

"It's your beauty. And your bravery. And your gorgeous legs. And those muscles in your arms. They're the most beautiful arms I've ever seen, Saffy. But you're not just strong in your body, you have an inner strength too. It's incredibly sexy. I can't keep my hands off you, and it's not because of a—"

"Stop. Please." I press my hand over his mouth. I don't want him to tell me I'm beautiful because he's under a spell. It's not real. And wanting his words to be true won't make them that way.

He tugs my hand away. "Saffy, I'm trying to tell you how I feel."

"Just look around. Is this normal?"

When he leans in for another kiss instead of doing what I say, I cup his chin and force his face away from mine.

"Look at all these people. This isn't a sex club. And even if it were, this is a little extreme, don't you think?" I point to a couple whose clothes are already on the floor. "Look at them."

"They're entitled to express their love." He tries to kiss me again.

"They're naked, and nobody's sparing them a glance. Come on, you're a policeman. You know when something's not right."

His body relaxes a little and he pulls away enough for his gaze to skim over the mass of writhing bodies around us. His expression changes, and I can see him struggling with himself. Finally, he nods. "Yeah, it's a little strange."

"It's magic. Somebody's making these couples forget about anything but each other."

"Who's doing it?" As though they have a mind of their own, his hands are still on me, moving under my T-shirt. And when he nuzzles my neck, I tip my head to allow him better access. I know we shouldn't be doing this, that we need to find out what's happening, but I can't make myself move out of his arms.

TWENTY-SIX

"Xander, cut it out." I have to say it three times before Xander groggily lifts his lips from my neck.

I put one hand up to his cheek. "Break out of it. I know you can."

His eyes, so dilated they seem black, stare at me with confusion. He leans in again and places his lips against mine in a searing kiss that sends my synapses spinning. I want to just let go, to surrender to the well of desire that's lying just out of my reach. Every cell in my body is raging at me to let go.

But I won't. I'm stronger than that. If Xander and I get intimate, it's not going to be because of magic.

Brick by brick, I build a stone wall around myself, pushing away the dark, tantalizing spell that's got its claws in us both. "Come on," I say, pinching Xander to drag his attention away from what he's doing to my body.

He smiles down at me like it's some kind of sexy game and pinches me back. It hurts, but it helps to clear my mind. Grabbing his hand, I lead him along the edge of the room toward the exit. He follows along obediently.

Then I spot the only movement in the room that's not a sex act. Some large men in suits are pulling a couple of barely-dressed partygoers into a back room. As they haul them away, the couple don't even struggle. Their sexual daze is enough to make them compliant as the men push them into the room and shut the door behind them.

"This way," I say, tugging Xander toward the room.

"Wait." Xander pulls me to a stop.

"What?"

In answer, he pulls me against his chest to kiss me. A surge of pure lust pulses through me, too strong to control. I don't want to control it, because Xander feels so good. I've been wanting to kiss him like this for the last few days, and now I'm not sure how much of the lust I'm feeling is the magic. It's intensified what was already there.

It takes me a long time to build my wall back up, using the stones inside my head to shield me from the spell's effects.

From the corner of my eye, I see the men come back out of the room and grab more people. Like the others, they're malleable, not protesting when the men haul them up and drag them off.

What could they be doing behind that closed door? Only one way to find out. We need to get inside that room. The only way I can think of to do that is to be the next romantic couple the goons manhandle in there.

I lead Xander as close to the door as we can get, pushing him onto the floor close enough that when they next open it, we'll be lucky if it doesn't hit us.

Once Xander's where I want him, I get into his lap, put my arms around his neck, and kiss him.

Hey, I may as well enjoy the wait.

The magic tears down my defenses until I have to pull back and take a fortifying breath of air.

The door opens. Rough hands grab me and haul me off Xander. I don't protest, just go along with him as though I'm as dazed as everyone else.

The men push us into the room and we stumble to a halt just inside. The smell of blood is the first thing that hits me. Lots and lots of blood.

A river of blood.

The Unseen's words come back to me, chilling my entire body. My magic surges in response to the blood that coats the floor. The last traces of the lust spell fall away and I feel the dark magic that's running underneath it.

Powerful magic.

Though I know it's evil, the magic is seductive. It calls to me, urging me to plunge my hands into the blood at my feet. To take whatever I want. To cast down all who would challenge me. To kill without conscience and revel in it.

I gasp in a ragged breath, trying to control the thoughts raging through my head. This is why dark magic is forbidden. It's cruel, and strong, and merciless. Giving into it corrupts the mind.

"Bring them here," intones a deep voice.

Then a foul stench hits me, so pungent it makes me gag. Rotting flesh. Dog hair.

Jeqabeel.

A figure is standing in the blood, bodies piled at his feet. He's wearing a long, black cloak that's soaked and heavy with blood, the hood drawn over his head. It's not until the men drag us toward him that I see what's under his hood.

A jackal's head.

Xander draws in a sharp breath. I think the spell must

have broken its hold on him, but I can't tear my eyes away from the creature in front of us to check.

In the library, it almost killed us. And now, how much stronger has it become? Now that it's standing in the river of blood it needed?

The jackal throws back its hood with human hands that are slicked with red. "Hello, Saffy." Its voice is half human, and half the rough growl of an animal.

As it watches the men drag us closer, its features start to change. Its hair becomes shorter as though retracting back into its skin. Its muzzle shrinks and becomes a nose. The smell lessens, then disappears as a human face emerges.

A face I recognize.

Uncle Ray.

I can only gape. My uncle? But how? Why?

"I'm glad you're here." Uncle Ray's voice is almost normal now. "You always were an annoying little busybody, but don't worry, you're about to be useful to me for the first time in years."

"Y-you..." I stutter as the truth hits me. "You were the one who attacked us in the library? You killed all those people? Sylvia and my parents? You murdered your own *sister*?" My voice rises. The horror is too much to bear. The only man who was even halfway decent to me after my parents' death was the man who killed them.

"Your mother wasted Jeqabeel's power for years, keeping the bone locked away. She didn't see that it could be used. She refused to see the *potential*."

His eyes burn and for an awful moment I see the demon alive inside him. Its madness has him in its grip.

"She loved you," I spit, struggling against the grip of the men holding me. "She and Dad were your family."

"They thought they were better than me. I proved them wrong."

I shake my head, trying to think. My brain is on a feedback loop. I picture the demon possessing him, my uncle welcoming it. I see him devouring my mother's heart. He already had animal magic. Did he intend to steal hers as well, because it was so much stronger?

Then the explosion that killed my father. Was it intentional? Did he mean to kill him?

I lunge at my uncle, rage filling me with a need for vengeance. The men hold me back though I try as hard as I can to wrench myself free.

All I want is to tear him limb from limb.

"Now, now, Saffy." My uncle gives me a smile so smug it makes me struggle harder with the overwhelming urge to wipe it off his face. "I'm glad you're here. I had thought to kill you months ago, but breaking the magical bindings around your magic may have alerted the council to my plans. Now I'm glad I resisted the urge. Jeqabeel wants to use your flesh for his rebirth into this world." He nods at his men. "We'll take them with us."

"Take us where?" I demand. "What am I in time for?"

"The Blood Moon ceremony, of course. You'll be my guest of honor, Saffy."

"You're going to use the ceremony to release Jeqabeel." I shake my head. "You can't do it. You don't understand—"

"It's going to be beautiful." My uncle's smile widens. "Magnus and the rest of those arrogant fools will finally see how strong my magic has become. I'm going to make them tremble. I'll make them *kneel*."

"Magnus doesn't know about the demon?" Xander sounds almost as angry as I am.

"He knows nothing. It will be a surprise for him when I take power over the council at the ceremony."

I make a furious, choking sound. "You mean, when *Jeqabeel* takes power and doesn't need you anymore."

"When I release Jeqabeel from his prison, I'll have everything I've ever wanted. I'll sit on the demon's right hand, with dominion over all. The most powerful witch who ever lived." His eyes glint and he clenches one fist. "Everyone's always called me weak. After tonight, they'll see the truth. They'll see how strong I really am."

"You're disgusting." It's probably not smart to antagonize the man who holds our lives in his hand, but I can't help myself. "You're not strong. You're *nothing*. So weak, you'll let a demon use you as its tool. I hope it kills you painfully. I hope it dances on your corpse—"

Uncle Ray lifts one bloody hand and I feel dark magic surround me so tightly, it's like being encased in clingfilm. I can't move. I can't speak. I can barely even breathe. It's like when he took me to the Veritas, only worse. The dark magic feels dirty, like there's something disgusting creeping over my body, seeping into my pores.

"Jeqabeel has been feasting. He's grown more powerful than you can imagine, and his power has filled me. I could kill you with a thought." My uncle smiles. "But both your body and your magic are strong, and Jeqabeel needs a vessel. Raw material for his rebirth into this world. He'll transform your flesh and use it to create his true form. The more powerful the clay, the better." He gives me an appraising look, up and down. "I was going to use Magnus's body after I take leadership of the council from him. But yours is younger and Jeqabeel finds it pleasing. I'll take Magnus as my slave instead. For years he refused me membership to the council, and now he'll obey my every command. He'll beg for every scrap of food or sip of water I allow him to take."

If I could control my body enough to shudder, I would.

Wet cloak dragging, my uncle walks close enough to run his bloody hand down my bare arm. The look in his eyes is so lascivious, my stomach clenches with disgust.

Xander must be bound with the same spell as I am, or I'm sure he'd do or say something. Instead, he's probably being forced to watch helplessly.

"It's almost a shame that Jeqabeel's transformation is going to rip you apart and remake you," my uncle murmurs. "You'll die screaming before Jeqabeel drinks the blood of your lover." He motions to Xander. "The mundane will have the honor of being Jeqabeel's first meal once the demon has achieved his true form. Your lover will get to watch you die, but his death will be just as painful as yours. I'll make sure of it."

I reach deep inside myself, desperately clutching at my magic. Trying with everything I've got to wrench it free and use it to strike my uncle down.

Uncle Ray gives me a small smug smile as though he knows exactly what I'm attempting. He shakes his head in a pitying gesture. Then he leans forward and licks my ear. His tongue feels raspy, like the tongue of a dog.

"Weak," he whispers. "Pathetic."

My magic is dead inside me. I can't move to draw any of my blood, and even if I could release it, both sides would be easily overpowered by the demon's dark magic.

As devastating as it is to admit, my uncle is right.

TWENTY-SEVEN

Once again, I'm taken to the council chambers while I'm helpless and vulnerable, propped up on the back seat of my uncle's car. This time Xander is next to me, just as helpless. After a while, I find I can move my eyes a little, but not enough to see his face.

The only thing that's working is my brain.

Uncle Ray.

I can't believe it was him the whole time. He stole the bone and invited Jeqabeel inside him. He thinks he's using the demon to achieve his own ambitions, but does he seriously think the demon won't kill him along with everyone else when it gets free?

When we arrive, my uncle gets out of the car, then leans in to talk to the driver. "When I'm ready for them, I'll bring them in myself," he tells the man. Then he straightens, brushes clean hands down his woolen overcoat, and starts up the stairs. Dread runs down my spine.

The Blood Moon ceremony is designed to reaffirm and strengthen the bonds between the council members. To give the council the ability to share their magic and do far more powerful magic together than they could ever do alone. United, they can make sure the magical world is kept secret, though it's in plain sight. If a witch is exposed, the council have the power to reverse the damage. Everyone trusts them to protect the community.

Because it's a super blood moon, the ceremony will be even more powerful than usual.

Individually, the council members are powerful witches. Bound by blood ties during the ceremony, their power is multiplied and magnified.

Could Uncle Ray control everyone in our community through the council bonds?

I don't even want to consider that possibility.

After what seems like a long time, I find I can move my face enough that I manage to see Xander. He's staring back at me, his eyes wide. I wish there was some way we could communicate. But although I'm getting a little more movement, it's not enough to be able to talk. Yet. I think the spell that's frozen us is gradually wearing off.

Not nearly fast enough.

The car doors open. I expect my uncle to come back out of the building, but he doesn't. Instead, I feel myself being tugged out of the car. My uncle doesn't need men to haul us around. His magic is so strong, he can control us like puppets. Xander and I jerk up the stairs and through the door. I think my own legs are propelling me forward, though I can't feel them or steer myself.

It's a terrifying feeling, this complete lack of control. Uncle Ray could bash our brains out on the council building's marble entrance or drop us down the stairs, and there's not a thing we could do to save ourselves. I can't even make a sound.

My uncle drags us into the circular room where the

Veritas invaded my brain just days ago. The full, red moon is positioned almost perfectly over the round skylight that's three full stories above me. Moonlight is the room's only source of illumination. It gives everything a red glow.

The council members are in their allotted places. Each is standing in one of the small circles carved into the floor, with the mysterious ninth circle still empty.

The spaces where Amber, Mireya, and Sylvia used to stand are now taken by other witches I don't recognize. There are eight witches in total, and my uncle is one of them. Magnus, Aunt Therese, Dallas, and the Veritas are all in their places, so we were wrong about Jeqabeel wanting to kill them to take their power. Has he killed others instead? Or is the ceremony going to give him the power he needs?

The ceremony has started, that much is clear. All eight witches are chanting in a haunting, single voice: one sound that's somehow created from all eight mouths. Each witch holds an identical empty glass goblet. In the center of their circle is a wide, squat bowl on a pedestal. The bowl contains a thick, dark liquid.

Magic coats the eight witches in an opaque layer, like a bubble of clear lightning. Their eyes are all pure white, like the Veritas's were when she questioned me. Nobody turns toward us, and they show no sign of noticing we're here. I don't think they can see us.

Xander and I are forced to a stop a little way from the circle, in full view of Uncle Ray. My uncle's eyes are pure white like the rest of them, but unlike the others, there's a creepy smile on his face.

Now we're so close, it hits me that Uncle Ray's wearing a thick black overcoat though the night's warm. The Unseen said he had to be touching the bone for the demon to control him. And sure enough, there's a bulge in the line of his coat. He must be carrying it.

Still chanting, the council members raise their goblets in perfect unison, as though they're connected to each other. My mother told me about this ceremony. It looks like every council member has already given blood into the bowl in the middle, and it's been topped up with wine. Next, they'll dip their cups in and all sip the blood and wine mixture at once, drinking it to share their power. It's the final part of the Blood Moon ceremony.

When they drink it, the entire council will be vulnerable. I can't let that happen.

I need to find a way to get my uncle to release his hold on us, or to use my magic to disrupt the ceremony. But my magic needs blood and I have no way to give it any without being able to move. How ironic, when a bowl of the council's blood is right in front of me.

If I could manage to knock it over, drain away the blood, maybe it would stop the ceremony. The council members wouldn't end up bonded to the demon, and it wouldn't be able to control them.

All I have to do is get my body to move.

But though the bowl of blood and wine is only feet away, it may as well be on the other side of the moon. There's no way I can move any part of my body close enough to make it count.

Chanting and moving in perfect synchronicity, the council members lean forward and dip their goblets into the bowl.

I strain against my uncle's magic, using all my muscle strength to attempt to get my arms and legs to move. My limbs are starting to awaken. I can curl my fingers a little and move my toes. It's not nearly enough. I can't even reach my fingernails to my palm to draw blood.

When I try to scream, all that comes out is a soft croak. Dammit, why can't the council hear me anyway? Surely they can read my uncle's evil intent? Can't they see that creepy smile he's wearing?

But the council members put the goblets to their mouths.

It seems like they're moving in slow motion. I'm straining so hard to move, I might bust an organ.

There's not a thing I can do to stop them as, in unison, all the council members sip the blood.

They swallow.

Nothing happens.

The moment seems to drag out. I feel like I'm stuck in between heartbeats. I'm so terrified of what my uncle might do that I can't bear to look, and I can't close my eyes.

Uncle Ray dips his hand into his goblet and coats his fingers with blood. The other council members stand as though frozen while he uses the blood to draw a complicated rune onto his forehead.

Eight goblets drop at once.

The goblets smash against the stone floor with a crash loud enough that I'd jump back if I could. Thick glass fragments skitter across the floor. Their arms now limp at their sides, the council members' eyes are still white. All except my uncle's.

Uncle Ray reaches into his overcoat and yanks out a bone. Holding it in his blood-covered hand, he draws runes on it, muttering words I can't hear. Then he holds it up, his arm outstretched in triumph. The blood slicked over the bone glints in the red moonlight and a black, smoky substance oozes out of it.

Whatever the substance is, it makes my skin prickle and my gut roil. The feeling of power in this room was already strong, but now there's a dark, terrible tang weaving through it. Its wrongness fills my senses.

The stench of the demon fills my nostrils as the thick black smoke coalesces into a menacing shape. Staring at the creature that's forming, ice runs down my spine.

It's Jeqabeel. Its form is still shadowy, not yet solid. Still, it fills me with sick dread. The drawing we saw was accurate. Its body is thickset and its clawed hands hang down to its thighs. Its jackal's eyes seem to glow, even with no substance to them.

I barely have time to gape at it before all the council members except my uncle collapse to the ground, as though flattened by an invisible hand. They lie limp and unmoving. I can only assume they're not dead, despite how it looks. My uncle said he wants them to grovel at his feet. Even if Jeqabeel is draining their magic through the shared link, my uncle will want them alive.

At least, I hope so.

A surge of power burns through my veins. The last of the council bonds have broken. My magic is free. Its tangled strands push against me, begging me to release them, to use their power.

The ritual is complete and there's no doubt in my mind as to what's just happened. The council wasn't ready for Jeqabeel and now the demon owns them. Through my uncle, it's stolen their power. That's why the bindings holding my magic have dissolved.

If Uncle Ray wasn't powerful enough before, now he has everything he wanted.

Ray turns his gaze onto me. His eyes hold a savage joy and madness.

"Your moment has come, Sapphira." Uncle Ray's voice booms from his stout frame, more powerful than I've ever heard it. "Jeqabeel has emerged from his prison. All he needs to make him whole is your flesh."

I can move my arms now. Big deal. All it means is that I can hold them in front of me, pretending I can somehow protect myself from what's about to happen.

The demon towers above me. I shrink back as it reaches for me.

I need my magic. I need blood, and lots of it. I need a way to kill an ancient demon that's at least a thousand times more powerful than I am.

I have nothing.

Jeqabeel reaches down, one black hand stretched out to envelop me.

Pain erupts inside me. My body is stretching. Growing. Being ripped apart.

The world becomes a bright, fiery place of pain. Nothing else exists. All I can do is scream.

TWENTY-EIGHT

The pain stops.

I collapse to the floor, so suddenly freed from the demon's grip that my legs don't get a chance to support me. Glass from the broken goblets crunches under me, and I feel the sharp shards digging into my flesh, scratching shallow wounds. My magic pushes against me, even a small amount of blood making it shudder for release.

Looking up blearily, I see Xander stumbling away from my uncle, his legs still stiff and clumsy, the bone clutched to his chest. He's managed to steal it from Uncle Ray.

The demon's form is shrinking, black smoke funneling back into the bone.

Jeqabeel must be drawing its power through my uncle and his link to the council, and when Uncle Ray isn't holding the bone, the demon can't sustain itself. For a moment, hope lifts inside my chest, and I think we might have a chance.

And then my uncle roars.

His eyes glow as he thrusts a hand at Xander. Animal magic crackles around him. Xander flies across the room and smashes hard against the wall. Incredibly, when he lands, the bone is still in his hand. But he looks like he's been knocked out, and his head bleeding.

Uncle Ray strides toward him. I have one chance to do something. No more than a few seconds to act. This is my last opportunity to save everyone. To save Xander.

My hand closes around one of the thick shards of glass from a broken goblet.

I don't know how to draw runes and the only spells I remember are harmless ones I learned in childhood. All I have is the uncontrolled magic inside me, with nothing to help direct or enhance it. Its power is raw, but if I feed it enough blood, it's guaranteed to create chaos.

There's only one question. How much blood is enough? But I already know what the answer has to be.

All of it.

I drive the glass into the brachial artery in my elbow. Blood spurts out with a force that shocks me. It hits my chest, soaking me in hot liquid.

My magic surges, hot and insistent. With this much blood, it's almost impossible to contain, but I struggle to hold it in anyway.

I'll only have one chance at this. I need to release the maximum amount of power at once, in one burst of magic, if I'm going to have any chance at all.

Time slows.

My heart pumps again and more blood floods from the wound.

Uncle Ray stops in front of Xander. In the library, not even bullets would stop him. But he was wearing Jeqabeel's head and carrying the bone. He hadn't seemed human then, not like he does now.

The demon's essence is still hanging in the air, a

menacing black shape that hovers over Xander, slowly getting smaller as it oozes back into the bone.

Another heartbeat. Another gush of blood.

Power burns through my body, tangled threads of lightning searching for a way out. I barely register how much it hurts.

I'm getting light headed, weakening faster than I would have believed possible. Falling toward death as though from a great height. My magic is barely restrained. As blood soaks my clothing and puddles under me, my power surges against my tenuous control, frantic to break free.

My blood feeds it, making it stronger than anything I've ever felt or imagined.

I'll only have one chance to release the magic. I'm dying fast. But if I can stop the demon and my uncle, my death won't be wasted.

Two enemies.

Two types of magic.

Somehow, I need to direct them both.

I'm cold. I can't feel my legs, so my body must be shutting down. But instead of being scary, this knowledge helps me focus my mind.

I'm in a dark tunnel that's slowly narrowing. All I can feel is the pain of holding my magic in. The only things I can see are my uncle and the bone, barely highlighted in the red glow of the moon.

I have one goal. A single-minded purpose.

Destroy my enemies.

I let my magic go.

In the darkness of my tunnel, the two clusters of magic are brilliant. Their strands are so bright, they hurt my eyes and overpower my senses. I *am* the magic. I have no mind or body. All that exists is the power. And now, totally absorbed in the strength of what I've unleashed, I can see how to keep the two strands of my magic from twisting together. It takes every scrap of what's left of my strength to keep them apart as my two magics launch toward my enemies.

My uncle's eyes glow bright. He blasts his own power at mine. When his magic and mine slam together, the collision is as hot as a bomb blast. It sears my flesh.

The magic my uncle stole from his victims is threaded inside his own, but it's far weaker than it was in the library and I can see gaps in it. The demon drank deeply from his power to escape the bone. It's all but drained him. And his magic has never been as strong as mine, let alone my mother's.

My animal magic forces its way through the gaps in my uncle's magic and pours itself into him. It turns him inside out.

Literally.

The bloody spectacle of seeing his insides turned out is so horrifying, I almost miss my earth magic pouring into the bone. It crumbles the bone, transforming it into gray dust.

The black smoke that had been a demon's shape lets out a terrifying sound. Not a scream, but a roar of rage so loud that it shakes the room and sends me sprawling.

The smoke swirls, suddenly homeless, but not destroyed. It dives into the nearest thing that's still whole.

The demon's insubstantial black form disappears into Xander. The noxious black smoke forces its way in through his nose, eyes and mouth.

"No!" With the last of my strength, I fight to turn my magic against that shadow. But it's too late. Xander has sucked in the last of the demon's form.

Stars fill my vision. I feel very light and completely numb. I'm panting and breathless. With my blood draining so fast, I'm not getting enough oxygen. A moment ago, hard stone and shards of glass were digging into me. Now I can't feel my body.

I've just killed Xander instead of saving him, but all at once it doesn't seem to matter.

My panting slows. The black tunnel of my vision narrows. My pain has slipped away. I feel almost peaceful.

There's nothing else I can do now. I have only one task left.

It's time to die.

TWENTY-NINE

I feel light and airy, like I'm floating.

Is this heaven?

No. My arm hurts. In fact, everything hurts, but my arm most of all.

I can't be dead. But how am I alive?

There's something on my lips and coating my tongue. The awful, thick coppery taste of blood. I'm choking on it. Am I back in the Unseen's basement, drowning in it?

I swallow and gag, struggling to force the stuff away. My vision is blurry and I can't seem to focus. All I can see is a bright silvery-red light.

"Drink," commands a male voice. "Hold it down."

More of the blood and wine mixture floods into my mouth and I cough and gasp for air. I'm too weak to fight. My limbs are full of lead.

I try to understand what's happening. Where I am.

And then I remember.

I killed my uncle with magic and now I really am a murderer.

I've killed Xander too.

Oh god.

Chanting starts. It's the same weird chanting the council members were doing during the ceremony. My mouth opens without my permission and I feel my own voice join in, blending with the others to make a single sound. Magic crackles through my body, lighting my veins with sizzling fire. For a moment I'm comforted, the familiar feeling of magic making me feel warm and at home.

But my magic has betrayed me yet again. My animal and earth magic have combined to do the unthinkable. I've destroyed the one person I was trying to help.

Xander.

A sob rises in my throat. I don't want the magic. I'll never use it again.

"Try to relax." It's the same male voice, only now it sounds different. *"The ceremony is almost over."*

A wave of grief and loss washes over me, the emotions so intense I gasp.

"They're dead," I choke out. But I'm no longer thinking of Xander. Two unfamiliar faces blend into my consciousness, and I feel their absence as though they've been carved out of my soul.

"You're feeling our loss," says the voice. *"Sharing the deaths of Valdis and Bryn. They were our newest members, inducted during the ceremony. They were too inexperienced to survive the demon's assault."*

I'm feeling pain for people I don't know? What about Xander?

The voice sounds like Magnus, and it seems too close for comfort. Did I hear his voice through my ears, or inside my mind?

What the HELL is going on?

The chanting stops abruptly.

"Ouch," grumbles a different voice in my mind. *"That was painfully loud."*

"We had to do it," says a woman's voice. *"You were all but dead. We couldn't have brought you back any other way."*

"We did it to save you." It sounds girlish. Like the Veritas.

I manage to lift my hands and clamp them over my ears, though the voices aren't coming through there. The council members are speaking directly into my head. Blinking to clear my vision, I discover that I'm lying on the stone floor in one of the circles in the ceremony room. The council members stand around me, their expressions ranging from worried to angry.

When I realize what they've done, my stomach lurches.

They made me drink the mixed blood of the council. They've forced me to join with the magic of the group.

"What have you done?" I croak, my voice like sandpaper on a grater.

"You were dying—"

"NOT inside my head," I say.

Above me, Magnus clears his throat. "It was the only way to save you. After your bravery, we couldn't let you die. It didn't seem right." He clears his throat again. "And the council needs strong witches like you..." He trails off as if realizing his words aren't exactly what I want to hear.

"You've forced me to join the Blood Council? Against my will?" Everything is churning inside me, my magic, my thoughts, my blood. I've gone from being a loner ex-witch hated by the establishment to being inextricably bound to the very people who cut me off from my magic all those years ago.

They're inside my *mind*.

Bile burns up my throat. I'm going to throw up.

"*We healed you.*" The voice is probably supposed to be soothing. A hand touches my shoulder and I flinch away.

The last thing I want is to be part of their circle. I've had nothing but contempt for them since my parents died and they threw me away like yesterday's garbage.

"Don't worry, the mind link is just a side effect of the blood moon ceremony." Magnus sounds tired and his voice is raspy. "In a few hours it'll weaken, and we'll lose the ability to speak without words."

"We need to bind her magic back up," snarls Dallas. "It's dangerous."

"We can't," says Magnus. "There's no way to bind her magic without restricting our own power. I'm not willing to do that."

"Can you feel our shared magic inside you, Saffy?" asks Aunt Theresa. "You need to be careful. You haven't had the training to be able to use it. It'll burn you if you draw on it."

I push myself up to sitting, too worried about Xander to think about anything else.

Two people lie on the floor next to me. Their faces are pale. Blood is caked around their nostrils and has leaked from their eyes like red tears. The two dead witches.

In the corner are the bloody remains of my uncle. Flinching, I turn quickly away.

"Xander," I demand. "Where's Xander?"

Then I see him, still lying by the wall where the demon hurled him. He's on his back, lying with his hands crossed over his chest like a man in a grave.

With a cry, I struggle to my feet. Though I'm healed, I'm so weak my legs barely support me as I stagger over and collapse beside him. He's alive. But when I try to touch him,

I run into a magic barrier. He's encased inside an invisible shield.

"What have you done to him?" I can already tell they've sedated him. Their spell is keeping him unconscious.

Magnus's expression is grave. "He carries the demon's essence. Now the bone has been destroyed, his body has become its vessel."

"What does that mean? Will he be okay?"

"I'm sorry. There isn't much we can do for him." Aunt Therese crouches next to me, her lined face kind. There's a lot more life in her eyes than there was before. She seems well again, with color in her cheeks. As if the ceremony healed her too.

"The demon was absorbing my power through Ray," she says, as though in answer to my thought. "It confused my mind and drew my life force like a leech. The demon was too strong to resist. It would have sucked me completely dry. You saved me." She waves her hand at the others who are still standing. "A little longer, and it would have done the same thing to all of us. We all owe our lives to you, Saffy."

I killed her husband. My uncle. The realization is like a punch to the gut. I turned him inside out. Why doesn't she hate me? I'm a murderer now.

"You had no choice," she says softly. "There was nothing left of the man I used to love, or the uncle you knew. The demon had consumed him."

She means well, but I hate that she can read my thoughts. The blood moon link had better wear off soon, because I can't stand having any of them in my head.

"How do we get the demon out of Xander?" My voice is gruff.

She shakes her head, her eyes creased with sadness. "I'm sorry," she repeats. "The demon will consume him too.

There's nothing we can do to stop it. We can only contain it."

"Contain it?"

"The Veritas will harden Xander's flesh. It'll keep the demon inert until we have a chance to—"

"Turn him into one of your statues? No way." I rake my gaze around the remaining council members. "Xander saved you all. You owe him your lives. There has to be a way to get the demon out of him."

"We should kill him." Dallas's voice is hard. "The demon hasn't been inside a mundane before. Killing him might destroy it."

Magnus shakes his head. "We can't take the chance of the demon escaping Xander and taking over a more powerful vessel. And we can't let a mundane walk around with a demon inside him. Jeqabeel's too dangerous to take chances with."

"I won't let you turn Xander to stone. You'll have to kill me first." My fists clench. *"And my magic is unbound now,"* I think at them. *"I'm strong. Maybe I can't control both strands of my magic so well, but that's all the more reason for you not to piss me off."*

They exchange glances, probably talking silently but cutting me out of the conversation.

With an impatient sound, Dallas draws a ceremonial knife out of his belt and stalks toward Xander. "I'm ending this now."

I leap in front of him and shove him backward. "Go near him with that knife and I'll stick it so far up your butt, you'll be able to cut your food and eat it at the same time."

"Stop," commands Magnus.

Dallas goes still and lowers the knife. But his glare is so furious, it singes my body hair.

"You don't understand, Sapphira," lisps the Veritas. "When we drank the blood, the demon gained access to our heads and we glimpsed its thoughts. It was like looking through an endless chasm into hell." The girl shudders, her face twisted with revulsion. "If you'd shared that experience, you'd be ready to do anything to stop it."

"You think I won't do what it takes?" My voice rises. "I stabbed an artery, remember? Are you really questioning how badly I want that thing dead or banished back to wherever it belongs? Because frankly, I'm the only one here who's done a single damn thing to keep it from taking over the world." I glare at her, then swing the glare around to include the rest of them, turning it into an equal opportunity glare-fest.

At least the Veritas has the courtesy to blush.

"Saffy's right," says Aunt Therese in a brisk voice. "We owe her."

Dallas's lip curls. "The demon will drive the mundane insane. Better for him if we kill him now. He'll beg us for death soon enough."

My heart contracts. Just touching the bone drove my uncle to do things I can't believe he would have been capable of if he hadn't been under the demon's influence. And Xander doesn't just have the demon whispering to him, he has the monster inside him.

Dallas is right. There's no way Xander can survive this.

My throat closes and I try again to touch him. My hands hit the magical barrier, so I can't take his hands or feel his skin. Even pushing as hard as I can, pouring all my frustration and despair into the effort, I can't manage to brush his fingers with mine. It makes me want to scream.

I can't lose him.

Aunt Therese puts her hand on my back. "The demon

will consume Xander eventually. But he's mundane, and Jeqabeel feeds on magic. Its strength comes from magical energy and Xander has none to give it. He's an inert vessel. So we may have time to look for another solution."

"How much time do we have?" I meet her gaze.

Instead of answering aloud, she opens her mind to me. The truth is, she has no idea. None of them do.

"There's only one way to find out," says Magnus. "We'll wake him."

He bends to put one hand just above Xander's arm, and Therese closes her eyes. Between them they unweave the magic that's surrounding Xander, and draw it back like a blanket. I can feel them do it, as clearly as if I were doing it myself.

It's so orderly that I gape. My magic has always been chaotic and difficult to control. It comes with pain and surges and bolts of lightning. Theirs is as structured as a neat piece of knitting.

Xander opens his eyes. His breath gets noticeably fast and shallow, but when he jerks himself up to sitting he doesn't move like someone who's been badly hurt. "What happened? Where am I?"

"It's okay. You're okay." Finally, with the barrier down, I can touch him. I reach out and grasp his hand.

The instant my skin touches his, my mind floods with darkness. A voice whispers in my mind. *"I can give you everything, Sapphira."* It's a deep, seductive whisper. *"Death is my mistress. Mine to command. I can give your parents back to you. Or I can make them suffer for all eter—"*

Chest tight, I snatch my hand away.

"The demon's voice," says Aunt Therese, her eyes sympathetic. "Do you hear it, Xander?"

"I hear *something.*" He puts one hand to his ear,

pressing it as though trying to get rid of an annoying noise. "What is that buzzing sound? How do I make it stop?"

I meet Magnus's eyes. "If Xander heard it as clearly as I did, he wouldn't need to ask."

The old man nods, his lips pursed. "Being mundane gives him a level of protection. The demon can't use him like it would use a witch. And if it could escape him, it would have already done so."

"Good. Then I'm taking Xander home." I stand up and motion Xander to get up too, hoping he has the strength to support himself because I'm afraid to touch him again. "We'll work on a way to destroy it."

"Wait," says Xander. "What's going on?"

"Are you insane?" Dallas ignores him, leveling an accusatory finger at me. "You can't take him anywhere. You can't even risk *touching* him. What if the demon gets out? Or it corrupts you and turns you into its tool, like it did your uncle? What if Therese is wrong about it needing magic to feed? It might get stronger feeding on the mundane. We've no way to know."

I clench my fists. My blood's pumping so hard, all I can hear is my heart beating in my ears. "The only reason you're not Jeqabeel's plaything right now is because of Xander and me. Over the last few days, I've been accused of murder, chased, shot at, drugged, and beaten. While you were sharing bodily fluids with the demon, Xander and I put our lives on the line to stop it. So, if I want to take him home so we can catch our breath and figure out what to do next, I'm damn well going to do it."

With an impatient noise, Dallas turns to Magnus. "You're not seriously going to let her waltz out of here with a mundane and the most dangerous creature that's ever walked our earth?"

Xander opens his mouth and then closes it again. He blinks, frowning. Is the demon whispering to him?

Magnus frowns at him, then at Dallas. "I will make the decision," he announces, lifting one hand in a 'wait' gesture. Then he drops his head, squishing his mouth into his long, gray beard while he thinks.

I was so sure he was the killer, perhaps because it would have explained why he turned his back on me after my parents died. Guess he's just a regular asshat rather than a demon-controlled one after all.

"What's with the dog smell?" I demand.

"What?" He lifts his head.

"You smell like a dog." I motion at his wrinkled gray shirt, noticing fine hairs that are almost the same color as the fabric.

He looks down and makes a half-hearted attempt to brush the hairs off his shirt. "I adopted a puppy."

As hard as it is to hate someone who adopts puppies, I manage it anyway. I scowl at him, and he gives a reluctant sigh as though he's being forced into something he doesn't want to do.

"I've made my decision. You have forty-eight hours, Sapphira."

The words etch themselves into my mind with a sharp sting of magic. He's used a spell to emphasize his words. I have no doubt it's a time limit I'll be forced to obey. Yet another reason the council sucks.

"But you can't—" starts Dallas.

Magnus cuts him off with a gesture, still frowning at me. "It's enough time for you to catch your breath, as you request. Though we think the demon will strengthen, I doubt it's enough time for it to drive the mundane insane. Or, more importantly, for it to find a way to escape its prison. But be very careful not to touch the mundane. I don't wish to kill you, but if you allow it to possess your mind, there may be no alternative."

"Great," I mutter. "Way to be reassuring. You ever considered a career in motivational speaking?"

Xander holds up both hands, his expression bewildered. "Wait a minute. Can you back up to the part where I'm going to be driven insane? And what's going to happen after forty-eight hours?"

He looks so confused that all I want to do is reach out and take his hand. The fact I can't is like a physical pain. I thrust my fists into my pockets.

"Jeqabeel's hiding inside you," I say gently, though I'm sure he's realized that much at least. "The council wants to turn you to stone so they can contain it." I keep my tone conversational, but my eyes narrow at the witches around me.

"Oh." Xander swallows. "Are we going to vote on the idea?"

"I'm not going to let them do it." I shoot them another don't-mess-with-me glare. "Here's what's going to happen. Xander and I are leaving now. I'm going to find a way to destroy the demon. And you're all going to stay out of my head until the link wears off."

"If we're going to vote, put me down for that plan." Xander limps toward the door, looking as shaky as I am.

The council members exchange glances, but nobody says anything, at least not out loud.

When I turn and follow him, to my relief, they let us go.

THIRTY

By the time we get back to my house, it's about three in the morning.

When we walk in, Xander asks in a too-casual tone, "You've got a way to get this thing out of me, right?"

I'd give anything to be able to touch him. I'd love to be able to put my arms around him and hold him close. It kills me that I can't.

I shoot him the most confident smile I can summon. "Absolutely. We'll do it together. We've made a damn good team up until now, haven't we?"

Xander rubs his face, smearing grime across his cheek, then collapses onto the living room couch. "Unfortunately, this isn't my area of expertise. You want a suspect chased or a statement taken, I'm happy to help. Demon stuff? That's your thing. I wouldn't know where to start."

I head purposefully to the kitchen, not wanting to let him know I don't have a clue where to start either. "First thing we need is something to eat and drink. I'll fix us something, then we can come up with a plan."

I'm almost at the kitchen door when I hear him give a grunt of pain. I glance back to see him wince and put a hand to his head. "No, I'm not doing that," he mutters, as though to himself. "You may as well shut up. I'm not going to listen to you."

A cold chill runs down my spine.

"You okay?" I ask.

"Fine. I can hear the thing whispering, that's all. Nasty bastard. Doesn't have anything good to say."

Shit. That's the last thing we need.

"Eating will help. Got to keep your strength up." I take off into the kitchen so he doesn't see my expression. I can't afford to fall apart now.

In the kitchen, I find a note propped up against the toaster. It's in Jess's messy handwriting, addressed to me.

Hey, Saff.

Where are you? I haven't seen you at home for a while.

We've got a gig in DC tonight so I won't be back 'til tomorrow.

Sylvia's rat and your chicken both looked hungry, so I've been feeding them. Boy, that chicken has a temper, doesn't she? Anyway, I hate to fuss, but give me a call to let me know you're okay. I'm worried about you.

Jess.

I put some bread in the toaster, then check Ratticus's cage. He's got food and water and seems happy enough. I hold out my hand for him to climb on and he rubs his whiskers against my palm.

Then I head out to the courtyard to check on Agnes, mainly because I'm putting off having to tell Xander that I have no plan. I don't have any idea what we're going to do about Jeqabeel.

When I accidentally blew up the concrete pavers in the courtyard, I exposed the bare dirt underneath. Agnes is asleep now, roosting on the back of the garden seat, but it's obvious she spent the day digging a tunnel. She's scratched out a deep hole and is angling it to go under the fence. Another few hours working on it and she'll probably be free, and at the mercy of any dog or person who decides she looks tasty.

I take a deep breath. I unleashed all my magical energy at the demon and really need a long rest before trying to use it again. On the other hand, my clothes are soaked with blood and I can feel the shared power of the council somewhere inside me. I don't want it and I'm not about to use it, but it's there in the background.

The shared power of the council is strong. When I search for my own magic, I have to tiptoe around it. It's like I'm trying to figure out how to light a propane tank without blowing myself up, and all I can hear is the hum of a nuclear power plant.

At least at night, chickens are docile, which means I won't get my hands torn to pieces trying to touch Agnes. Moving behind her, I pick her up. She lets out a surprised squawk.

I close my eyes and reach out with my newly-unbound magical senses. The magic keeping Agnes in her current form is a tangle that's knotted and snarled into an impossible mess. It's mostly made up of animal magic, but earth magic is snagged inside the spell like barbed wire in wool. No wonder Mireya couldn't unravel it.

Agnes pecks my hands while I concentrate on the all-but-exhausted magic inside me, trying to direct it at the mess I've made. Her sharp beak hurts like hell, but every time she draws blood, my scraps of magic glow a little brighter.

The fibers that make up the spell are an angry shade of red. I can barely remember how furious I must have been when I cast it. Now, I feel close to the end of my endurance. I've lost so many people I loved. Will I lose Xander too? What if I can't save him?

With a desperate effort, I force out the last traces of animal magic I have left. The meager scraps trickle slowly into the spell, unbinding it and letting the twisted mess of magic fall away.

A small amount of earth magic escapes with it, slipping out of my control before I can stop it.

My focus is split between the two branches of magic, and even though there's only a tiny amount of each, trying to control them both is like juggling with sparks. My earth magic has nowhere to go. It's looking for an outlet and I try desperately to guide it away from anything electrical.

While I'm concentrating on that, the spell falls away from Agnes.

Instead of a chicken, I'm holding a woman. A confused, old, woman.

Agnes is still wearing brown slacks and a brown cardigan, but the sharp creases and fresh linen smell are gone. She looks like she's been scratching in the dirt. Her face and hands are dark with grime, and her hair is as tangled as my spell was.

Losing my concentration at the last moment was a bad mistake. Tiny traces of the spell still cling to her, caught like burrs in her flesh. Feathers coat one side of her neck.

"Agnes?" I ask gently. "Are you okay?"

As she turns wide, frightened eyes on me, I feel my earth magic seep into the porch light. It explodes with a noise loud enough to make me duck with my arms around my head.

My neighbor makes a strangled sound that's half human and half a chicken's squawk. She flaps her arms and hops, as though trying to flee.

"Agnes." I grab her shoulder. "You're okay. Nothing's going to hurt you."

She stops, frowning. Her terrified eyes dart to me and away again.

From behind us, I hear a long, low whistle. "I thought I'd seen some things today," says Xander. "But that was one of the weirdest."

"Agnes?" I say again. "Can you answer me?"

If I could summon any more magic, I'd try to clean all the spell off her. But the only power I feel now belongs to the council. What if I can't manage to clean up my mess, and she can only cluck like a chicken for the rest of her life?

Agnes swallows hard, her hand held to her mouth. "What happened?" Her voice is croaky.

I blow out a relieved breath. At least she can speak.

"What do you remember?" I ask.

"I asked you to turn your music down. Then I came in to do it for you, and..." She puts a shaky hand to her forehead, frowning at a feather poking from the skin on her arm. "Did I hit my head?"

"Yes, you did. You hit it hard. I think you must have been knocked out for a while and had strange dreams. Isn't that right, Xander?"

"Strange dreams," he agrees, nodding. "I've been having them myself."

"It's dark now. Maybe you should go home to sleep. I'm sure you'll feel better after a long rest." I take her arm to lead her toward the door. Trying to get those feathers off her neck and arm will be the first thing I'll attempt tomorrow.

Agnes snatches her arm out of my grip and sniffs. She may not be completely sure what's happened to her, but it looks like she's just remembered how much she hates me.

"Keep the music down," she snaps. Then she stalks to the door.

When it slams behind her, I turn back to Xander. "At least that's one problem solved. Mostly." I blow out a relieved breath.

"Why didn't you tell me you could do that?"

"I did. I told you I turned her into a chicken."

"No, I mean turning her back."

"Because I couldn't. But now my magic's unbound, I can use it again. I'm not great at controlling it, though. I have to be careful."

He shakes his head, looking more cheerful than he has since he woke up with a demon inside him. "You really did turn her into a chicken. And you changed her back again. Watching her change was incredible. If you can do that, you'll be able to fix me." The smile he shoots me is way more confident than I deserve.

Oh-kay. So maybe he didn't see the leftover feathers?

"Piece of cake," I say breezily, wiggling my fingers. "Just let me get my strength back."

"Once you've banished the thing that's squatting inside me, what do you think about making plans to have a quiet night in?"

"A quiet night?" I wrinkle my brow. "What, like watching TV or something?"

"TV. Yeah." He shrugs. "I'm craving a boring night in for a change. Just the two of us. You up for it?"

I wouldn't have thought I could manage a smile, but

incredibly I feel my lips twitch up. A night on the couch with Xander sounds like bliss.

Jeqabeel had better be afraid. If I was determined to destroy him before, I'm doubly determined now. No centuries-old demon is going to stand in the way of a night of Netflix and chilling with Xander. That's a promise.

"It's a date," I say.

Dear Fabulous Reader,

Thank you so much for reading The Trouble With Magic!

Writing this series has been a bit like stepping through the portal into a hidden athenaeum full of grimoires. When we started, we had no idea how the magic would change us and what terrible dangers we'd uncover...

Dangers like the one threatening Xander.

The Blood Council's time limit is ticking down fast, and Saffy's unbound magic is a total chaos-factory. What if Saffy can't find a way to save Xander, or Jeqabeel gets loose?

And what does the Unseen plan to do with Saffy's ring?

In her search for answers, Saffy finds herself caught in a web of dark magic. The next step in her journey will be far more dangerous than anything she's faced so far.

What's on the other side of the next portal may shock you. We hope you'll take a deep breath and leap through it with us.

Trudi and Tania. x